Jean Marteilhe

Autobiography of French Protestant

Translated From the French. With a Pref. by H. Paumier

Jean Marteilhe

Autobiography of French Protestant
Translated From the French. With a Pref. by H. Paumier

ISBN/EAN: 9783337009588

Printed in Europe, USA, Canada, Australia, Japan

Cover: Foto ©Raphael Reischuk / pixelio.de

More available books at **www.hansebooks.com**

MEMOIRES

D'UN

PROTESTANT,

Condamné aux

GALERES DE FRANCE

POUR CAUSE DE

RELIGION;

écrits par lui même :

Ouvrage, dans lequel, outre le récit des souffrances de l'Auteur depuis 1700 *jusqu'en* 1713; *on trouvera diverses Particularités curieuses, relatives à l'Histoire de ce Temps-là, & une Description exacte des Galeres & de leur Service.*

A ROTTERDAM,

Chez J. D. BEMAN & *Fils.*

M. D. C. C. LVII.

CONTENTS.

—◆—

NOTES.

PREFACE.

—✦—

EVERAL years ago, one of our friends at Lyons discovered hidden, at the bottom of an old family library, the book which we here reprint. Attracted by the title, he read it, and gave it to some of his friends to read ; the interest it excited was so lively and so universal, that all desired the republication of the narrative.

But one question had first to be solved, What was this book ? Was its harrowing narrative of the odious consequences of religious persecution authentic ? Could it be accepted as a picture, sadly faithful, of the truth ? Or was it merely a romance, destined to excite the reader's pity on behalf of an imaginary hero ? The matter was investigated ; two copies of an edition later than that of 1757 were discovered in Holland, which furnished the key to all the names, which, in the first edition, were only denoted by initials. There was now no doubt that these memoirs (perfectly authentic, and revised by Daniel de Superville, one of the pastors who received the poor fugitive) contained the real history of the sufferings of a young man, Jean Marteilhe, of Bergerac.*

Amidst more pressing labours, the project of reprinting the book was postponed, and would, perhaps, have been forgotten altogether, if the publication of M. Michelet's work on the " Revocation of the Edict of Nantes," by

* See note at end of volume.

fully confirming the investigations already made, had n
excited a more lively desire for the appearance of the
memoirs, unknown for the most part to the descendan
of those who had so severely suffered for their faith.]
one of the most touching chapters of his book, N
Michelet, after having rapidly analysed these memoir
adds, " It is a book of the first order, distinguished t
the charming *naivete* of the recital, by its angelic swee
ness, written as if between earth and heaven. Why h:
it never been reprinted?" We are glad to be able
length to realise the wish of our eminent historian.

If we try to revive these glorious recollections of tl
past history of our church, it is not to excite anew tho:
religious conflicts in which our ancestors so ardent
engaged. We know, and we bless God for it, how tl
times are changed. Children of the same country, y
free to profess our faith publicly, we are happy to car
into practice the counsel of the prophet to the people
Israel, " Pray for the peace of the city in which ye dwe
for in the peace thereof ye shall have peace."* But
is good to remember, at all times, those lessons of ste:
obedience to conscience, of fidelity to duty, and
self-sacrifice, which, in the days of trial, our fathers :
courageously gave both to us and to their persecutors.

Our sole desire is to revive the spirit of the fathe
in the children, reminding them by these salutary e
amples, that " man doth not live by bread alone, b
by every word that proceedeth out of the mouth
God."

HENRY PAUMIER.

PARIS: *October*, 1864.

* Jer. xxix. 7, French version.

TRANSLATOR'S PREFACE.

O the foregoing preface, by the French editor, little needs to be added. By the Edict of Nantes, Henry IV., in the year 1598, guaranteed to his Protestant subjects liberty of conscience and of worship, absolute security to person and property, and equal rights and privileges before the law. The Edict continued in force for nearly ninety years, though its stipulations were often violated, and, under one pretence or another, the Protestants suffered frequent persecutions. But on the 22nd October, 1685, it was revoked by Louis XIV. The Reformed pastors were commanded to leave the kingdom within fifteen days, under pain of the galleys. All Protestant worship was interdicted, both in public and private, and the temples were ordered to be razed to the ground. The Protestant schools were to be closed forthwith; and all children born after the date of the Revocation were to be baptized by the parish priests, and brought up as Roman Catholics. Refugees were enjoined to return and abjure their faith within four months, under penalty of confiscation and outlawry. Protestants attempting to escape from the kingdom were sentenced to the galleys. Adults who had been brought up in the reformed faith were allowed to remain "*until it shall please God to enlighten them.*"

These stern and cruel enactments were at once put into force, and a regular *stampede* from the kingdom commenced. Though every effort was made to guard the frontiers, yet multitudes escaped, and reached England, Switzerland, Holland, or Germany. The number of fugitives will never be fully known. The estimates vary widely. Probably not fewer than a quarter of a million succeeded in flying from their homes, and finding liberty to worship God in foreign lands. The fugitives were from every class in society, and adopted every variety of disguise—pilgrims, cattle-drovers, soldiers, footmen, beggars. Some bribed the guards who lined the frontiers, some crept along byways and through forests under cover of the night, others, who could afford it, paid guides to conduct them by intricate and unwatched passes. Those near the coast concealed themselves on board ship, by the connivance of the merchants and sailors, amongst bales of goods or in empty casks. Many ventured out to sea in open boats, in the desperate hope of reaching England, or being picked up by some passing vessel. The Count and Countess de Marancè, with forty companions, amongst whom were several aged and sick persons, and pregnant women, embarked in a fishing-boat of only seven tons burden. Driven from their course by a violent storm, they were on the point of perishing from hunger. For some days they subsisted upon melted snow, and at last reached the English coast more dead than alive.

Many of the most eminent men in France—men in the first rank of the nobility—vainly implored permission to quit the country. The Marquis de Ruvigny and Marshal Schomberg were almost the only exceptions. Admiral Duquesne, the founder of the French navy, was urged by the infatuated monarch to change his religion. The veteran, now eighty years of age, pointed to his hoary hairs, and replied, "For sixty years I have rendered unto Cæsar the things that are Cæsar's; let me still render to God the things which are God's." As a special favour he was allowed to remain without molestation.

Whilst many succeeded in making their escape from the kingdom, many less fortunate were seized and sent to the galleys. Amongst these were David de Caumont, —connected with the Duke de la Force, whose name appears in the following narrative,—and Louis de Marolles, one of the king's council. The former was sixty-five years of age at the time of his arrest; the latter, after an imprisonment of some months in the Chateau de la Tournelle,* was marched to Marseilles, with the great chain of galley slaves, where he died in 1692. Within a year after the Revocation of the Edict, there were more than six hundred Protestants in the galleys at Marseilles, as many at Toulon, and a proportionate number at the other ports. "On all the roads of the kingdom," says Benoît, "these miserable wretches might be seen, marching in large gangs, burdened by heavy chains, often weighing more than fifty pounds, and so fixed as to give the greatest amount of discomfort. Sometimes the prisoners were conveyed in waggons, in which case these fetters were riveted to the cart. When they sank down from exhaustion on their long marches, the guards compelled them to rise and resume their journey by blows. Their food was coarse and unwholesome, and insufficient in quantity, for the guards put into their own pockets half the amount allowed for the expenses of the escort. When they halted they were

* For a description of this horrible dungeon and the great chain of galley slaves, see p. 202 *et seq.*

lodged in foul dungeons, or in barns where they lay upon the bare earth, without covering, and weighed down by their chains."

But it would only weary the reader to narrate in detail the cruelties of the persecutors, and the sufferings of the oppressed. Abundant illustrations will be found in the histories of the period.*

There is little need to point the moral of the following narrative. Its lessons are obvious. If this life were all, these martyrs for the faith might seem to be " of all men most miserable." But " after this I beheld, and, lo, a great multitude, which no man could number, of all nations, and kindreds, and people, and tongues, stood before the throne, and before the Lamb, clothed with white robes, and palms in their hands ; and cried with a loud voice, saying, Salvation to our God which sitteth upon the throne, and unto the Lamb. . . . These are they which came out of great tribulation, and have washed their robes, and made them white in the blood of the Lamb. Therefore are they before the throne of God, and serve him day and night in his temple : and he that sitteth on the throne shall dwell among them. They shall hunger no more, neither thirst any more ; neither shall the sun light on them, nor any heat. For the Lamb which is in the midst of the throne shall feed them, and shall lead them unto living fountains of waters : and God shall wipe away all tears from their eyes."

* Special reference may be made to the *History of the French Protestant Refugees from the Revocation of the Edict of Nantes.* By CHARLES WEISS. Blackwood and Sons. 1854.

AUTOBIOGRAPHY

OF A

FRENCH PROTESTANT

CONDEMNED TO THE GALLEYS.

———•———

HERE are few of my fellow-countrymen, refugees in these happy Provinces,* who could not bear witness to the calamities which persecution has inflicted upon them in every part of France. If each of them had written memoirs of all that they had suffered, as well· in their common country as after they had been forced to leave it, and then a collection of all these memoirs had been made, such a work would be not only very curious, on account of the different events which would be related therein, but at the same time very instructive for a large number of good Protestants, who are quite ignorant of a great deal which has taken place since the year 1684 in this bloody and cruel persecution. Divers authors have written about it in a general way ; but not one of them (at least to my knowledge) has particularised the different kinds of hardship and torture which each of my dear companions in suffering has experienced.

* The Netherlands.

B

It is far from my design to undertake such a work, only knowing imperfectly and by tradition an almost infinite number of facts which many of my dear fellow-countrymen daily relate to their children. I shall therefore only impart to the public, in these memoirs, that which befell myself, from the year 1700 to 1713, when I was happily delivered from the galleys of France by God's mercy, and by the intercession of Queen Anne of England of glorious memory.

I was born at Bergerac, a small town in the province of Perigord, in the year 1684. My parents were in trade. By the grace of God they had always maintained, even unto death, the doctrines of the true reformed religion ; their conduct was such as never to draw down any reproach upon these doctrines. They brought up their children in the fear of God, continually instructing them in the principles of true religion, and in aversion to the errors of popery.

I will not weary my reader by relating the events of my childhood up to the year 1700, when persecution tore me from the bosom of my family, forced me to fly from my country, and to expose myself, notwithstanding my tender age, to the perils of a journey of two hundred leagues, which I made in order to seek a refuge in the United Provinces of the Netherlands. I shall only relate, briefly and in simple truth, what has happened to me since my sorrowful separation from my parents, whom I left enduring the most cruel persecution.

Before detailing the story of my flight from my dear country, it is necessary to speak of what occasioned it, and kindled the most inhuman persecution in my native province.

During the war which was terminated by the peace of Ryswick, the Jesuits and priests had not been able to indulge in the pleasure of dragooning the Reformed in France, because the king had all his troops upon the frontiers of his kingdom ; but no sooner was peace concluded, than they wished to indemnify themselves for the repose they had been obliged to give us during the war. These pitiless and inveterate persecutors then made their rage felt in all the provinces of France, wherever there were any of the reformed faith. I shall confine myself to detailing some of the best authenticated facts which took place in Perigord.

In the year 1699, the Duke de la Force, who proved that he by no means shared the sentiments of his illustrious ancestors with regard to the reformed religion, at the instigation of the Jesuits, requested permission to go to his estates in Perigord, *in order* (as he expressed it) *to convert the Huguenots.* In doing this he flattered the views and principles of the court too well not to obtain such an honourable and worthy employment. So he set out from Paris, accompanied by four Jesuits, a few guards, and his servants. Arrived at his castle of La Force, about a league distant from Bergerac, he began, in order to give an idea of the gentleness of his mission, and the spirit of his counsellors, to exercise unheard-of cruelties against those of his vassals who belonged to the reformed faith, carrying off, daily, peasants of every age and of both sexes, and making them suffer in his presence, and without any form of trial, the most frightful tortures, continued upon some till they died, to compel them to abjure their religion upon the spot, without any reason but his own will. Then, by means as diabolical, he obliged all these poor wretches to take the most fearful oaths to remain inviolably attached to the Roman religion. To testify the joy and satisfaction which he felt at his happy success, and to terminate his enterprise in a manner worthy of the motives and counsels which had caused him thus to act, he celebrated public rejoicings in the village of La Force, where his castle was situated, and made a bonfire of a magnificent library, composed of the pious books of the reformed religion which his ancestors had carefully collected. The town of Bergerac this time was exempt from persecution, as well as several other towns in the neighbourhood, but this repose was only a calm which was to be followed by the most terrible tempest.

Before relating what the Reformed in this province had to suffer, I must amuse my reader with a rather diverting scene which took place at the castle of La Force, while the duke was reposing after the fatigues of his successful expedition, and receiving the praise and homage of the priests and monks of the neighbourhood. There was an advocate of Bergerac, named Grenier, who had a good deal of wit, but was really a little cracked, and who never had much religion, though he was born in the reformed faith ; this man wished to show off his wit, and to range himself among the flatterers, by making a speech to the duke. He asked permission, which was readily granted him. The duke seated in his chair of state, having his four Jesuits by his side, admitted Grenier to an audience, who began in these words :—"Monseigneur, your grandfather was a great warrior, your father a great saint, and you, monseigneur, are a great huntsman." The duke interrupted him, to inquire how he knew that he was a great huntsman, for in reality he had no great passion for the chase. "I judge of it," replied Grenier, as he pointed to the four Jesuits, " by your four bloodhounds, who never quit you." These fathers, as good Christians, began to demand that Grenier should be punished for his insolence, but it was represented to the duke that Grenier was not right in his mind, so he was content with driving him from his presence.

I resume the thread of my narrative, and must explain what gave rise to my flight, and made me attempt to escape from the kingdom.

The Duke de la Force, proud of the fine conversions which he had made, went to give an account of them to the court. We can easily judge whether he and his Jesuits exaggerated the effect which their mission had produced. However that might be, he obtained permission to return to Perigord, in the year 1700, to convert, by means of a pitiless dragonade, the Huguenots in the royal towns of that province. He came then to Ber-

gerac, where he took up his residence, accompanied
by the same four Jesuits, and by a regiment of
dragoons, whose cruel mission—for they were
allowed full license among the towns-people—made
a great many more converts than the exhortations
of the Jesuits.   There were no conceivable cruelties
which these booted and spurred missionaries did
not exercise to oblige the poor citizens to go to
mass, make their public abjuration, and swear,
with horrible oaths, never to abandon the practice
of the Roman religion.   The duke had a form
of this oath filled with imprecations against the
reformed faith, which he made them sign and
swear to, either by their consent or by force.
Twenty-two of these execrable dragoons were
quartered in my father's house.   I do not know
for what reason the duke caused my father
to be taken to prison at Perigueux.   Two of my
brothers and my sister, who were but children,
were seized and placed in a convent.   I had the
good fortune to escape from the house.   My poor
mother found herself left the only one of the
family, in the midst of those twenty-two wretches,
who caused her to undergo horrible tortures.
After having consumed and destroyed everything
in the house, they dragged my poor unhappy
mother before the duke, who, by the infamous
treatment to which he subjected her, accompanied
by horrible threats, forced her to sign his formulary.
This the poor woman did, weeping abundantly, and
protesting against the act to which she was compelled.   She resolved that her hand should join in

the lamentable protestations of her lips, so, the duke having presented the form of abjuration for her signature, she wrote her name on it, and at the bottom added the words, "(la) Force made me do it"—alluding doubtless to the name of the duke. They tried to make her efface these words, but she persisted in refusing; so one of the Jesuits took the trouble of erasing them.

I had escaped from the house (October, 1700) before the dragoons entered it. I was then just sixteen years of age. It is not a time of life when one has much experience, especially in getting out of such a critical position as mine was. How was I to escape the vigilance of the dragoons, by whom the town and all the approaches to it were filled, in order to stop the flight of any of the inhabitants? Nevertheless, I had the happiness, by the great mercy of God, to leave the town at night without being perceived, accompanied by one of my friends, and after walking all night through the woods, we found ourselves the next morning at Mussidan, a small town four leagues from Bergerac. There we resolved, whatever the perils might be, to continue our journey as far as Holland, resigning ourselves wholly to the will of God in the prospect of all those dangers which presented themselves to our imagination; and as we implored the Divine protection we made a firm resolution not to imitate Lot's wife in looking back, and that, whatever might be the result of our perilous enterprise, we would remain firm and constant in confessing the true reformed religion, even at the risk of the punishment of the galleys, or of death. After this resolution we implored God's gracious help and mercy, and then proceeded cheerfully along the high road to Paris. We consulted our purse, which was not too well supplied. Our whole capital consisted of about ten pistoles. We formed economical plans to make our little money last, and lodged every day at the humblest inns to save expense. We had not, thank God, any unpleasant adventure as far as Paris, where we arrived on the 10th of November.

We expected at Paris to see some of our acquaintances who would tell us the easiest and least dangerous route to the frontier. A good friend and good Protestant wrote out for us a little itinerary as far as Mezières, a garrison town on the Meuse, which at that time was the frontier of the Spanish Netherlands, and on the borders of the formidable forest of Ardennes. This friend informed us that the only danger we should have to guard against was on entering this town—for on going out no one was stopped; and that the forest of Ardennes would favour our journey to Charleroi, six or seven leagues distant from Mezières, and that once at Charleroi we were safe, for then we should really be out of the French territories. He added that there was also at Charleroi a Dutch garrison and commander, who would protect us from all danger. This friend, however, warned us to be prudent, and to take the greatest precaution in entering the town of Mezières, because they were extremely particular in stopping at the gates all those whom they suspected to be strangers, and that if they were found without passports they were taken at once before the governor, and thence to prison.

At last we started from Paris for Mezières. We had no disagreeable adventure during the journey, for within the French dominions no one was stopped. The strictest attention of the government was only directed to guarding all the roads across the frontiers. We arrived then, one afternoon about four o'clock, at the summit of a little hill, about a quarter of a league from Mezières, whence we could see the whole of this town and the gate by which we should have to enter it. One can easily judge of our feelings of suspense and dread as we considered the near and imminent peril which presented itself before our eyes. We sat down for a moment upon the hill to take counsel concerning an entrance into the town. In narrowly observing the gate, we perceived that a long bridge over the Meuse led up to it, and as it was very fine weather, a number of the inhabitants were walking about upon this bridge. We thought that by mixing with the citizens, and walking with them upon the bridge, we should be able to enter the town with the crowd without being recognised as strangers by the sentinel at the gate. Having decided upon this stratagem, we emptied our knapsacks of the few shirts which we had, putting them all on, and the knapsacks into our pockets. Then we cleaned our shoes, combed our hair, and finally took all the precautions requisite in order not to look like travellers. We had no swords, for it was then forbidden in France to carry them.   Thus equipped, we descended the hill and betook ourselves to the bridge, walking up and down there with the citizens till the drum beat for the closing of the gates.   Then all the inhabitants hastened to return into the town, and we with them, the sentinel not perceiving that we were strangers.   We were filled with the greatest joy at having avoided this great peril, believing that it was the only one we had to fear; but we were reckoning, as the saying is, without our host.   We could not leave Mezières at once, the gate opposite to that by which we had entered being shut.   We must then lodge in the town.   We entered the first inn which presented itself.   The landlord was not there; his wife received us.   We ordered supper; and whilst we were at table, about nine o'clock, the master of the house arrived.   His wife told him that she had received two young strangers.   We heard from our chamber her husband ask her if we had a ticket of permission from the governor.   His wife having replied that she had not inquired, " Jade," said he, " do you wish that we should be utterly ruined ? You know the rigorous prohibitions against lodging strangers without permission. I must go at once with them to the governor."

This dialogue which we overheard made us shudder.   The landlord soon entered our chamber, and asked us very civilly if we had spoken to the governor.   We told him that we had not thought this was necessary for lodging one night only in the town.   " It would cost me a thousand crowns,"

said he, "if the governor knew that I had lodged
you without his permission. But have you a passport to enable you to enter the frontier towns ?" he
asked us. We replied boldly that we were well
furnished with papers. "That changes the whole
affair," said he, "and saves me from incurring the
blame of lodging you without permission; but
still you must come with me to the governor to
show your passports." We replied that we were
very weary and fatigued, but that the next morning
we would willingly accompany him there. He was
satisfied with this. We finished our supper, and
though our bed was a very good one, it did not
induce us to sleep, so troubled were we by anxiety
at the peril which threatened us. How many
counsels we held through that long night! How
many expedients did we propose with regard to
the answer which we should make to the governor!
But alas! they were all counsels and expedients
without result. Seeing nothing which could protect us from going straight from the governor's
house to prison, we passed the remainder of the
night imploring in prayer the help of God in such
a pressing hour of need, and asking him that, to
whatever his Divine will might think fit to expose
us, he would grant us the firmness and constancy
necessary to confess worthily the truth of the
Gospel. The dawn of day found us in this pious
exercise. We got up quickly and went down to
the kitchen, where the landlord and his wife slept.
As we were dressing we thought of an expedient
to avoid appearing before the governor, which

we put into practice, and it succeeded admirably. It was as follows :—We formed the design of leaving our lodging clandestinely before our host was up and able to observe us. When he saw us so early in his kitchen he inquired our reason for such early rising. We said that having to go to the governor with him, we wished to breakfast at once, so that on leaving the governor's house we could continue our journey. He approved of our scheme, and ordered his servant to fry some sausages, whilst he was getting up. This kitchen was on the ground-floor, and close to the street door. Having perceived that the servant had opened the street door, we made a pretext that we wished to go out for a few moments. The host suspecting nothing, we went out of this fatal inn, without saying farewell or paying our reckoning, for the trick seemed absolutely necessary.

Once in the street, we found a little boy, of whom we asked the way to the Charleville gate, that by which we were to leave the town. We were very near it, and as the gate was open we went out without any obstacle. We entered Charleville, a small town with neither gate nor garrison, which is within gunshot of Mezières. We breakfasted here quickly, and then left it to enter the forest of Ardennes. It had frozen during the night, and the forest appeared terrible to us; the trees were covered with hoar frost and icicles. As we penetrated this vast forest we perceived a great number of roads, and did not know which to take to lead us to Charleroi. While we were in this embarrassment a peasant met us, of whom we asked the way to Charleroi. This peasant answered us, shrugging his shoulders, that he saw well enough we were strangers, and that our enterprise of going to Charleroi by the Ardennes was a very dangerous one, seeing that we did not know the roads, and it was almost impossible that we should follow the right one, as the farther we advanced, the more roads we should meet; and that as there was neither village nor house in this great wood, we should run the risk of so losing ourselves that we might wander about for twelve or fifteen days; that moreover the forest was full of ravenous animals, and that if the frost continued we might perish there of cold and hunger.

These words alarmed us, and made us offer the peasant a louis d'or if he would serve us as guide as far as Charleroi. " Not if you were to offer me a hundred," he said. " I see very well that you are Huguenots escaping from France, and I should be putting the rope round my own neck if I rendered you this service. But," said he, " I will give you a piece of good advice, leave the Ardennes, take the road which you see upon your left; you will arrive at a village (which he named), you will sleep there, and to-morrow morning continue your journey, keeping to the right of this village. You will then see the town of Rocroy, which you will leave upon your left, and pursuing your road, always to the right, you will arrive at Couvé, a small town; you will pass through it, and in leaving it will find a road to your left; follow it; it will lead you to Charleroi without peril.   The route by which I have directed you," continued this peasant, " is longer than that by the Ardennes, but it is without any danger."

We thanked this good man and took his advice. In the evening we arrived at the village of which he had spoken ; we slept there, and next morning found the road to the right ; we took it, leaving Rocroy to the left.   But the peasant had not told us, perhaps through ignorance, that this road led us straight to a gorge between two mountains, which was very narrow, and where there was a guard of French soldiers, who stopped all strangers who had no passports, and took them to prison at Rocroy.   We, like poor straying sheep, walked with rapid strides into the jaws of the wolf. However, without seeing or knowing the inevitable danger that we ran, we avoided it by the most favourable chance in the world ; for, at the very moment we entered this gorge, called the Guet du Sud, the rain fell so heavily that the sentinel on duty before the guard-house had gone into it for shelter, and we passed by very innocently, without being noticed, and pursuing our way arrived at Couvé.   At that moment we were safe, had we only known that this little town was not on French territory.   It belonged to the Prince of Liége, and contained a castle garrisoned by Dutch troops.   But alas ! to our great misfortune, we did not know this, for had we done so, we should have gone to this castle at once, the governor of which granted an escort to all refugees who requested it to conduct them to Charleroi.   But it was God's will that we should remain in this ignorance, so that our constancy and our faith should be put to trial during thirteen years of the most frightful misery in dungeons and in the galleys, as will be seen in the course of these memoirs.

We arrived then, as I said, at Couvé. We were wet to the skin. We entered an inn to dry ourselves and get something to eat. Having sat down to table, they brought us a pot of beer with two handles, without giving us any glasses. On asking for some, the host said that he perceived we were Frenchmen—for the custom of that country was to drink out of the pot. We at once conformed to it. But this request for glasses, which seemed a mere trifle and of no consequence, was, humanly speaking, the cause of our ruin; for in the same room with us were two men, one a citizen of the place, the other a gamekeeper of the Prince of Liége. The latter noticing the observation of the landlord, that he had perceived at once that we were Frenchmen, began to examine us very minutely, and at last made free to accost us, and declared that he was quite ready to lay a wager that we did not carry rosaries in our pockets. My companion, who was taking a pinch of snuff, showing him his snuff-box, said, very imprudently, that that was his rosary. This reply confirmed the gamekeeper in his opinion that we were Protestants escaping from France. And as the spoils of those who were arrested belonged to the informer, he conceived the design of having us arrested, if, in leaving Couvé, we passed by Mariembourg, a league

distant in the French territory. This was not our
intention, for, following the instruction of the good
peasant, in leaving Couvé we were to take a road to
the left, by which we should have avoided touching
upon any French territory. But who can avoid his
destiny? Going forth from Couvé we walked
along the road to the left, but perceiving in the distance an officer on horseback coming towards us,
we were afraid, as the least thing increases fear, lest
this officer should stop us, which made us turn
back and take the fatal road which led us to
Mariembourg. This town is small, and has only
one gate, so there is no passage through it. We
knew this, and resolved to leave it upon our right
and to proceed to Charleroi, keeping to the left, according to our previous plan. But we did not know
that the treacherous gamekeeper was following us
in the distance ready to pounce down on us. At
last we arrived before Mariembourg, and as it was
almost dark, and we saw an inn opposite the gate
of the town, we decided to stop there for the night.
We went in ; they gave us a room, and we had a
good fire made to dry ourselves. We had scarcely
been there half an hour when a man came in who
we thought was the landlord. He saluted us very
civilly, and then asked us whence we came and
whither we were going.

We told him that we came from Paris, and were
going to Philippeville. He said that we must go
and speak to the Governor of Mariembourg. We
thought to quiet him as we had done our host
at Mezières, but in this we deceived ourselves, for

he replied immediately, and sharply enough too, that we must follow him thither at once. We met this bad luck with a good heart, and, without showing any fear, prepared to follow him. Speaking in *patois* to my companion, so that the man should not understand, I said that as it was such a dark night we might escape from our conductor between the inn and the town ; so we followed the fellow whom we took for the landlord, but who was really a sergeant of the town guard accompanied by a detachment of eight soldiers with fixed bayonets, whom we found in the court-yard of the inn. At their head was the treacherous gamekeeper of Couvé; these soldiers seized us in such a way that it was impossible for us to escape. We were led to the governor, M. Pallier by name, who asked us what countrymen we were, and whither we were going. To the first question we told him the truth, but to the second we prevaricated, telling him that we were hairdressers' apprentices, and that we were making the circuit of France ; that our design was to go to Philippeville, from thence to Maubeuge, Valenciennes, Cambrai, etc., and thus to return to our own country. The governor had us examined by his valet, who knew something about a barber's work, and who fortunately began with my companion, who really was one. He was convinced that such was our business. The governor then asked us of what religion we were : we told him plainly that we were of the reformed religion, for on this question our conscience would not allow us to disguise the truth. Alas! that we were weak

C

and foolish enough not to tell the whole truth to the other questions which the governor asked us : for this may God pardon us ; for to be faithful followers of the Christian religion we ought never to lie. But such is the weakness of human nature, which never performs a good work perfectly. The governor having asked us whether our design was not in reality to leave the kingdom, we denied it.

After this examination, which lasted a good hour, the governor ordered the major to conduct us safely to prison, which he did with the escort which had arrested us. On the way from the government house to the prison, the major, named M. de la Salle, asked me if it were true that we were from Bergerac. I told him that indeed it was. "I was also born half a league from Bergerac," said he ; and having asked my name and my family, he exclaimed, "Why your father is my best friend ; be comforted my children," he added ; "I will get you out of this unhappy affair, and you will be free after two or three days." Thus discoursing he arrived at the prison. The gamekeeper asked the major to have us searched, that he might have his reward, believing that we had a great deal of money ; but all our capital consisted of about one pistole, which the major told us to give to him without having us searched. The major, who was touched with compassion at our unhappy fate, and who wished to be of service to us, feared lest we had much more money, which circumstance would have been to our detriment, as it would have been a sign that we wished to escape from the kingdom, for it is well known that wandering apprentices are not overburdened with cash. Besides, he feared that the wicked gamekeeper, of whom he had a perfect horror, because he caused us to be arrested, would receive from our spoils too lucrative a recompense for his perfidy. The major then, fearing this, would not have us searched, but kept the little money which we had given him, to remit it afterwards to the governor. The gamekeeper seeing that we were not searched, had the impudence to tell the major, " That was not the way Huguenots were treated when they fled to Holland. I shall know how to find their money," said he, attempting roughly to search us himself. " Rascal," said the major, " if you are not off at once, I'll have you well thrashed. Do you think you are going to teach me my duty?" At the same time he drove him from his presence. Such was the reward which this wretch received for all the trouble he had taken in causing us to be arrested, added to which, a few days after, the Prince of Liége, at the solicitation of the Dutch Governor of the Castle of Couvé, dismissed him from his service, and banished him from his dominions, on account of this wicked and treacherous action. A fit recompense for this worthless and cunning fellow.

We were now placed in a frightful dungeon. With tears in our eyes, we asked, " What crime have we committed, sir, that we should be treated as criminals who have deserved the gallows and the wheel?" " These are my orders, children," said the major, much affected, " but I will take care you don't sleep here!" He went immediately to give in his report to the governor, telling him that he had caused us to be very strictly searched, and that he had only found about a pistole on us, proving clearly enough that we had no design of leaving France, without reckoning other proofs which we had given him to the same effect, and that he thought it would be just and right to set us at liberty. But, unfortunately, it was the evening of the day on which the courier left for Paris, and while we were being conducted to prison, the governor had written to the court about our detention. Owing to this mischance, he could not now liberate us without an order from the court. The major was mortified at this obstacle, and entreated the governor to release us from this terrible and infamous dungeon, and to grant us the gaoler's house for our prison, promising to place a sentinel at the gates to watch us, and that he would be responsible, even to his head, that we did not escape. The governor acquiesced, and we had not been an hour in the dungeon when the major returned to the prison with a corporal and a sentinel, to whom he consigned us. He gave orders that we should have full liberty within the gaoler's house, and chose himself a bedroom for us. Moreover, he gave the little money which we had given up to him to the gaoler, ordering him to provide us with food as long as the money lasted, not wishing that we should appear to be criminals fed by the Government. He told us, with deep regret, that the governor had already written to the court about our detention, but that he would do his best with the governor that our *procès-verbal* should be favourable. The major's kind treatment consoled us a little.

Soon after, the governor sent our *procès-verbal* to the court ; it was strongly in our favour. But the declaration we had made that we were of the reformed religion, prejudiced the Marquis de la Vrillière, the minister of state, so strongly against us, that he would pay no attention to the remarks contained in this *procès-verbal*, which indicated that we had no intention of leaving the kingdom, and he ordered the Governor of Mariembourg to prose-cute us and condemn us to the galleys for being found on the frontiers without a passport. Mean-while the curé of Mariembourg was to use every effort to bring us back within the pale of the Roman Catholic Church. If he succeeded, after we had been instructed and had made an ab-juration, by the favour of the court, we might be set at liberty and brought back to Bergerac. The major had these instructions of the Marquis de la Vrillière read to us. "I shall give you no advice," he said to us, "as to what you ought to do ; your faith and your conscience must decide you. All that I can say is, that your abjuration will at once open the door of your prison, and that unless you make it, you will certainly go to the galleys." We replied, that we placed our whole confidence in God, and that we resigned ourselves to his holy will ; that we did not expect any human help ; and that by God's grace, which we should never cease to implore, we would never deny the Divine and true principles of our holy religion ; that he must not believe it was through obstinacy or infatuation that we continued steadfast ; that it was, thank God, through a firm conviction of the goodness of our cause, and that our parents had taken all possible care to instruct us in the truth of our religion and the errors of the Roman faith, that we might boldly profess the one, and avoid falling into the dangers of the other. We thanked him very affectionately for all the pains he had taken to be of service to us, and assured him that not being able by any other means to testify our gratitude, we would always pray to God for him. This good major, who was in his heart a Protestant like ourselves, though outwardly a Roman Catholic, tenderly embraced us, confessing that he felt less happy than we did, and left us weeping bitterly, entreating us not to think it unkind of him if he did not see us again, for he had not the courage to do so.

Our pistole which had been given to the gaoler was exhausted. They gave us a pound and a half of bread a day, the king's bread, but the governor and the major, by turns, sent us every day enough to eat and drink. The curé, who hoped to make proselytes of us, and the nuns of a convent in the town also, sent us occasionally things to eat ; so that we in our turn fed the gaoler and his family.

The curé came to visit us nearly every day, and gave us a controversial catechism to prove the truth of the Roman religion. We opposed to this the catechism of M. Drelincourt, which we had.

This curé was not very clever, and having found us quite masters of the subject, he soon desisted from his enterprise of converting us, for, having given us the alternative of discussing by tradition or by Holy Scripture, and we having chosen the latter, our friend found himself quite out of his depth, and, after three or four conferences, he gave up the attempt altogether. He then confined himself to tempting us with temporal advantages. He had a young and beautiful niece, whom he brought one day under the pretext of a charitable visit. He promised her to me in marriage, with a large dowry, if I would conform to her religion, making sure that if he gained me my companion would soon follow my example. But I had such a great dislike to all priests and their families, that I rejected his offer with contempt, which so greatly enraged him, that he went at once to declare to the governor and the judge that he had no longer any hope of our conversion ; that we were obstinate fellows, who would listen to neither proof nor reason ; and that we were reprobates under the influence of the devil.

Upon his deposition it was resolved to commit us for trial. The judge of the place and his registrar came to interrogate us judicially in the prison, and two days after our sentence was read to us, the substance of which was as follows :—" That being found upon the frontier without passports from the court, and that being of the pretended reformed religion, we were suspected and convicted of having intended to escape from the kingdom, against the ordinances of the king, who has forbidden it; and, as a punishment, we were therefore condemned to be taken to his majesty's galleys, to remain there in penal servitude for life, with confiscation of our property, etc."

Our sentence read, the judge asked us if we wished to appeal to the parliament of Tournay, in the jurisdiction of which the town of Mariembourg is situated. We replied that we would only appeal from his iniquitous sentence to the tribunal of God; that all men were against us; and that we looked to God alone, in whom we reposed our confidence, and who was a righteous Judge. "Do not, I pray you," said he, "attribute to me the rigour of your sentence; these are the king's orders which condemn you." " But, sir," said I, " the king does not know if I am suspected and convicted of intending to leave the kingdom; and the ordinance does not state that for professing the reformed religion one is sent to the galleys, it is only a conviction of the intention of escaping from the kingdom which condemns to this kind of punishment; but you, sir, have introduced into the sentence, *suspected and convicted of having intended to escape from the kingdom;* not only having no proof of this, but not even having examined if there was any." " What would you have?" said he. " It is a formality required to obey the king's orders." " No longer call yourself a judge, then," said I, " but simply an executor of the king's orders." " Appeal to the parliament," said he. " We will do nothing of the kind," we replied, " for we know well enough that the parliament is devoted to the king's orders, and that it will not examine the proofs in our favour any more than you have done." "Very well," said he, "then I must appeal for you." We knew this before, as no inferior judge can carry into execution a sentence which involves corporal punishment without its being ratified by parliament. "Therefore prepare," said the judge, "to start for Tournay." "We are ready for anything," we replied.

The same day they shut us up again in the dungeon, and we only left it to set out for Tournay, with four archers, who put fetters on our hands, and bound us together with cords. Our journey on foot was very painful. We went by Philippeville, Maubeuge, Valenciennes, and thence to Tournay. Every evening they placed us in the most frightful dungeons that they could find, giving us only bread and water, neither bed nor straw to rest on; and if we had deserved the wheel or the gallows, we could not have been treated more cruelly. At last, arrived at Tournay we were confined in the prison of the parliament. We had not a sous; and as no charitable person entered this prison to assist the prisoners, as is the custom in so many gaols, and having only a pound and a half of bread a day, we soon nearly died of hunger. The curé of the parish obtained the consent of the parliament that our act of indictment should not be revised till he had exercised his mission upon us, hoping, as he said, to convert us. But the curé, either by idleness or to constrain us

by famine, only came to see us every eight or
fifteen days, and then he spoke so little to us about
religion, that we had not even the trouble of de-
fending ourselves ; and when we wished to tell
him our sentiments upon the truths of the reformed religion, he cut us short. " Another time,"
said he, and off he went. Meanwhile we became
so thin and attenuated, that we could no longer
stand, and were obliged to lie down upon a little
damp straw, filled with vermin, close to the door of
our cell, through a hole in which our bread was
thrown to us as if we were dogs, for if we had
stayed farther away from the door we should not
have had the strength to go and take it, so weak
were we. In this extremity we sold to the turnkey,
for a little bread, our coats and waistcoats, as well as
a few shirts which we had, only reserving the one
which we wore, and which soon fell into rags. In
this state, the most miserable which can be imagined, we saw no one but the curé, who sometimes
paid us a visit, rather to mock us than to show us
any compassion. The object of his mission was to
ask us if we were not weary of suffering thus, and
to tell us that we were not to be pitied, since our
deliverance and welfare depended upon ourselves
and our renouncing the errors of Calvin. At last,
his discourses were so wearisome to us that we did
not deign to answer him.

Such was our situation in the prisons of the
parliament at Tournay during nearly six weeks ;
at the end of which, one morning, about nine
o'clock, the gaoler threw us a broom through

the door, telling us to sweep out our dungeon
well, as they were just about to bring two
gentlemen to keep us company. We asked him of
what they were accused. "They are," said he,
" Huguenots, like you ;" and then he left us. A
quarter of an hour afterwards the door of our cell
opened, and the gaoler and some soldiers armed
with swords and muskets, led into it two young
gentlemen covered with lace from head to foot.
As soon as this escort had thrust them into our cell
they shut the door and went away. We recognised
these gentlemen as being two of our fellow-towns-
men, sons of well-to-do citizens of Bergerac, with
whom we had been very intimate, having been
schoolfellows together. They on their part did
not recognise us, for the misery in which we were
made it absolutely impossible for any one to do
so. We were the first to salute them, calling
them by name. One was named Sorbier, the other
Rivasson. But they pretended to be nobles :
Sorbier called himself Chevalier, and Rivasson
Marquis, titles which they had assumed to facilitate
their escape from France. I think my reader will
be interested in hearing their story ; but before
relating it I must continue the account of what
occurred upon their entrance into our cell. Hearing
themselves addressed in our patois, they inquired
who we were ; we told them our names and our
country. They were very much astonished, and
told us that our relatives and friends, during the
six or seven months since we had left Bergerac,
hearing nothing of us, believed us to be dead or

assassinated on the road.   Indeed, since our detention we had not been allowed to write.   Then we
all four embraced each other, shedding abundance
of tears at the sad situation in which we found
ourselves.   These gentlemen asked us if we had
anything to eat, for they were hungry.   We gave
them our wretched morsel of bread intended for the
whole day and the pitcher of water for our drink.
"Good God!" they cried; "shall we be treated in
this manner? and cannot we by payment have something to eat and drink?"   "Certainly," said I, "for
money; but there is the difficulty; we have not
seen a coin for nearly three months."   "Oh, oh!"
said they, "if we can have what we want for money,
it is all right."   At the same time they cut the
seams of their belts and trowsers and the soles of
their shoes, and nearly 400 louis d'or fell out.   I
confess that I never felt greater joy than the sight
of the gold caused me, for I foresaw that we should
eat a good meal and no longer languish in hunger.
Our friends now gave me a coin, requesting me
to try and get something to eat.   I knocked with
all my strength at the door.   The gaoler came
and asked us what we wanted.   "To eat," I said
to him, "for money," giving him the louis d'or
at the same time.   "Very well, gentlemen," said
he, "what would you like to have?   Will you
have soup and boiled beef?"   "Yes, yes," said I;
"a good thick soup, and a 10-lb. loaf, and some
beer."   "You shall have it all in an hour," said he.
"In an hour!" I replied.   "What a long time!"
The two gentlemen could not help laughing at

my eagerness to get something to eat. At last the long-desired hour arrived. They brought us a thick cabbage soup, a dish of boiled beef, and a 10-lb. loaf. The two gentlemen ate very little; but as for my companion and myself, we fell upon the soup in such a ravenous manner that I suffered greatly in consequence, having so long been accustomed to a spare diet. An apothecary was sent for, who gave me an emetic, without which I should probably have died.

When I had recovered, they asked me through what bad luck we had been reduced to this miserable condition. I told them all which had passed since our departure from Bergerac up to the present time, just as it is written in these memoirs. They began to weep on account of their own weakness, confessing to us that they had resolved to abjure their religion rather than be condemned to the galleys. "What an example, gentlemen," said I, "do you bring us here! We should wish rather never to have seen you than to find you holding sentiments so opposed to the education which your parents gave you, and to the faith in which you have been instructed. Do you not tremble for fear of the just judgments of God, who declares that those who know their Master's will and do it not, shall be beaten with more stripes than those who are ignorant of it?" "What would you have us do?" they replied. "We cannot make up our minds to go to the galleys. You are very fortunate in having courage to do so, and we praise you for it; but speak no more about it—our resolution is taken." We could do nothing but lament and sigh over their weakness, and pray God to bring them to a better mind. We asked them to tell us their adventures since their departure from Bergerac, and the way in which they had been arrested, which Rivasson did as follows.

NARRATIVE

OF

MESSIEURS SORBIER AND RIVASSON.

———◆———

MY friend Sorbier and myself (said Rivasson) escaped from the Duke de la Force's great persecution by flying into the country, where we remained concealed ; and as the duke at his departure left very strict orders against us, we saw no other way to avoid falling into our enemy's hands than by flight into Holland. For this purpose we sent for a famous and experienced guide from Amsterdam, who gained his livelihood by these perilous enterprises ; for if these guides are captured they are hanged without mercy. He was cunning and adroit, very prudent, and had the map of all the roads and bye-ways at his fingers' ends. He was generally called the Gasconnet, for he was, in fact, of Gascon origin. The Gasconnet having arrived at Bergerac, we made arrangements for our departure. Our parents, who consented to our flight, gave us as much money as they could, that we might not suffer want in foreign countries. We dressed ourselves as officers going to rejoin their regiment near Valenciennes. The Gasconnet passed as our valet. In this way we crossed France without the least obstacle. The Gasconnet went on foot and we on horseback ; but as a precaution he rarely kept close to us on the road; he directed us to the inns where we were to dine or sleep, in which places he never failed to meet us. Thus we arrived at Paris, where we stopped a few days to see the curiosities of that fine city. One day at Versailles we met an officer of our acquaintance who had married a Protestant lady of Bergerac, though he was a Papist himself. This lady had two brothers, refugees abroad ; and as the king's agents had confiscated their property because of their escape, this captain, named De Maison, was petitioning the court that it might be made over to him. We greeted him ; he treated us to good cheer, and so succeeded in gaining our confidence that we told him the secret of our flight from the kingdom. He applauded our design in order to extract from us all the particulars of our enterprise, which we candidly related to him. We separated from him at Paris, when we started for Valenciennes.

De Maison wished us a successful journey, and professed great friendship for us on parting. But the treacherous fellow took the road to Versailles ; and in order to gain favour with M. de la Vrillière, minister of state, and thus have a better chance of obtaining what he was soliciting from the court, he discovered our flight to this minister, with the exact route which we were to take as far as Mons, where we hoped to be in safety, it being a town of the Spanish Netherlands with a Dutch garrison. The minister did not fail at once to despatch a

courier to Quievrain, between Valenciennes and
Mons. Quievrain belongs to France; and here
there is a bridge across a little river which forms
the boundary of France and the Spanish Netherlands. As there was no garrison in this place,
the minister ordered the mayor to have this bridge
guarded by peasants, with orders that when two
officers and their valet, who said they belonged to
the regiment of La Marche, and were going to join
their garrison, presented themselves there, they
should be arrested at once and led to prison at
Valenciennes. The Mayor of Quievrain assembled
his well-armed peasants and placed a guard of
twenty-five men at the head of the bridge on the
French side. We were in perfect ignorance of what
was going on at Quievrain. Our guide assured us
that we had no danger to fear there ; and he was
right in one sense ; for had it not been for the
treason of the perfidious De Maison we should have
passed through without any obstacle.

Well, in the obscurity of the evening we arrived at
this fatal bridge. The sentinel of the guard cried out,
" Who's there ?" " Officers of the king," we replied.
" Of what regiment ?" he asked. " Of the regiment
of La Marche." " Halt, then," said the sentinel.
At the same time the whole guard, with guns
pointed at us in good order, barred the entrance to
the bridge. Our guide, surprised at this unprece-
dented opposition, encouraged us, saying that our
safety depended on passing this bridge, for once on
the other side of the river, we were undoubtedly
saved, for we should then be on Spanish territory,

where France could in no way molest us. Animated with this hope, we then seized our pistols. The guide having jumped on my horse behind, we fired several pistol shots at the peasants without however wounding any of them ; nevertheless a panic seized them ; each fearing for his life, they fled precipitately, leaving us masters of the bridge, which we now crossed. Our guide congratulated us, assuring us that we were now as safe as if we were at Amsterdam. As part of the town of Quievrain is situated on that side of the river where we now were, we entered an inn to lodge for the night. We supped very merrily, and we all then went to bed in an upper room. Next morning our guide got up very early, as was his habit, and putting his head out of the window to see what sort of weather it was, beheld more than one hundred armed peasants who surrounded the house. Surprised at this apparition, he came to wake us in great alarm. When we heard this terrible news, we jumped out of bed, and when I looked through the window and saw what the guide had told us of, I felt inclined to break the poor man's head, thinking that he had betrayed us, and led us into the jaws of the wolf. But the poor fellow fell on his knees, imploring my mercy, and swearing that we should be soon convinced that it was not his fault, and that certainly some recent change in these states must have taken place.

During this conversation, the landlord of the inn came up to our chamber and informed us that these peasants who surrounded the inn were about to arrest us by the order of the king. " What king ?" said I. " Of the King of France," replied he. " How, of the King of France ?" I inquired, " we are not in his dominions." The landlord perceived at once our ignorance of what had occurred during the last four or five days, viz., that the French, by the consent of the King of Spain, had taken possession of the whole Spanish Netherlands in one day and at the same hour ; that they had entered all the towns, and driven out the Dutch. This event happened in 1701, as everybody knows. Our landlord told us of it, and we at once confessed that our guide had not been in the wrong. We took counsel to consider what could be done in such imminent danger. We determined to ask the commander of these peasants, from our window, what he wanted. He was the mayor of the village. On demanding his business, he replied, " To arrest you, gentlemen, by order of the King of France, and take you prisoners to Valenciennes." " But here we are in the district of Mons," said we. " Yes," said the mayor ; " but lately everything is changed, and the French are at Mons as well as at Valenciennes, and I must obey the orders of the King of France, to conduct you to Valenciennes." " You will do nothing of the kind," said we ; " and you will only have us as dead men, after selling our lives very dearly." " You will die then of hunger, gentlemen," he replied, " for we shall not take you by assault ; but no food will be given you till you surrender." We fired some pistol shots upon the peasants, but without effect, for they took refuge in the lower part of the house, so that we were obliged to suspend our operations, seeing no enemy to attack.

In this extremity, upon reflection that we must yield sooner or later, we thought it best to know what was the nature of the order of the king for our arrest, so we called the mayor and assured him that he had nothing to fear, that he could come up alone and unarmed to our chamber to show us his orders, to which he consented, and came up to the top of the staircase and opened the *lettre de cachet* which contained the king's orders. But when he began to read, my friend Sorbier very imprudently, and contrary to our word of honour given to the mayor not to do him any injury, fired a pistol-shot at him, which happily only pierced his hat which he held in his hand, and burned and rent in pieces the king's *lettre de cachet*. The mayor descended, or rather tumbled down the steps, much faster than he had come up, and excited by my friend's act, which I avow was a most unworthy one, as he, too, thinks at present, the mayor swore to give us no quarter nor favour.

He posted his men in such a manner that it was impossible for us to force a passage through. After having skirmished for nearly an hour without any results, we began to reflect that seeing no way to save ourselves, we must negotiate to obtain the most favourable capitulation under the circumstances. For this purpose we called for the mayor, who came to the foot of the stairs, fearing a second insult. We told him that being in the district of Mons, he must send an express to the governor of that town (who was a Spaniard—there was only a French commandant for the French garrison), and that if this governor thought it right to have us brought to that town we would yield, otherwise we would rather be cut to pieces, or die of hunger, than surrender.

The mayor reflecting that as we were in the department of Mons, it was, in some sense, his duty to inform the governor of our arrest, despatched an express with all haste. The governor, vexed that the French had given such orders within his jurisdiction, without asking his permission, sent a detachment of ten horsemen, under a lieutenant, who commanded them, to Quievrain. The lieutenant was very civil to us, and, according to his orders, discharged the mayor from his commission to take us to Valenciennes, and conducted us to Mons himself. The governor was most friendly to us, assuring us that he would only surrender us to France by the order of the King of Spain, and that he would send a courier immediately to petition his Catholic Majesty in our favour. Meanwhile, we were well guarded. The French court was not backward in urging that of Madrid to surrender us into its power. But through the governor's solicitation the balance turned in our favour; the King of Spain consented, indeed, that we should be given up to the King of France, but on the condition that we should not be rigorously treated, only punished by a few months in prison, after which we were to be sent back at liberty to the place of our birth. And it was arranged that the Governor of Mons should have us sent to the castle of Ham, in Picardy, to be imprisoned there for a short time, according to this convention.

Our guide was not included in the convention ; but it was agreed that he was to share our fate. The governor having received these orders, communicated them to us. You can well imagine the joy with which we heard this decision. The governor sent us with an escort of six horsemen to Ham. We were placed in the hands of the governor of this place, who gave us the castle for our prison, and was so kind to us that we dined every day at his table, and our guide ate with his servants.

We expected to remain prisoners in this castle a few months, according to the convention. But we were sadly deceived when, at the end of three weeks, the governor received orders of the court to send us, under a good escort, to the prisons of the parliament at Tournay, till we should take our trial there. The good governor, with whom we had contracted a great friendship, was so sensibly touched by our misfortune, that he could not adequately express to us the grief which he felt. He took us aside, and told us that he consoled himself with the thought that we had two doors of escape open to us from this trouble. The first, that we had only to become Roman Catholics ; as to the second, it was contrary to his duty to tell us what it was, but that we should find it out in time, and perceive how willing he was to be of service to us. We understood very well that he meant to give us an opportunity to escape on the road, which was confirmed by the way he afterwards acted, and that we had only to profit by it. Before leaving Ham, my friend and I held counsel together as to whether we should try to escape or change our religion. We decided on the latter course, considering the dangers we should run in trying to escape from France, our previous experience of which made us tremble. In a word, our courage and our faith abandoned us, and we formed the firm resolution of allowing ourselves to be led like lambs to Tournay, and then to make our abjuration. The day after this resolution, the Governor of Ham chose from among his garrison, which was composed of a company of pensioners, the escort which he gave us, and which consisted of an old and decrepit sergeant and three soldiers, of whom one had only one arm, and the other two were completely lame. He particularly charged the sergeant not to let the guide escape. "As to these two gentlemen," said he, "they have no notion for making the attempt, it is a pure formality conducting them with a detachment to Tournay. They would go themselves without an escort, as it is to their own advantage." After these instructions, he embraced us, wishing us every possible good fortune on our journey. "Profit, gentlemen," he said, "by any opportunities which appear advantageous to you, and let me hear from you if you can. I shall with pleasure receive good tidings of you." We

very well understood what was hidden beneath
these words, but our determination was fixed to
become Roman Catholics. The governor gave us
each a good horse, whilst our lame guards walked
with the guide, who was manacled and bound with
cords.   In fact, Sorbier and I performed this journey as if it were a party of pleasure. We often
made our horses gallop to the right and the left,
and out of sight of our guards, who did not trouble
themselves about it, for all their attention was
turned upon the poor guide. You see how easily
it would have been for us to have escaped without
trouble or risk, but we never thought of it.   It was
not the same with our guide; he never lost an
opportunity, whether in the road or in the inns
where we lodged, when he thought he should not
be overheard by the guards, to supplicate us with
clasped hands and tears in his eyes to have compassion upon him and upon ourselves, and to profit
by the frequent opportunities which presented themselves for all three of us to escape.

"I cannot do it alone," said he, "bound and
manacled as I am ; but if you will only aid me a
little, I shall be able to make myself master of the
sergeant, and as to the other three soldiers, they
would submit at the least threat you made to them.
Reflect, gentlemen, if I am brought to Tournay,
I shall be hanged without mercy." We paid no
heed to his supplications, for, having no desire
to make our own escape, we did not wish to make
ourselves more guilty by facilitating his. Passing
through Valenciennes, we were led by a soldier of

the guard to the governor's house, as is the custom in garrison towns. M. Magaloti, the governor, having heard our case, said, " That is only a trifle, gentlemen ; you will wash it all away with a little holy water, and by going to mass." Then, perceiving the guide, he at once recognised him. " Ah ! it is you, Gasconnet, is it ?" said he. " You have been a long time spinning your rope." And then, addressing our sergeant, he said, "My friend, you and your detachment are not fit to conduct that sly rogue to Tournay. Last year he was condemned to be hanged in this town, but the rascal escaped from our strong prison the night before the execution. It will be best to strengthen your detachment by a few grenadiers, for I am afraid he will escape from you." The sergeant, piqued at this remark, replied that he had conducted quite as cunning fellows as Gasconnet, and that the Governor of Ham had considered him quite capable of undertaking this expedition. "Very well," said M. de Magaloti ; " only take good care of him."

The next morning we started with our usual detachment for Tournay, which is seven leagues from Valenciennes. As it was too long a distance for our escort on foot to perform in the day, we arrived in the evening at St. Arnaud, a little walled town, two leagues from Tournay. Here, just at the end of our journey, the Gasconnet succeeded, by a clever trick, and without any assistance on our part, in making his escape during the night. Our escort made ineffectual efforts to recapture him, and then came to us very crestfallen and downcast, not knowing what to do. They proposed that we should do as we liked ; as for them, they had no wish either to go to Tournay or to return to their garrison, fearing to be summoned before a court-martial, and to receive a severe punishment. But we, who were as eager to go to Tournay as they were to avoid it, dissuaded them from this resolution, and wrote at once an exaggerated declaration in their favour, which we signed. They were content with this, and so were we, and they brought us this morning, as you see, to this prison (said M. Rivasson), where we hope not to make a long stay.

Such was the story which M. Rivasson related to us. I will continue the remainder of it up to their deliverance at Lille, of which we were witnesses. Two days after the arrival of these gentlemen in our dungeon, they were summoned to appear before the parliament. They were questioned very leniently. After which the president asked them if they wished to change their religion, and to become good Roman Catholics. They did not hesitate to say that they desired it with all their hearts. "Very well," said he ; "you shall be instructed in order to make your abjuration, after which we will proceed to your deliverance." They were then sent back to our dungeon, delighted at having taken this step, which promised them in a short time not only their liberty, but some recompense from the court as the price of their abjuration, which several of the councillors of the parliament had led them to expect. They never ceased congratulating themselves in our presence, and we did not cease to detest their cowardice and their apostacy. But a few hours had passed since their return to our cell when the chaplain of the parliament entered, and after having highly praised their pious intention, put into their hands a catechism, telling them that their release depended on their diligence in learning it by heart, and then took leave of them. Day and night they studied, till at the end of three days they ceased their studies by a fatal mischance for them ; for two huissiers of the parliament came to take them before the Criminal Court. The huissiers put fetters on their hands, which we thought augured no good ; but they were not affected by it, persuading themselves that it was only a formality of justice. They appeared then before the assembly of the parliament, when the president at once addressed them : " Gentlemen, three days ago, you promised before this assembly to abjure your errors, and to embrace the Roman Catholic religion ; in consequence of which we promised you your deliverance. We do not wish to deceive you. We are no longer in a condition to be able to set you at liberty. It is this," said he, showing them a *lettre de cachet,* " which prevents us. The court orders us to prosecute you rigorously for breach of the ordinance which prohibits attempts at escape from the kingdom, and you are very fortunate that there is no mention made of your imprudent conduct at Quievrain, where you fired a pistol-shot at the *lettre de cachet* containing the order for your arrest.

The king's orders command us to condemn you to the galleys, without any reference to the action which you committed at Quievrain, for in that case the punishment would have been still more severe. Thus, gentlemen, whether you make your abjuration or not, it is the king's wish that you should be condemned to the galleys for life. It is, however, free to you to make your abjuration ; we shall indeed praise so pious an action, but at the same time we declare to you that it will not save you from going to the galleys." Upon which these gentlemen replied that if such was the state of affairs, they would give up the design of making their abjuration. "Good Catholics!" replied the president, and he ordered them to be taken back to their cell. We beheld our former would-be proselytes return with an air of extreme consternation, making pitiful lamentations, and remorseful reflections upon their weakness in every respect. The parliament expedited their prosecution, and in less than a week their sentence was read, condemning them to the galleys for life. The day after four archers came to conduct them to Lille, in Flanders, where the chain of galley slaves assembled. It was a strange and pitiful sight to see these gentlemen, all laced and in scarlet coats, manacled and bound with cords, traversing on foot, between the four archers, the large town of Tournay, which they could scarcely get through on account of the large concourse of people assembled in the streets to see this tragic occurrence, for every one firmly believed that these two gentlemen belonged to the highest nobility in France. Thus, on foot, were they conducted to Lille, five leagues from Tournay. They were placed in the dreadful dungeon of the galley slaves, in the town of St. Pierre, which frightful prison I will describe in its proper place. These gentlemen, however, did not remain there long. The Jesuits of Lille (for these fathers know everything) came to visit them, and having asked them whether they would become Roman Catholics, if in such case they could obtain their pardon from the court, they consented at once. Upon this the Jesuits requested the provost of Lille, who had charge of the galley slaves, to give these gentlemen up to their convent, to be instructed there and make their solemn abjuration, guaranteeing that after this ceremony they would deliver them back to prison. The provost willingly consented. Thus these weak and lukewarm souls again fell into apostacy.

They were three weeks with the Jesuits. These fathers, after having instructed them in the principles of the Roman religion, and having made them utter the most horrible blasphemies against the reformed faith, and the most fearful imprecations against Calvin and his doctrines, obliged them to make a public and very pompous abjuration, having invited to it the *elite* of the garrison of Lille, and all the persons of consideration in the town. After this they brought them back to the prison, not to the dungeon of the galley slaves, but into a comfortable and well furnished room, which cost six pistoles a month with board, all at the expense of the Jesuits, or, rather, of those people of distinction in the town among whom these good fathers made a collection for that purpose. Next they petitioned the court for their pardon, thinking to get it by main force. But they were deceived in this, for the king flatly refused, and ordered that the sentence should be rigorously carried out. The Jesuits did not rest here. They moved heaven and earth to obtain the pardon. Their solicitations reached Madame de Maintenon. To this lady they exaggerated, saying that these gentlemen belonged to one of the highest noble families in Perigord, that their offence at Quievrain, which had so incensed the king, was rather an act of youthful folly, than a premeditated design to insult his majesty, and finally that these two gentlemen were the two best Catholics in France. This lady, thus persuaded by the Jesuits, asked their pardon from the king, who granted it to her with an infantry lieutenant's commission for Rivasson, and one in the dragoons for Sorbier ; but, at the same time, with this restriction towards the latter, that he should remain in prison six weeks after the pardon, while his friend was set at liberty immediately. It appeared that the most guilty was the best rewarded, for a lieutenancy of dragoons is worth more than one in the infantry ; but perhaps the king considered Sorbier's audacity fitting to the dragoons—at least such was the judgment passed upon the affair at Lille. Rivasson kept his friend company during his six weeks in prison, although he was free to go out when he

wished ; but he desired to show this mark of generosity to his friend, which everybody praised and
approved of. When the six weeks had expired,
they were set at liberty, visited their friends and
benefactors, and set off for their regiments. Afterwards we learned that they were both killed at the
battle of Hekeren. Such was the end of these two
gentlemen, whose honourable death, in my opinion,
is the only glorious incident in their history.

Persons of talent and penetration who read this
narrative may find food in it for just and useful reflection, in considering the conduct of MM. Rivasson and
Sorbier, and the judgments of God, who sooner or
later punishes scandalous crimes, especially that of
apostacy, which is the most atrocious of all those
which can be committed against his Divinity. For
myself, I am content with writing down the facts
simply and truthfully, leaving to each of my
readers to form his judgment as he pleases. I now
resume the thread of my narrative, as regards my
dear companion in suffering and myself.

[The Autobiography is here resumed.]

ORBIER and Rivasson prevented us from dying of hunger, as I have already said. We knew that they had plenty of money, and the fear that we should be again reduced to starvation after their departure, made me supplicate them with clasped hands to leave us three or four louis d'or. I told them that I would write out an order, so that my father would repay them at Bergerac. But they were so hard-hearted that they would only leave us half a louis, which I gave back to them when we met in the prisons of Lille, in Flanders, a few days before their release. We economised this half louis d'or extremely, eating nothing but bread. However, we had no time to spend it in the parliament prison, for we were transferred to the prison of the town, named Le Beffroi, for the following reasons :

The river Scheldt traverses the town of Tournay. On the south side of this river stands the parliament house, and this side is in the diocese of the Archbishopric of Cambrai ; the other part of the town, to the north of the river, is in that of the Bishop of Tournay. I have already said that the curé of the parish in which the prison was situated sometimes came to visit us, rather to see if our opinions on religion were changing, than to exhort us by good reasons to renounce them. The Bishop of Tournay having heard of the indifference, or, rather, the negligence and ignorance of this curé in converting

us, sent one of his chaplains to visit us. This chaplain was a good old priest, who had more honesty
than theology—at least so it seemed to us—for
after having told us that he was sent by the bishop,
he added, "it was in order to convert you to the
Christian religion." We replied that we were
Christians, both by baptism and by our faith in
the Gospel of Jesus Christ. "What!" said he,
"you are Christians? And what are your names?"
taking his tablets, in which our names were written,
out of his pocket, thinking he had made some
mistake. We told him our Christian names and
surnames. "It is you indeed!" said he, "to whom I
am sent; but you are not what I thought, for you
say that you are Christians, and his lordship sent
me to convert you to Christianity. Repeat to me,
if you please, the articles of your faith." "Very
willingly, sir," said I, and at the same time I repeated the Apostles' Creed. "What!" cried he,
"you believe that?" and having replied in the
affirmative, "And I too," said he; "his lordship
the bishop has been trying to make an April-fool
of me,"—for that day was in fact the 1st of April,
1701. He took leave of us very quickly, much put
out that his bishop should have played such a trick
on a man of his age and character. My readers
may judge whether this good ecclesiastic had
studied and examined the different sects of Christianity. However that might be, we saw him no
more. But the next day the bishop sent us his
grand vicar, M. Regnier, a very different kind of
theologian from the good old chaplain. He found

E

us better instructed in the evidences of the reformed religion and in the errors of the Roman Church than he had expected, for which reason he took the matter all the more to heart, determined, as he said, to convert us. Scarcely a day passed that he did not visit us. He was an acute rhetorician, full of sophistry, wishing only to argue from tradition, as we did only from Holy Scripture ; thus it was impossible to come to any conclusion, so that he always retired without having made any progress in his object. In other respects he was a very good man, full of probity and Christian charity. I remember that having noticed that we were in want of linen and clothing, and even of necessary food, he secretly gave us linen without wishing us to know that it came from him; and being the Holy Week, during which the bishop bestowed charity on the prisoners, the grand vicar came to the parliament prison, and visiting all the prisoners, of which there was a large number, he gave them each two coins from the bishop. He then came to our cell, and after requesting us, on the part of the bishop, to accept his generosity, as a mark of esteem and distinction, he made us a present of four louis d'or. We felt some difficulty in accepting them, but as he begged us so kindly to take them, representing to us that his lordship would consider our refusal as a mark of pride, it was impossible for us to refuse, and in truth this assistance came very opportunely to help us in our great necessity.

I have said before that the curé of the parish

sometimes came to visit us. One day he found the grand vicar with us. He was much offended at this, asking him how he dared to come into his parish to perform duties which only belonged to the curé of the place. The grand vicar replied very modestly that he came there for the same reasons as he did, to bring back the lost sheep into the Saviour's fold. "I can bring them back well enough without you," answered the curé rudely, "and his grace of Cambrai will never allow you to intrude into his diocese. I order you in his name to leave the place at once, and never venture to return to it." The grand vicar in fact departed, and did not return; but having told the affair to his bishop, the latter requested the procureur-general of the parliament to transfer us to the prisons of the town, which were in his diocese: this request was at once granted.

Here we were then in the prison of the Beffroi, where we were much better off than in that of the parliament. Many Protestants, respectable citizens of Tournay, had permission to visit us. They "greased the paw," as the expression is, of the gaoler, who at their solicitation opened our cell-door every morning that we might take the air in a small court-yard close by for several hours, often till the evening. There our zealous friends frequently came to see us, consoling us as much as they could, and exhorting us to perseverance. The grand vicar, Regnier, often met them there, but without taking the least offence at it; on the contrary, he was very civil to them; and when, out of

respect, these charitable persons were about to
retire, he at once and very kindly begged them to
remain and listen to our conversation; and I make
bold to say that these good Protestants were
delighted to hear the manner in which, by God's
grace, we were able to defend ourselves in these
controversies, as well as by the gentleness and be-
nignity with which the grand vicar explained to us
his pretended evidences in favour of his religion.
Often after an hour or two of discussions which
settled nothing, he had a bottle of wine brought in,
and we drank together as good friends, without
speaking of controversy.   Finally, after having discussed all the points by which we thought to prove
to him the errors of the Roman religion, he proposed to us a plan of conversion to decide our
disputes.   "We will dispense with our belief," said
he, " in the greater part of those doctrines which
seem to you to be errors, such as the invocation
of saints and of the Virgin, respect for images,
belief in a purgatory, faith in indulgences and
pilgrimages, if you will only submit to believe
faithfully in transubstantiation and the sacrifice
of the mass, and will abjure the errors of Calvin."
But we gave him to understand that we saw the
slippery step which he proposed to us, and that we
should never be the dupes of it.   After this he
gradually diminished his visits, so that he only
came to see us every week or fortnight, and at last
he let us quite in peace, and since then neither
priest nor monk has come to trouble us, which has
given us much pleasure.

One day, about nine in the morning, our gaoler put five persons into our cell, and then retired. We looked at each other, and soon recognised three of these gentlemen as being from Bergerac, but we did not know the other two, who burst into tears on embracing us, as each of the three first did, calling us by name, and appearing to know us intimately. Surprised at not knowing these two persons, who did not cease to embrace us, and to lament our condition as much as their own, we asked Sieur Dupuy, who was one of the three, who these two persons unknown to us were. "One," said he, "is Mademoiselle Madras, and the other Mademoiselle Conceil, of Bergerac, your good friends, who have exposed themselves to the perilous journey of escaping from France with us, in men's attire, as you now see them, and who have endured the fatigue of this painful journey on foot with a firmness and constancy extraordinary for persons brought up in refinement, and who previous to this expedition would not have been able to walk a league." We saluted these two ladies, but represented to them the impropriety of their remaining thus disguised, and continuing in the same cell with five young men, which our enemies would certainly magnify into a scandalous crime. I begged them to allow me to acquaint the gaoler with their disguise, which could in no way serve them at present, and that they ought now to declare their names and sex, and confess the truth with firmness and constancy. The gentlemen were of my opinion, and the ladies consented. I called the gaoler, and having told him about it, he made these ladies leave our cell, put them into a private room, and told the judge, who gave them clothes suitable to their sex. We have not seen them since, for they were condemned for the remainder of their days to the convent of the "Repentants," at Paris, to which they were taken at the same time that their three companions in suffering were condemned to the galleys for attempting to escape the kingdom.

After mingling our lamentations and regrets with those of these three gentlemen, named Dupuy, Mouret, and La Venue, we begged them to tell us the history of their flight, which Dupuy did as follows :—

"Nothing particular occurred to us after our departure from Bergerac ; with a good guide, we crossed France without any accident or obstacle till we came to the passage of the Scheldt, two leagues from Tournay, where we were arrested through the treachery of a wretched peasant, in whom both our guide and ourselves had trusted to convey us across the river.

"When we arrived near the river Scheldt, which separates France from the Spanish Netherlands, our guide took us for the night to the house of a peasant of his acquaintance, who made it his business to convey the refugees across the river in a little boat. This peasant was delighted to see what a windfall had come to him, for we agreed each to pay him in advance two louis d'or to take us over the river. He gave us something to eat whilst we waited for a fit time to cross, as just then it was not safe on account of the patrols who were walking along the banks of the Scheldt. The peasant noticing a gay mantle of good material which M. Mouret wore, coveted it, and asked him for it. Mouret said he would not give him that mantle for anything in the world, because it belonged to his father, who was a refugee at Amsterdam, and he was looking forward to the pleasure of bringing it to him. The peasant made many entreaties for this mantle, but Mouret constantly refused him. This fatal mantle, indeed, was the cause of our ill fortune; for the peasant, out of spite at this refusal, formed the resolution of having us arrested, in which he succeeded only too well, and this is how he managed it.

" He amused us in his house till about midnight, after which he told us to follow him to the place where the boat was. We did so, our hearts full of joy at the prospect of being so soon in safety. This villain led us to an inn, which was not far from his house, telling us that we must still wait a little longer while he took his boat to the spot whence we were to cross the river. We were all in a room of this inn ; our guide, who was with us, suspected nothing, no more than ourselves. The peasant remained absent a good hour, at the end of which he entered the room, and, taking the guide aside, went out with him, and made him cross to the other side of the river. Then he returned accompanied by a score of armed peasants, who arrested us and brought us here."

Such is the story of the detention of these gentlemen. But whilst I am upon this subject, I must relate how this peasant, named Batiste, received the just reward of his perfidy in the town of Tournay.

At that time a great deal of smuggling took place, almost daily, between the towns of Ath and Tournay. Batiste and one of his comrades, hearing that a tradesman of Tournay was coming from Ath with a cart laden with smuggled goods, determined to waylay and stop him. They pointed their muskets at his head, and threatened to take him to the custom-house, where his goods would be confiscated. He offered them ten pistoles if they would let him go on his way. This was just what these vagabonds wanted. They received the money and went off. But it happened that the cart was stopped by the douaniers at the gates of Tournay, and its contents confiscated. The tradesman, now that he had lost his goods, thought only of vengeance upon these two peasants who had robbed him on the high road. He denounced them to M. Lambertie, the Grand Provost of Flanders, who sent to arrest these two wretches, and they were brought to the prisons of the Beffroi, but not into our cell. The provost had known for some time that Batiste was a villain capable of committing all sorts of crimes, and he suspected him of favouring the Protestants in the passage of the Scheldt, in order to get money from them, a crime punishable with death. Hoping, therefore, to get him convicted for robbery and violence against the tradesman, and have him broken alive upon the wheel, he summoned him and questioned him very strictly. But Batiste, who was a cunning rogue, knew his lesson very well, and cleverly defended himself against the accusation of highway robbery, alleging that every one ought to act as he had done, that the laws promised a reward to all informers, and that, in truth, he and his companion had no other intention than that of merely informing against the trades-man, but that he, of his own accord, without being asked, had tempted them by his present of ten pistoles, and that out of gratitude they had allowed him to continue his way. The provost was disappointed in his hope of being able to condemn this bad fellow to death, for his defence had such a plausible air, that they were obliged to give up prosecuting him for the crime. But a circum-stance occurred connected with this affair which I must now narrate.

Soon after the arrest of the three gentlemen and two ladies, of whom I have already spoken, they underwent their trial before the magistrates of the town of Tournay; and whilst they were waiting for the parliament to confirm their sentence to the galleys, a space of five or six weeks, they were left in our cell. During this time the gaoler often came to smoke his pipe with us, and one day, in the course of conversation, Dupuy told him the story of their capture through the perfidy of Batiste. He told him, too, how this wretch had mentioned the names of several of their fellow-countrymen and acquaintance whom he had taken over in his boat,

praising them very much for having paid him so
well; also how, before having them arrested, he
had sent his good friend the guide over the river,
either through friendship, or, what is more probable,
lest the guide should accuse him for his wicked
practices.   However that might be, Batiste, according to the laws of France, deserved death,
had he committed no other crime than that
of taking the guide across the Scheldt.   Now it
happened that the provost, in descending to the
chamber where he held his tribunal, spoke to the
gaoler, enjoining him to guard Batiste very strictly
in one of the strongest cells, while he sought proofs
of certain crimes of which the wretch was suspected.
The gaoler told him at once that he could have
certain proofs that Batiste had often taken persons
of the reformed religion across the Scheldt, who
were flying from the kingdom, informing him of
what Dupuy and his companions, who were still
in prison, had said.   The provost was delighted
to get such a deposition.   He soon after came to
our cell, and told those gentlemen that at ten o'clock
the next morning he would cite them to appear
before his tribunal, to tell the truth upon their oath
on the subject of this Batiste, by whose means they
had been arrested.   "But, gentlemen, I exhort
you," he added, "not to cherish in your hearts any
sentiment of vengeance against this wretched man,
but to tell the pure truth when you are asked."
After this he retired.   The three gentlemen at
first appeared delighted at the idea of being able to
avenge themselves on Batiste by declaring all they

knew. At first I was of the same way of thinking, but then, having reflected upon the consequences of their deposition, I changed mind, and told them so, as follows :—

"It is certain, gentlemen, that if you tell the whole truth on the subject of Batiste, he will be hanged without mercy; but, I pray you, let us consider two things which will result from it. In the first place, it will do you no honour among our friends, and will be a subject of reproach on the part of our enemies, for both one and the other will conclude that there was love of revenge in your action, for every one is naturally inclined to speak evil of his neighbour. In the second place, you will commit an act of injustice in having this rascal hanged, for then you will cause the death of a man who, according to Protestants, has not committed any crime in facilitating the escape of our brethren ; for when any one performs this service for us, we pay him as meriting a recompense, not for his trouble, but for the risks which he runs in rendering us this service, which is regarded by the Papists as a crime worthy of death, and by the Protestants as a virtue worthy of a reward. However sincere and truthful your deposition may be, it will expose you to this, which, if you take my advice, you will avoid." "But," exclaimed they, "are we to perjure ourselves to save this man's life, and avoid the two dangers which you have shown us ?" "No," said I, "for no reason in the world ought you to perjure yourselves." "What is to be done then ?" said they. "It is that which embarrasses me," I replied. "However, I have an idea in my head, but I do not know whether it can be carried into execution, not being sufficiently acquainted with the laws of civil and criminal procedures. I have been told that the witness borne by a man condemned to the galleys is invalid, and no magistrate nor judge can force him to give any testimony upon oath. In your place, then, I should try to avoid bearing witness on oath, alleging as a reason to the grand provost what I have just said, that a galley slave is incapacitated from performing such an act. If I am wrong, and they can, according to law, force you to tell the truth upon oath, well, then you must tell the truth. To my mind that would be a proof that you ought to do so; at least this course of conduct will prevent you from being accused of desiring vengeance, since it will be seen that you only bear witness against Batiste because you are forced to do it."

This advice was approved and followed. The next morning, at ten o'clock, the gaoler and two huissiers came to conduct these gentlemen before the provost and his councillors assembled. In the criminal dock, bound and fettered, sat the miserable Batiste, more dead than alive, at the sight of those on whom his life depended, and who had so great reason to revenge themselves for the treachery he had been guilty of. The provost first asked him if he knew these gentlemen. He first said he did not. "We will make you know them well enough," replied the provost, asking these gentlemen at the same time if they knew the criminal. They answered that they recognised in him the man who had caused their arrest. "Lift up your hand," said the provost, "and swear before God and the Law to answer the truth to the interrogations put to you." They replied boldly that they would do nothing of the kind, for that, by their sentence to the galleys, they were placed out of the world, and that they were not obliged to bear witness, still less to take an oath. The provost said to them with a less gentle air, "What! you say you make a profession of the truth, and you refuse to tell it!" "We make profession, sir," replied Dupuy, "of the Gospel, but we are not obliged to have a man hanged when the laws excuse us." "What virtue!" said the provost, raising his eyes to the sky. Then turning to Batiste, who was delighted to hear his enemies defend his cause instead of taking vengeance on him, the provost said, "Wretch, kiss the footsteps of these honest people who have taken the rope from your neck. Through you they are condemned to the galleys; you shall keep them company." Then rising from the judicial bench, he broke up the assembly, and each of the prisoners was led back to his cell. Sentence was pronounced against Batiste and his companion; they were condemned to the galleys for life for highway robbery upon the tradesman.

The sentence of these three gentlemen being now confirmed, six archers came to conduct them to Lille, where the chain of galley slaves assembled. They were bound, two and two together, by their hands, and then all the five together; and fate willed it, or perhaps it was an order of the provost, that Batiste should be tied to Dupuy.   Thus bound, at ten o'clock in the morning they took them out of prison to lead them to Lille.   The whole town of Tournay knew what had taken place, and the generous and Christian action of these gentlemen which had saved the life of their perfidious and treacherous enemy.   A concourse of people assembled before the Beffroi ; the streets, too, were filled with crowds to see, as they said, virtue bound to crime.   Each uttered hootings and horrible imprecations against the villain and traitor Batiste, and wished every kind of blessing to these three gentlemen.

Thus, for the second time, were we deprived of our fellow-prisoners, which much afflicted us.   Their piety edified, and their conversation cheered us. It was a long time since the grand vicar had been to see us ; at last he came after the departure of these three gentlemen.   "I came to see," said he, "if our former conversations have not caused you to make some reflections favourable to your conversion."   We told him that all the reflections we had made justified us more and more in those sentiments which we had already expressed to him. "If such be the case," said he, "my visits are useless, and I shall only come to learn if I can be useful to you in anything ; but his lordship the bishop must now fulfil his promise to the procureur, and allow you to be taken back to the prisons of the parliament."   At these words we turned pale for fear of returning to that hideous dungeon where we had suffered so much. "I see," said he, "you fear to return there; if you like, I will beg the procureur to leave you here, and that, when the parliament has completed your prosecution, he will not have you transferred to its prisons, and I will come and tell you his answer to-day." We told him how grateful we were to him for his kindness, for we feared the parliament prisons as we did fire. The same day he came and told us not to disturb ourselves—we should not be removed. We thanked him for his great kindness towards us. He went away much moved with compassion for us. I saw him even shed tears. Some days after a parliament councillor came to see us in prison, and told us that we had been very strongly recommended to him, and that he would see if he could not some day rescue us from our sad plight. We could not imagine whence came this recommendation, unless our parents, to whom we had written since we had been in the Beffroi, had procured it through persons of consideration among their friends. But, as we had heard nothing of our parents, this did not seem likely, so our suspicions rested on our good friend, the grand vicar, who had assured us, in a manner which appeared to us most sincere, that he ardently desired to see us at liberty. However that might be, this councillor remained a good hour with us, questioned us about our route, at what place we had been arrested, and in what way. We satisfied him upon all these points. He made us repeat the occurrence at Couvé, and he asked us if we could prove that we had lodged at an inn in that town.   We replied that nothing was easier than to verify it, upon which he said, "Take courage, my lads ; I hope you will get out of this affair.   To-morrow I will send a lawyer to you, who will give you a requisition to sign ; sign it, and you will see its effects."   After which he departed, and we only saw him again seated among our judges in the court, where we appeared a few days after.

The day after his visit, the lawyer of whom he had spoken came to our prison, and read to us the requisition which he had drawn out, and which we signed.   This requisition, addressed to our judges in the parliament, was to the effect, that for professing the reformed religion we were not liable to the punishment which the law pronounces against all who try to escape from France without the permission of the government, and that we offered to prove how we were not escaping from the kingdom, because we had already left it, and returned to it again, having passed through Couvé, a town of the Prince of Liége, where there was a Dutch garrison, under the protection of which we could at once have placed ourselves had we had any design of escaping from France, and have been sent under their escort to Charleroi.   This requisition was placed on the table of the criminal court of the parliament.

Two days afterwards three huissiers of the parliament came to take us before the president, who, showing us the requisition, asked us if we had signed and presented that document.   We replied that we had, and that we prayed the venerable assembly to regard it favourably. The president said that they had examined it, and perceived thereby that we wished to prove that we had passed by Couvé ; but this was quite useless, as it was a well-known fact that we could not reach Mariembourg without passing through that town. "But," said he, "you have another thing to prove, without which the first is null and void ; you must prove that, when at Couvé, you were fully informed that that town was outside the French territories." This was a question which certainly we had not expected. However, we replied boldly enough, and without hesitation, that we knew it perfectly well. "How could you know it ?" said he ; "you are young lads who have never before left your firesides, and Couvé is more than two hundred leagues from your home." As far as I was concerned I did not know how to reply, for if I said we had learned it at the frontier it would be impossible to prove it. But my companion at once said that he knew it before he left Bergerac, because, having served as a barber in a company of the regiment of Picardy, which, at the time of the peace of Ryswick, was garrisoned at Rocroy, he had witnessed the arranging of the boundaries in that part of the country, that from thence his regiment was transferred to Strasbourg, where he joined the reformed religion, and that if he had wished to escape from France, either to go into Holland or Germany, it would have been very easy to have done so when in the service. "If you have been in the service, and left it, you ought to have your discharge." "So I have, my lord," said he ;

F

and, taking out his pocket-book, he produced the said discharge, printed and in due form, and handed it to the president, who sent it round among the assembly, after which the register attached it to the requisition ; we were then taken back to prison.

To make this matter clearer, it is as well to say that in truth my companion, Daniel le Gras, had been a barber in the regiment of Picardy, and that, after the peace of Ryswick, he had become a Protestant at Strasbourg, but he had never been at Rocroy nor its neighbourhood. He asserted this fact in our defence, leaving the parliament to investigate whether it was true that this regiment had been at Rocroy at the peace of Ryswick. This they did not take the trouble to do, for our patron the councillor had gained several votes in our favour, and the majority, indeed, was inclined to acquit us.

Two hours after our return to the prison, the gaoler ran quite out of breath into our cell to congratulate us upon our approaching deliverance. A clerk of the parliament had come to announce it to him, having seen with his own eyes the resolution of the assembly, which fully absolved us from the accusation of attempting to escape from the kingdom. Our good friends of the town at once came in crowds to congratulate us, and we thought the fact so real that we expected our release every hour. However, it was nothing of the kind, though it was true that the parliament had acquitted us. But as we were state criminals, the parliament could not set us at liberty without the orders of the

court. The procureur-general then wrote to the
Marquis de la Vrillière, minister of state, acquaint-
ing him that we had perfectly proved our inno-
cence of the offence of attempting to escape from
the kingdom, and that the parliament awaited his
orders for the destination of the prisoners. The
minister replied that he was to be careful that these
proofs were not equivocal, and to examine them
well. The parliament, unwilling to contradict itself, wrote that the proofs were complete and un-
answerable. A fortnight passed before the final
orders of the court arrived. They came at last to
deprive us of the flattering hope of our approaching deliverance, and to leave us no longer in doubt
about our fate, for the parliament, having summoned us before their full assembly in the criminal
court, the president asked us if we could read, and
on our replying in the affirmative, he said, giving us
the letter of the Marquis de la Vrillière, "Read this,
then." Owing to its brevity, I have always remembered its exact words, which were as follows :—

"GENTLEMEN,
        "Jean Marteilhe, Daniel le Gras, having been found
upon the frontiers without passports, his majesty decides that they
shall be condemned to the galleys.
            "I am, gentlemen, etc.,
                "THE MARQUIS DE LA VRILLIÈRE."

"Here, my friends," said the president and
several of his councillors, "is your sentence, which
has emanated from the court, and not from us; we
wash our hands of it. We pity you, and we wish
you the mercy of God and of the king."

After this we were taken back to the Beffroi, and the same evening a councillor and a registrar of the parliament came to the prison, and having made us enter the gaoler's room, the councillor told us to "kneel down before God and the Law and to listen to the reading of our sentence." We obeyed, and the registrar read it, the substance, after the preamble, being as follows :—

"The said Jean Marteilhe and Daniel le Gras having been suspected and convicted of professing the pretended reformed religion, and of attempting to escape from the kingdom in order to profess freely the said religion, for punishment of which crime, we condemn them to serve as convicts in the king's galleys, for life," etc.

The reading of this sentence being finished, I said to the councillor, "How, sir, can such a just and venerable body as the parliament make the conclusion of this sentence *(suspected and convicted)* agree with their decision to acquit us?"—as in fact they had done. "The parliament," said he, "has acquitted you, but the court, which is superior to parliaments, condemns you." "But where, sir, is justice, which ought to direct both tribunals?" "Do not go on so fast," said he; "it is not for you to fathom these things." We were forced then to be silent and bear our wrongs with patience. I begged the councillor to give us an authentic copy of our sentence, which he promised to do, and subsequently did.

Three days later the archers of the grand provost came to take us, and after we had been bound and had fetters put on our hands, they brought

us to Lille, in Flanders, where the chain of
galley slaves assembled. We arrived at that town
in the evening, exhausted with the fatigue of
walking these five leagues, and much inconveni-
enced by our bonds. They took us to the town
prison, where the tower of St. Pierre is set apart
for the galley slaves, on account of the thickness
of its walls. On entering the prison the gaoler
searched us all over, and as, either by chance or
prearranged design, there happened to be two
Jesuit fathers there, they took from us our books
of devotion and the copy of the sentence, and
never returned either the one or the other, and I
overheard one of these fathers say to the other,
after having read this sentence, that it was a great
imprudence of the parliament to give authentic
copies of such documents.

After this examination they led us to the dungeon of the galley slaves in the tower of St. Pierre,
one of the most frightful prisons I have ever seen.
It is a spacious dungeon, but so dark, although
it is on the second storey of the tower, that the
unfortunate persons there imprisoned never know
whether it is day or night, except by the bread
and water which is brought to them every morning ;
and what is worse, neither fire nor light is allowed
them. One has to lie down upon a little straw
torn and gnawed by rats and mice, of which
there are great numbers here, and who ate with
impunity our bread, because we could not see them
to drive them away. On arriving in this cruel
dungeon, where there were about thirty villains of

every kind, condemned for divers crimes—we could only know their number by asking them, for we could not see each other—their first compliment was to demand money from us, under the penalty of tossing us in a counterpane. Rather than experience this game, we preferred giving them two crowns, to the amount of which these wretches taxed us without mercy. It was performed two days after upon a wretched new comer, who endured it rather through want of money than of courage. These fellows had an old counterpane of coarse cloth, upon which they stretched their victim, then four of the most robust convicts each took a corner, and raising it as high as they could they then let it fall down upon the stones which formed the flooring of the cell; this was done as often as the poor wretch's sentence decreed, according to his obstinacy in refusing the money for which they had taxed him. This horrible punishment made me shudder. The miserable victim had good reason to cry out, there was no compassion for him. Even the gaoler, to whom all the money which this execrable game produces goes in the end, did nothing but laugh. He looked through the hole in the door and cried to them, " Courage, comrades." The poor wretch was so bruised by his repeated falls that they thought he would have died. Nevertheless, he recovered. A few days after, I had, in my turn, a terrible experience to undergo.

Every evening, the gaoler, accompanied by four great rogues of turnkeys, and the guard of the

prison, came to visit our dungeon to see if we were
making any attempts to escape. All these men, to
the number of about twenty, were armed with
pistols, swords, and bayonets. They examined the
four walls and the floor very minutely, to see if we
were making any holes there. One evening, after
they had paid their visit and as they were retiring,
one of the turnkeys remained the last to lock the
door. I addressed a few words to him, and as he
answered me amiably enough, I thought I had
conciliated him a little, and made bold to ask him
for the bit of candle which he held in his hand,
that we might rid ourselves of the vermin which so
tormented us, but he would do nothing of the kind,
and shut the door in my face. I remarked aloud,
not thinking that the fellow was near enough to
hear me, that I was sorry I had not snatched the
candle from his hand, as I easily could have done.
He overheard me, however, and reported me to the
gaoler.

The next morning, when all my companions were
awake and singing their litanies as usual—which if
they had neglected, the priests would have given
them no alms, as they were accustomed to do
every Thursday—and I was sleeping on my bit of
straw, I was suddenly awoke by several blows from
the flat side of a sword. I started up and saw the
gaoler, sword in hand, the four turnkeys, and all
the soldiers of the guard, armed to the teeth. I
asked them why they ill-treated me thus. The
gaoler only replied by giving me twenty more blows
of the sword, and the turnkey with the candle-end

gave me such a terrible box in the ear that he knocked me down. Having got up again, the gaoler told me to follow him, and perceiving that it was to do me more injury, I refused to obey him until I knew by whose orders he treated me thus, for that if I deserved it, the grand provost alone could order me to be punished. Then they gave me so many blows that I fell down a second time. The four turnkeys now took me up, two by the legs and two by the arms, and carried me out of the dungeon, dragging me like a dead dog down the steps of the tower into the court-yard, where they opened the door of another stone staircase which led underground. Then they pushed me down these steps, of which there must have been twenty-five or thirty ; at the bottom they opened a cell with an iron gate, called "the dungeon of the sorceress." They forced me in here, shut the door on me, and went away. I could see no more in this horrible dungeon than if I had my eyes shut. I groped a few steps to find a little straw, and then sunk down to my knees in water as cold as ice. I turned back and leaned against the door, where the ground was higher and less damp. By groping about I found a little straw, upon which I sat, but I had not been there two minutes, when I felt the water coming through the straw. I then firmly believed that they had buried me alive, and felt that this dungeon would be my tomb if I remained there twenty-four hours. Half-an-hour after the turnkey brought me some bread and water. I rejected his pitcher and his bread, saying, "Go tell your butcher of a master that I will neither eat nor drink till I have spoken to the grand provost."

The turnkey went away, and in less than an hour the gaoler came alone with a candle in his hand, armed with nothing but a bunch of keys ; and, opening the door of the dungeon, he told me, quite kindly, to follow him up-stairs. I obeyed. He led me into his kitchen. I was dirty, covered with blood, which had run from my nose and from a contusion on the head, which these barbarous turnkeys had given me when they let me fall and dragged my head down the stone stairs. The gaoler washed off the blood, put a plaister on my bruise, and then gave me a glass of Canary wine, which revived me a little. He reprimanded me slightly for my imprudence about the turnkey's candle, and, after having made me breakfast with him, he led me into a cell in the court-yard which was dry and light, as, he said, he could not put me back with the other galley slaves after what had happened, " But let me have my comrade with me," I said to him. " Patience," said he, " that will come in time." I remained four or five days in this cell, during which time the gaoler sent me my dinner from his table. One day he proposed to place my comrade and myself in a chamber in the prison where there was a good bed and every necessary comfort, for two louis d'or a month. We were not very well provided with money. However, I offered him a louis and a half up to the time when the chain started. He refused, but afterwards changed his mind, for a few days after we were placed in a large good room, with comfortable beds, where we were well fed without its costing us anything, as I will presently relate. One day he told me that my comrade had entreated him to bring me back to him, and that he had promised to do so. "Very well," said I, "but why not bring him down to me?" "No," said he, "you must return with the other galley slaves to the tower of St. Pierre." I saw that he wished to oblige us to give him the two louis a month to put us into a room; but, consulting our purse, and considering that if the chain did not start for two or three months, we could by no means afford it, I kept strictly to the offer that I had made him, so that he put me back into the tower with the others. My companion, who thought me lost, was delighted to *feel* me near him. I say *feel*, for we could not *see*, we had no light for that.

One morning, about nine o'clock, the gaoler came to open our dungeon, and calling my companion and myself, told us to follow him. We thought that he was going to put us into the chamber for one louis and a half; but we were soon undeceived, for when we were out of the dungeon he said, "It is M. Lambertie, Grand Provost of Flanders, and who is master here, who wishes to speak with you. I hope," said he, addressing me, "that you will tell him nothing about what happened recently." "No," said I; "when I have pardoned I forget, and do not seek revenge." Thus speaking, we arrived at an apartment where we found M. de Lambertie, who gave us a most gracious reception. He held in his hand a letter from his brother, a good gentleman of Protestant origin, who lived three leagues from Bergerac. My father had procured this recommendation for us. M. de Lambertie told us how sorry he was not to be able to procure our release. "For any other crime," said he, "I should have sufficient influence and friends at court to obtain your pardon, but no one dares to exert himself for those of the reformed religion. All that I can do is to make you comfortable in this prison, and to keep you here as long as I can, though the chain is just starting for the galleys." Then he asked the gaoler what good and comfortable chamber he had empty. The gaoler mentioned two or three which he rejected, and said, "I not only desire that these gentlemen have every comfort, but, also, that they enjoy some recreation ; and I therefore order you to place them in the alms room." "But, sir," said the gaoler, "there are only civil prisoners in that department, who have liberties which we dare not give to condemned criminals." "Well," replied M. Lambertie, "I command that you give them those liberties ; it is your business, and that of your turnkeys, to take care that they do not escape ; give them good beds and all they desire for their comfort, putting it all to my account, and not daring to take a sous from them. Go, gentlemen," said he to us, "to this alms room, it is the largest, the best ventilated, the most cheerful in the whole prison, and, besides having good cheer, which will cost you nothing, you can make some money there. I order," said he to the gaoler, "that you make M. Marteilhe provost of that room." We thanked M. de Lambertie as well as we could for his great kindness. He told us that he would often come to the prison to inquire after us, and see if the gaoler performed his orders with respect to us, and then he retired.

We were placed in the alms room, and I was installed provost, to the great regret of my predecessor, who was removed elsewhere. This alms room was very large, and contained six beds of twelve civil prisoners, who were generally people of some consideration and respectability ; and besides these were one or two young scapegraces, pickpockets, or prisoners for some light offences, whose business it was to make the beds, to cook, and keep the room clean. They slept upon a mattress in a corner of the apartment ; they were, in fact, our *valets de chambre*. The provostship with which I was invested, was a sufficiently onerous employment. He who possesses this office in the alms room has to distribute all the charitable donations which are made to the prison. They are generally considerable, and are all brought into this room. There is a box which hangs by a chain from the sill of the window to receive the charity of the passers by. The provost, who has the key of this box, opens it every evening to take the money out and to distribute it to all the prisoners, as well to the civil (if they wish it) as to the criminal. Besides this, every morning the turnkeys go with carts or barrows throughout the town to collect the offerings of bakers, butchers, brewers, and fishmongers. They go also to the different markets, and all that they collect is brought to the alms room to be divided and distributed in all the apartments and cells by the provost, in proportion to the number of prisoners in each, of which the gaoler gives him a list every day, and of which the total when I arrived there was from five to six hundred.

Although I had become the distributor-general of these alms, I was unable to remedy one abuse which prevented any of this charity reaching the prisoners condemned to the galleys. The gaoler received their share of the money from the box, to use it, he said, in making soup for them ; but, alas ! what soup that was ! It was generally composed of bad and putrid pieces of beef which he cooked for them with a little salt, the very smell of which made me sick. Six weeks after we had resided in this happy apartment, M. de Lambertie came to see us, and told us that the chain was to start to-morrow for Dunkirk, where were six of the king's galleys, but that he had got us exempted from going, passing us off for sick ; we must therefore remain that day in bed till the chain had started, which we did, and this procured us the blessing of remaining in this comfort three months longer. After which another chain set out, and with this we went, as I will now narrate.   •

In January, 1702, M. de Lambertie came to see us, and told us that the chain would start the next day—that he could still procure our exemption from joining it, but that he must warn us (so that we might have the choice of going or remaining) that this would be the last chain which would go to the Dunkirk galleys—that all the subsequent ones would go to Marseilles, a journey of more than three hundred leagues, which would be much harder and more painful for us—that we should be obliged to do it all on foot, with the chain round our necks ; moreover, he should have to go himself into the country in the month of March, and would no longer be able to render us any service at Lille. He advised us, therefore, to start with the chain which to-morrow began its journey to Dunkirk. This chain was under his orders as far as that town ; he would have us conveyed apart from the other galley slaves in a cart, as comfortably as possible, the distance being about twelve leagues.

These plausible reasons of M. Lambertie decided us to choose the latter alternative. This good nobleman kept his word, for, instead of chaining us to the twenty-five or thirty galley slaves who composed the band, and who went on foot, he put us into a cart, and every evening they gave us a good bed. The officer of the archers who guarded the chain made us take our meals at his table at Ypres, Furnes, and other places which we passed through, so that we were taken for people of great distinction. But, alas ! this comfort was only a smoke which soon disappeared ; for the third day after our departure from Lille we arrived at Dunkirk, where we were all placed in the galley, *L'Heureuse*, commanded by the Captain de la Pailleterie, who was the head of the squadron of six galleys which were in the port. They put us at once each on

separate benches, by which means I was parted
from my dear companion. The very day of our
arrival, they administered the bastinado to an
unfortunate convict, for what offence I know not.
I was terrified at witnessing this punishment, which
takes place without any form of trial and immediately. The next day I was upon the point of
receiving the very same treatment which had
caused me so much horror, and that through the
malice of a great rascal of a convict who was at
the galleys for robbery. I had, happily, not
replied a word to all his insulting speeches, but to
his demand for money I replied that I would only
give it to those who did not ask for it. I had
already paid for five or six bottles of wine for those
on my bench who had not asked me. This wretch,
who was named Poulet, told the *sous-comite* (under
officer) of the galley that I had uttered execrable
blasphemies against the Virgin Mary and all the
saints of Paradise. This *sous-comite*, who was a
brutal barbarian, as all his class are, credited
Poulet's story, and came to my bench, telling me
to begin to strip at once to receive the bastinado.
One can judge of my emotions. I did not know
that Poulet had spoken to him. Besides, I had
neither said nor done anything which could draw
down on me this punishment. I asked my companions on the bench why they were going to treat
me thus, and if it was the custom to make all new
comers pass under this ordeal. They, as surprised
as I was, told me they did not understand it.
Meanwhile the *sous-comite* went to the quay to

give in his report to the major of the galleys, who was there, and in whose presence the execution of the bastinado always took place. While then this *sous-comite* was on the plank which connected the galley with the quay, he met the first *comite*, to whom he said that he was going to speak to the major to have the bastinado given to a new comer, a Huguenot, who had poured forth horrible blasphemies against the Catholic Church, the blessed Virgin, and all the saints. The *comite* asked him if he had heard him. He said, No ; but that Poulet had given the information. "Very good testimony !" replied the *comite.* This first *comite* was a tolerably honest man, and very serious for a man of his profession. He came up to my bench and asked me what reason I had had to blaspheme against the Catholic religion. I replied that I had never done so, and that my religion even forbade such a thing. Upon which he called Poulet and asked him what I had said and done. This rogue had the impudence to repeat the same things which he said to the *sous-comite,* who was present, as the first *comite* had made him return with him. Not wishing to receive Poulet's deposition, he questioned the six galley slaves on my bench, then those on the bench before and behind. These, from twenty to twenty-eight persons, all testified to the same thing, that I had never uttered a word good or bad when Poulet had grossly insulted me, and that all that I had said was that I would not treat those who asked me to do so. This testimony having been given, the head *comite* severely belaboured the wicked Poulet, had him bound with a double chain to the criminal bench, and strongly reprimanded his under *comite* for having decided so promptly upon the information of this rascal. Thus was I delivered from the bastinado, which is a frightful punishment.

The manner in which this barbarous punishment is inflicted is as follows:—The unfortunate victim is stripped naked from his waist upwards; then they make him lie upon his face, his legs hanging over his bench, and his arms over the bench opposite. Two convicts hold his legs and two others his arms, his back is bare and exposed, and the *comite*, who is behind him, every now and then strikes with a whip a muscular Turk, who is also stripped, to urge him on to scourge the back of the poor victim with all his strength, which he does with a coarse thick rope. As the Turk knows that there will be no mercy for him if he spares, in the least, the poor wretch who is to be so cruelly punished, he applies his blows with his whole force, so that each cut raises a bruise an inch in height. Those who have to suffer this punishment can rarely endure more than ten or twelve blows without losing the power of speech and motion. This does not hinder them from continuing to strike the poor body, which neither moves nor utters a cry till the number of blows ordered by the major are accomplished. Twenty or thirty blows are only for slight offences ; I have seen fifty, eighty, and even a hundred given; in such cases the victims scarcely ever recover. After the poor patient has received the appointed

G

number, the barber or surgeon of the galley comes, to rub his lacerated back with strong vinegar and salt, to make the miserable body regain its sensibility, and to prevent gangrene from coming on. Such is the cruel bastinado of the galleys.

I remained about a fortnight on the galley where I had first been placed. As with the rest of mankind, there are some *comites* who are more malicious and cruel than others. By the side of my galley was one, the *comite* of which was a very demon. He always had the *bourrasque*, or cleaning out of his galley, done every day, instead of only every Saturday, as all the others did. During this *bourrasque*, strokes from the whip fell like hail upon the galley slaves, and this exercise lasted two or three hours. I used to see this cruel treatment, because the distance from one galley to the other was not great. The convicts on my bench constantly were saying, "Pray God that in the distribution which will shortly be made of the new comers you may not fall to the galley *La Palme :*" the name of that commanded by the wicked *comite.* I trembled with fear, We new comers were about sixty in number. The time for distributing us in the six galleys arrived. They took us first to the arsenal, where we had to stop, and were examined. We were then divided into classes, the strongest and the weakest together. Six lots were thus made, and the six *comites* drew for us as in a lottery. They had placed me in the first class, and I was at the head of a lot. The *comite* to whom I had fallen told us to follow him to his galley.

Curious to know my fate, and ignorant that this man was a *comite*, I prayed him to tell me to what galley I had fallen. "To *La Palme*," said he. I made an exclamation deploring my bad fortune. "Why," said he, "are you more unfortunate than the others?" "Because, sir," said I, "I have fallen to a galley whose *comite* is a perfect fiend." I did not know that I was talking to this very *comite*. He looked at me with a frown. "If I knew," said he, "who told you that, and I had them in my power, I would soon make them repent of it."

I saw that I had said too much; but the evil was done, and there was no remedy. However, this wicked *comite* wished to show that, with regard to me, he was not such a demon as he was accused of being. He led his lot to his galley, where he at once showed a mark of his favour toward me, for as I was young and strong, the *argousin** had put an iron ring round my leg, and a chain of excessive weight and thickness. The *comite* perceived this, and, with a rude and brutal air, said to this *argousin*, that if he did not take off that enormous chain he would complain to the captain—that he would not allow him to spoil the best subject for the oar he had in his lot. The *argousin* at once took off the thick chain and put on me one of the lightest which he had, and which the *comite* chose himself. He then ordered the *argousin* to go and chain me to his (the *comite's*) own bench. I must mention that the *comite* eats and sleeps on a bench of the galley, upon which a table standing on four little

* Under officer charged with guarding the galley slaves.

iron pillars is erected ; and this table is both long enough for him to take his meals at and also to spread his bed upon, surrounded by a tent of coarse cotton cloth ; so that the convicts of this bench are under the table, which can easily be removed when they want to row or perform any other manœuvre. The six convicts of this bench compose the domestic establishment of the *comite*. Each has his special employment in waiting upon him ; and when the *comite* takes his meals or is seated on his table (for it serves both as bed-room and dining-room), all the convicts of this bench, and of the benches on each side, always stand up, with heads uncovered, out of respect. It is the great ambition of all the convicts in the galley to be on the bench of the *comite* and *sous-comite*, not only because they eat the remnants of their meals, but principally because they never get any stroke of the lash there while they are rowing or performing other manœuvres ; so these benches are called "reserved seats." I, then, had the privilege of being on this bench ; but it did not last long, which was owing to my own fault, for feeling the remains of worldly pride, I could not dance attendance as the others did ; for when the *comite* was at table I laid down or turned my back upon him, my cap on my head, pretending to look at the sea. The convicts often told me that he would take offence ; but I let them say so, and went on still in my own way, contenting myself with being the slave of the king, without being that of the *comite* as well. Nevertheless, I ran the risk of falling into disgrace with him, which

is the greatest misfortune that can happen to a convict. The *comite*, however, demon as he had been
painted to me, was very reasonable. He inquired
of the convicts of his bench if I ate with them the
remains of his meals, and hearing that I would
never taste them, he said, " He has not forgotten
his former good living ; leave him alone."

One evening, after he had gone to bed in his tent,
he called me to his bedside, and speaking in a
whisper, that the others might not hear, he told me
that he perceived I had not been brought up as a
vagabond, and that I could not submit to cringe to
him like the others—that he did not esteem me less
for it, but that for an example he should put me in
another bench, and that I might reckon, in all the
labour and fatigue of the galley, on never receiving
a blow from him or his *sous-comites*. I thanked
him for his kindness as well as I could ; and I can
truly say that he kept his word, which is a great
thing, for while we were rowing or making manœuvres, he would not have regarded his own father,
and would have belaboured him like any one else.
In a word, he was the cruellest man, in the exercise
of his authority, I have ever seen ; but, at the same
time, when not in a passion very reasonable and just
in his judgment. There were five of the reformed
faith in his galley. He treated us all equally ; not
one of the five ever received the least ill-treatment
from him. On the contrary, when the opportunity
presented itself he rendered us service. This I
have experienced, as I shall relate at the proper
time.

The captain of our galley, the Chevalier de Langeron Maulevrier, held the most Jesuitical sentiments. He hated us extremely; and never failed when we were rowing, with our bodies naked, as was the custom, to call the *comite* and say to him, " Go and refresh the backs of those Huguenots with a salad of strokes of the whip." But these blows always fell upon some one else. This captain was very magnificent and extravagant in his table, for the five hundred francs a month which the king gave to each of the captains for their table was not half enough for him. The captains have generally for their pantry or provision-room, which is in the hold of the galley, a cabin-boy or waiter; a convict generally holds this office. It is a very desirable occupation for him who can get it, for he is then exempt from rowing, and from all other fatigue, and makes good cheer in the captain's kitchen. Now it happened that M. de Langeron's waiter had stolen fifty or sixty pounds of coffee, which the steward missed from the store-room. He told the captain, who, without any form of trial or examination, at once ordered that fifty strokes of the bastinado should be given to this poor rogue of a waiter, and that he should be placed on the criminal bench, which was punctually carried into effect. After this the captain ordered the *comite* to find him an honest waiter among the convicts of the galley. The *comite* cried out at the word *honest*, saying that it was impossible for him to guarantee the honesty of any of these malefactors; but that he knew one galley slave, of advanced age, and scarcely capable of rowing, for whose honesty he could answer, "but," said he, "I know that you will not have him." "Why not," said the captain, "if he is as you describe?" "Because," said the *comite*, "he is a Huguenot." The captain frowned and replied, "Have you no other to propose to me?" "No," said the *comite*, "none at least that I can answer for." "Well," said the captain, "send him to me; I will try him." This was done. He was a venerable old man, named Bancilhon, whose candour and integrity were imprinted on his countenance. The captain asked him if he would serve him as waiter. The air and prudence with which he replied pleased the captain, who had him at once installed by his steward in the pantry. The captain soon became so fond of his waiter that he liked no one else. He even entrusted his purse and his expenses to him. When the money was exhausted, Bancilhon brought him the bills and memoranda of how the money was spent. And so great confidence had the captain in him that he often tore up these memoranda in his presence without looking at them, and threw them into the sea. The captain's extreme confidence in Bancilhon, and the great economy which he practised to his master's profit, soon made for him many jealous and mortal enemies. The captain had two stewards, a purveyor, and a cook, who took their meals at the second table.

These men often wished to regale themselves with champagne and other delicacies entrusted to the care of Bancilhon, who as often refused them, being forbidden to touch them except for the captain's table. Upon which they both conceived such a hatred against him, that they determined to ruin him. To effect this, they planned that on a day when the captain was going to have a dinner party, and there would be hurry and confusion in the party, they would steal some piece of plate (with which article the captain was well provided) and accuse Bancilhon of the robbery. The matter being thus arranged between these four, one of the stewards, either out of good will to Bancilhon or to supplant his colleague, secretly communicated the plot to Bancilhon, telling him that he would take his part if it were necessary. Bancilhon, informed of the hatred of these men against him, resolved not to wait for the storm which sooner or later would ruin him, and decided that he would rather row all his life on the slaves' bench than remain thus exposed to their malice. With this determination, with his bills in his hand, he went to the captain one morning while he was in bed, and begged him instantly to discharge him from the burden of his office, protesting that his age, which was enfeebling his memory and his sight, no longer permitted him to profit by his kindness. The captain, very much surprised, told him that there must be some other reason which induced him to make this request, and that he wished to know immediately, under penalty of his indignation. Bancilhon, not being able to excuse himself, confessed the truth, and told him that Moria, the second steward, had discovered the plot to him.

"Call these gentlemen to me immediately," said the captain.

This being done, he threatened to throw them all at once into the sea, if they did not confess the truth. They very soon confessed, begging for pardon a thousand times. "Well, gentlemen," said he, "I shall not impose any other punishment than to declare to you that from this moment if anything is missing of which Bancilhon has the charge, you will all three be responsible." They exclaimed at this, saying that in such conditions Bancilhon could ruin them at any moment. "He is an honest man," said the captain, "and you all a set of rogues, who deserve to be thrashed and put in chains." These fellows retired quite confused, and never after attempted to supplant Bancilhon, who continued the favourite servant of M. de Langeron, whose kindness to him was reflected upon us other four Protestants in the galley.

This same year, 1702, in the month of July, we went with our six galleys to the fort of Ostend. From thence we cruised, when the sea was calm, along the coast of Blankenbourg and L'Ecluse, in Flanders. Then we returned towards Nieuport, and the entrance of the channel.

One day we perceived from the heights of Nieuport, at the distance of four or five leagues in the offing, a squadron of twelve Dutch vessels of war, stopped by a calm. We went to reconnoitre them, and seeing that one of their ships was about a league distant from the others, all six galleys advanced abreast to cannonade it. The captain of this ship was certainly a great simpleton, for when he saw us coming up to him, as the galleys are low in the deck, and do not appear at a distance to be very large, he said, boastingly, to his crew, " Let us prepare our tackle to haul these six boats on board." His head surgeon, who was a French refugee, named Labadoux, who knew the strength of the galleys better than he did, made bold to tell him that if he allowed the galleys to approach his vessel they would take it, owing to the great number of men they carried. Notwithstanding this advice, the captain made no effort, either to defend himself by his artillery, or to approach the squadron, which he might have done by having his vessel towed by his boats, in which case we should have been between two fires, and obliged to relinquish our prize. At last, by hard rowing, we approached this vessel, making the *chamade*, a cry which galley slaves raise to terrify the enemy. In truth, it is a terrible thing to see on each galley three hundred naked men, who all row in good time and shake their chains, the noise of which is mingled with their yells and shrieks, and makes those who have never before witnessed such a sight shudder. Thus was it with the crew of this ship ; so frightened were they at the sight, that they all rushed down to the bottom of the hold crying out for quarter, so that the soldiers and sailors of the galleys had no trouble in boarding and seizing the vessel, which had fifty-four guns. The crew, indeed, was too weak to resist, being composed of only one hundred and eighty men in all. She was called the *Unicorn of Rotter-*

dam. We quickly towed her off, in sight of the
other ships of the squadron, who could not follow
us for want of wind, and we brought her into the
port of Ostend. We made no other expedition
during the remainder of the campaign, and returned
to winter in the port of Dunkirk.

The year 1703 also passed without our doing
anything but alarming the English coast in the
channel by firing cannon-shots, and this only when
the weather permitted it, for it must be quite calm
for the galleys, and every winter we went to dis-
mantle at Dunkirk.

In the year 1704 we were at Ostend, watching a
Dutch squadron which cruised off this harbour, and
when it was calm we worried their vessels by firing
heavy cannon at them, being out of the range of
their artillery, which was much less than that of the
galleys. Their ships not being able to move in a
calm, we always chose such days for these expeditions, and whenever a little breeze arose we returned
to Ostend. One day, when Admiral Almonde was
cruising with five Dutch men-of-war off Blankenbourg, he met a fisherman of that coast, to whom
he gave some ducats, on the condition that he
would go at once to Ostend, and tell the commander of the galleys that he had just met five
large Dutch vessels, returning from the East Indies,
so heavily laden, and their crews so invalided, that
they would scarcely be able to make for any Dutch
port. This fisherman, following his instructions,
came to Ostend to make his report to our commander, accompanying it with several incidents

which seemed plausible.   Among other things, he said that he had been on board these vessels and made a good thing of it, having sold all his fish there.   One easily believes what one wishes.   Our commander fell into the trap, and, as the tide flowed, about ten o'clock in the evening our six galleys put to sea in search of this rich prize.

There was a little easterly breeze, rather fresh. We rowed all night, and in the morning at daybreak we saw our six Indiamen, which, immediately they perceived us, pretended to put on all sail, proceeding, all five in file, one after the other, so that we could not see which was the rear guard and which the admiral's.   These ships were well masked, their stern ornaments covered up, their portholes closed, their topsails lowered,—in fact, they were so well disguised as merchant vessels returning from a long voyage, that they quite deceived us, and we really took them for five ships returning from the Indies.   All our officers, sailors, and soldiers, felt nothing but joy, in the firm hope of enriching themselves by this great booty.   Meanwhile we continued to advance and to approach this fleet nearer, which only put up all sail to make us believe that they were afraid, and to draw us more surely within range of their guns, with the design of giving us a warm reception ; for though they seemed to crowd all sail, they found means not to advance by dragging a large double cable behind their ships.   Our six galleys rowed with all their might, in line of battle, and with perfect confidence that the Indiamen were so heavy that they could not make way. Being within range, we discharged our artillery at them. The vessel which formed the rear guard replied by firing a small cannon from below the quarter-deck, which did not reach half way to us, and which encouraged us more and more. We still advanced, pouring forth a terrible fire from our artillery, which they endured with constancy. At last we found ourselves so near to the rear guard ship that we prepared to board it, axe and sabre in hand, when, all of a sudden, their admiral made a signal. Immediately their rear guard veered round upon us, the others did the same, so that in a moment we were surrounded by these five great ships, which, having had all this time to prepare their guns, opened their ports and poured upon us a terrible fire, which cut down the greater portion of our masts and rigging, and made great slaughter among our crews.

We now perceived that these pretended Indiamen were nothing less than good and formidable men-of-war, which by their stratagem had allured us beyond the sand-bank which lies two or three leagues from the coast, and which large vessels, that draw much water, cannot pass, while galleys can easily do so. Perceiving that we were thus taken in, and fearing worse than we had already suffered, our commander gave the signal for instant flight towards the sand-bank, which our enemies could not prevent us from reaching. But they escorted us thither in line of battle, with such a terrible fire that we ran the greatest peril in the world of being all sunk. At last the proximity of the sand-bank saved us. We regained Ostend by force of our oars, very much battered, having had more than two hundred and fifty men killed in the combat, and a great number of wounded. Arrived at Ostend, the first thing to be done was to seek for the fisherman who had so much deceived us. If they had found him, he would have been hanged immediately, but he had not been foolish enough to wait for us.

Our commander was not much praised by the court ; everybody spoke of his credulity, but, above all, of his imprudence in risking the loss to the king of six galleys of three thousand souls (for these galleys have five hundred men each). I say his imprudence, for when we were within sight of the enemy, and he was holding a council of war with the other five captains, he insisted that they were Indiamen. One of the captains, however, M. de Fontête, strongly suspected that it might be a trick, and said he thought it would be well to make sure by sending our brigantine to reconnoitre the fleet. But the commander telling him it was fear of the cannon-shots which made him think so, M. de Fontête replied without hesitation, " Now, gentlemen, let us attack the enemy at once, and you will see if I am afraid." Words which cost us a great deal of blood, at least, to the commander's galley, for when he had given the signal to retreat, M. de Fontête, stung with the reproach which the commander had made to him at the council of war, did not retire from the battle, acting as if he had not seen the signal to retreat ; and the five galleys having retired to the sand-bank, the commander, seeing this galley in danger of being sunk, exclaimed, "Does Fontête wish to challenge me to be as brave as he is ? Come," said he to his *comite*, "row up again to the enemy." The *comite*, who seemed to foresee his death, fell on his knees before him, entreating him not to go, but the commander, pistol in hand, threatened to break his head if he did not execute his orders immediately. The poor *comite* obeyed, and rowed out again to take the order to M. de Fontête to retire. The commander thus placed himself again in the midst of the enemy's fire, and the first ball which struck the galley carried off the head of the poor *comite*. The commander being near enough to make M. de Fontête hear him, cried out to him to retire, which he did at once, and, by means of the sand-bank, escaped, as well as the commander, from the pursuit of the Dutch. During the remainder of the campaign, he had no desire to undertake new expeditions ; that of the five sham Indiamen had quite cooled our courage, and we were in great fear of Vice-Admiral Almonde, who, with his feints and stratagems, we imagined to be everywhere, as the following fact will show.

I have already said that in 1702 we took a Dutch man-of-war, named the *Unicorn of Rotterdam*. I have also spoken of one Labadoux, a French refugee, who was surgeon on board this vessel. The ship having been brought into Ostend, the crew were put into the prisons of the town. Labadoux, to avoid going to the galleys as a refugee, took his place as a soldier in the commander's galley, but soon after he deserted to return to Holland. He was taken and brought back to the galley, where he was chained down till his trial could take place. The council of war questioned him to know whither he designed to escape. " To Holland," said he, "to bear arms against France." The commander, surprised at this reply, said to him, " If you had replied that you were deserting to remain in France, you would only have been condemned to be a convict ; but now you are yourself putting the rope round your neck." " Yes, sir," replied he ; " I declare here to the council, as is the truth, that I have deserved, according to the king's commands and the laws of war, to be hanged, and if you sentence me otherwise you will commit an injustice." The commander, perceiving that it was fear of the punishment of the galleys which made him prefer death, said to him, " And I, to punish you more rigorously, remit the sentence of death which you desire, and condemn you to the galleys." And to the galleys he was in truth condemned, but he only remained there a little more than a year.

Admiral Almonde knew and esteemed Labadoux,. who. had been surgeon on board his ship. Labadoux found means of writing him a letter, in which he represented to him that, having been taken by the French upon the *Unicorn*, they had forced him to serve as a soldier in the galleys, by the threat of making him work as a convict, and having deserted in order to return to Holland, his legitimate country, he had been arrested and condemned to the galleys for life, which punishment he was now suffering, with a hope, however, that the favour and good-will of the admiral, whose aid he implored, would procure his deliverance.

We were in Ostend after the expedition of which I have just spoken, when one evening a boat, carrying an express, arrived. This express brought a letter from Admiral Almonde to the commander of the galleys, praying him to release Labadoux, considering the great injustice they had already done him by obliging him, as a prisoner of war, to bear arms on the side of France. The admiral concluded that if Labadoux was not given up immediately, he would be obliged to take other measures which might not be so agreeable, by which he probably meant that he would come and burn the galleys in the fort of Ostend, which was easy enough to do, and which at that time we greatly feared. This letter had its effect. Never before had a convict or a Turkish slave been released from the galleys except by the king's warrant. However, the commander of the galleys, either through fear of the threats of Admiral Almonde, or because he was glad to find an opportunity of obliging him, set Labadoux at liberty the same day in the following manner. He called him alone into his cabin, and told him that, in order to please Admiral Almonde, he was going to give him his liberty, but that this must be done as if he had escaped, and that he, the commander, would facilitate the thing that very evening in the dusk, by ordering the *argousin* to forget to chain him on his bench;

H

that Labadoux was to keep outside the galley seated on his oar ; the boat of the galley would then come and take him off, landing him on the side of the town which leads to L'Ecluse, in Flanders. This plan was perfectly carried out. Labadoux, with whom I was very good friends, requested, after this conversation with the commander, to go to the galley *La Palme*. He came, and after embracing me, took leave of me, telling me in what manner he was to be released that very evening. After the boat had landed him, the *argousin*, coming to see if all were chained, found, as he knew very well he should, that Labadoux had escaped. He informed the commander, who stormed against the negligence of the *argousin* in the presence of the crew and the officers. He had him put in chains for twenty-four hours only, and sent several detachments to the opposite side of the town from that at which Labadoux had landed to pursue him. The next day no more was said about it. From this circumstance the impression can well be understood which the request, or rather the threat, of Admiral Almonde made upon the commander of the galleys.

It was during the following campaign that the allies laid siege to Ostend. Our six galleys were ready armed in the port of Dunkirk, and M. le Chevalier Langeron, my captain, was made head of the squadron, his predecessor being raised to the dignity of Grand Master of the Knights of Malta. Our new commander received, one evening, a despatch from the court, with orders to go as soon as possible with his six galleys to Ostend to strengthen the garrison, this town being threatened with a siege. We immediately started thither, and, having sailed all night, morning found us before Nieuport, three leagues from Ostend. We perceived along the coast a great number of people with waggons and horses heavily laden escaping from Ostend. We sent the boat on shore to gain intelligence from these people, who told us that the army of the allies was within sight of Ostend, and that the town would be invested that very day.

Soon after we saw an extremely large naval armament advancing from the north, and crowding all sail to cut us off from the channel of the sand-bank which is between Ostend and Nieuport. We were more than an hour in advance of them, and could easily have entered Ostend before the fleet arrived there. But our commander reflected upon the extreme peril to which we should be exposed in that port, which is only protected from the army on one side, added to which the fleet could very easily send fire-ships among us, which might have destroyed us ; besides that the allies, if they took the town, would take the galleys also, which would vex the king extremely. Everything considered, and a council of war having been held, it was resolved to return to Dunkirk, which we did, rowing as hard as we could. The Chevalier de Langeron was praised and rewarded by the court, because he had not executed its orders. Ostend was besieged by land and sea, and was obliged to surrender at the end of three days, not for want of a sufficient garrison, but because there was too large a one, for

Count de la Motte, who was in the neighbourhood
with a camp of twenty-two battalions and several
squadrons of cavalry, threw himself with all his
troops into the town, which was a great blunder, for
the allies, only having attacked the place by firing
bombs, red-hot shot, and shell, so many people,
pressing one upon another in this little town, could
neither move nor obtain shelter from these infernal
machines, which rained down upon them ; so they
were obliged to surrender on condition that they
might depart sword in hand, and not take arms
again for a year.   During the three days that they
bombarded the town, we went at night, without
light or fire, creeping with our six galleys among
the allied fleet, trying to seize some transport
or gunboat, but we did not succeed.   No retreat
now remained to us but the harbour of Dunkirk.
Here we passed all the summer, only venturing out
in calm weather, or with an east, north, or north-
east wind, for if a west or south-west wind had
caught us at sea, we should not have known where
to run into.   We always disarmed in the month of
October for the winter, and in April we armed
again to enter on the campaign.

The following year, 1707, we had many hardships
to endure.   As there was a great deal of east wind
we cruised all over the channel.   We took a small
English privateer, and burned one belonging to
Ostend, on the coast of England.   We were one
day in very great danger of perishing with two
galleys.   Being in the port of Dunkirk in the finest
weather possible, with not a cloud on the sky,

M. de Langeron, who was impatient to go and visit
the English coast, called all the most experienced
pilots to ask them their advice about the weather,
and if they saw any sign of its soon changing.
They were all agreed that the weather was settled,
and promised to continue fine.   Great precautions
were always necessary when we put out, now that
Ostend was in the hands of the allies, for if a storm
from the west or south-west had overtaken us at sea,
and we had missed the port of Dunkirk, we should
have been obliged to run to the north, or to run
aground on the coast of some province belonging
to the allies ; for in bad weather the galleys cannot
keep at sea.

We had on board our galley as pilot, a fisherman
of Dunkirk, named Peter Bart.   He was brother of
the celebrated Jean Bart, Admiral of the North; but
Peter was only a poor fisherman, much given to dis-
sipation and drunkenness—indeed he drank gin like
water.   But otherwise he was well acquainted with
the coasts, and a great observer of the weather, for
I have never known him to be wrong in his prognos-
tication as to what wind and weather we should
have two or three days hence.   This pilot, however,
had no great credit with the other pilots, nor with
our commander, because he was nearly always
drunk.   They summoned him, however, to this
council to give his advice.   He spoke very bad
French, and expressed his opinion to be quite opposite to those of the other pilots.   "You want to
go to sea," said he to our commander: "I promise
you a good storm to-morrow morning."   They

laughed at his opinion, and, notwithstanding all his entreaties to remain in shore, the captain would not consent. So our galley and that of M. de Fontête put to sea with such calm, beautiful weather, that we might have held a lighted candle at the top of the mast.

We cruised along the shores of Dover, making our guns roar along the coasts during the night, after which we returned to the French coast to the roadstead of Ambleteuse, a village situated between Calais and Boulogne. There was a cove here between two cliffs, which sheltered the vessels which anchored in it from the east and north-east winds. I do not know what fancy took our commander, who persisted in anchoring in this cove. M. de Fontête was wiser, he remained in the open roadstead. Directly Peter Bart saw the movement we were making to go and anchor in this cove, he shrieked out like a madman that we should beware of doing so. They asked him the reason. He assured them that at sunrise we should have as violent a storm from the south-west as we had ever seen in our lives, and that the entrance of this cove being exposed to this wind, we should not be able to get out of it, nor to avoid running upon the rocks of which the cove was full, when the galley would be broken to pieces and not even a cat could be saved. They laughed at him and his counsel, and we entered this fatal cove a little before dawn. We cast out two anchors, and every one thought of taking a little sleep. Peter Bart, however, wept and sobbed at the approach, as he said, of inevitable death. Day at last dawned, the wind blew from the south-west, but so softly that we took no notice of it.   But as the sun rose higher the wind increased, which awakened attention to Peter Bart's prophecy.   We were about to make an attempt to go out of the cove, when a most furious tempest arose, so suddenly, that instead of weighing our anchors we were obliged to cast out two others to sustain us against the violence of the wind and waves, which were driving us upon the rocks, which the retreat of the waves made visible every instant, quite close to the stern of the galley.   The worst of all was that the anchorage in this cove was good for nothing, and that the four anchors we had cast were dragging, and could find no hold, so that we were clearly driving upon the rocks.   The commander and all the pilots seeing that our anchors could not hold, tried to row towards the anchors so as to relieve them ; but immediately we dipped the oars into the sea, the huge waves carried them away far from us.

Then every one knew that shipwreck was inevitable ; each one cried, groaned, and prayed. The chaplain exposed the Holy Sacrament, gave the blessing and absolution to those who felt a real contrition, and had neither time nor opportunity to go to confession.   The most singular thing in this great calamity, was to hear these wretched convicts, condemned for their crimes, cry aloud to the commander and officers, " Come, gentlemen, we shall soon be equal, for it won't be long before we shall all drink out of the same glass." Judge what contrition and repentance they had for their crimes! At last, in this horrible extremity, when every one was expecting that instant death which was visible to all eyes, the commander caught sight of Peter Bart, who was weeping and lamenting. " My dear Peter," said he, " if I had believed you, we should not have been in this desperate plight. Have you no expedient to save us from this inevitable peril ?" " What good is it," said Peter, " for me to counsel or to act if I am not listened to? Yes, I have, by God's grace, a means of escaping from this perilous position. Now, I declare to you that if my own life was not involved in it, I would leave you all to drown like pigs, as you are !" This impertinence was readily pardoned him, in the hope that he might save our lives. " But," added he, " I must stipulate not to be contradicted or opposed in any manœuvre which will appear ridiculous to you at first ; you must obey my commands, or you will all perish."

The commander at once gave orders, by beat of drum, that Peter Bart was to be strictly obeyed, on pain of death ; after which Peter asked the commander if he had a purse of gold. " Yes," said he, " here it is, dispose of it as if it were your own." Peter, after taking out four louis d'or, gave it back to him. Then he asked the sailors of the galley if there were four among them quite prepared to do what he ordered them, promising that each should receive a louis for drink-money. More than twenty presented themselves. He selected four of the most determined, whom he put into the large boat, called the *caique*, which is always kept on board the galleys when they go to sea. He made them take an anchor in this boat, but the cable remained in the galley to be told out as they got farther from us. This being done, the boat was let down into the sea with its four men and the anchor. Peter ordered them to take it from the stern of the galley, and cast it upon the rock upon which we were driving. At this order every one shrugged their shoulders, not being able to understand what this anchor could do from the *stern* of the galley, as it was from the *bows* that it ought to be held. The commander could not help asking him what was the use of this anchor. Peter replied, "You will see, please God." The four sailors succeeded, though with great difficulty, and in danger of being swamped, and cast the anchor against the rock. Then Peter, seizing the commander's hand, exclaimed, "We are saved, thank God!" But still no one understood his manœuvre.

Peter now lowered the yard-arm, to which he fastened the large sail, which he reefed, tying it with such knots that when he pulled the sheet of the sail the knots would loosen, and the sail be at once unfurled. The yard-arm was then hoisted up again, and he ordered four men with axes to be ready to cut the four cables of the anchors which were cast from the bows of the galley when he commanded them ; then he hauled in and tightened the cable of the anchor which he had cast from the stern against the rock, and told a man with an axe to be ready to cut it at his command. This done, and everything being prepared in the manner that I have described, he ordered the four men at the bows to cut the cables of the four anchors. As soon as the galley was released at the bows she began to turn, because she was held firmly by the anchor at the stern, and if they had given her time she would have turned right round. When Peter saw that the galley had turned sufficiently to take a quarter wind into her sail, he drew the sheet of the sail. Immediately the knots were loosened, and in a twinkling the sail was unfurled and took the wind. At the same moment the cable of the stern anchor was cut, and Peter, himself holding the helm, made the galley fly out of this fatal cove like an arrow from a cross-bow. Thus by God's great mercy, and through the skill of Peter Bart, we were saved from this great and manifest peril of being dashed upon the rocks of this cove, and once more found ourselves in the open sea.

We now had to run for the nearest port to obtain shelter from this furious tempest, which continued with greater violence than ever. Dunkirk was the only one to the leeward that we had. The difficulty of reaching it did not disquiet us ; we were only twelve leagues from it, and the furious wind which was blowing, being from the south-west, was favourable to us, and took us there in less than three hours, with only one small 'sail. But our officers were still in the greatest anxiety, fearing lest the tempest should so drive us as to force us to pass Dunkirk. Then we should have had to run to the north, and, by reason of the bad weather, been obliged to run aground on the Dutch coast. This was what the convicts ardently wished, but what the officers and the rest of the crew exceedingly dreaded.

We ran then into the roadstead of Dunkirk. Our galley had left all her anchors in the cove of Amble-teuse, but M. de Fontête, who followed us, gave us two which we cast in this roadstead, where the anchorage is very good and sound. Here we were obliged to remain for six hours, till the tide was high enough for us to enter the harbour. During these six hours we were constantly between life and death. Waves, like mountains, continually covered us. We had to take great care to keep the hatch-ways well closed, otherwise the hold would in a moment have been filled with water, and we should have sunk. Every one was at prayer, as well in our galleys as in the town of Dunkirk, where the inhabitants saw us in this great danger. The Holy Sacrament was exposed in all the churches, and they ordered public prayers to be offered for us. It was all that they could do to help us, for no boat, neither small nor great, would have been able to leave the harbour to render us assistance. Another difficulty and danger threatened us. The harbour of Dunkirk is formed by two long and high jetties, which extend nearly half a league into the sea. The heads of these jetties form the entrance to the port. This entrance is difficult for vessels which must approach it from the south, because of a bar of sand in front of it, which makes it necessary to keep quite close to the southern shore, and by very careful steering to turn sharp round between the heads of these two jetties, the space between which is narrow, and, consequently, very difficult in rough weather, especially for galleys, which are of extreme length and cannot easily be turned. All these difficulties greatly puzzled us ; moreover, the heads of these jetties were quite covered by the sea, on account of the horrible tempest which was still ·increasing, and we only saw the entrance in the intervals between the retreat of the waves. But what was to be done ? We must enter the harbour or perish. All our pilots quite lost their presence of mind. They went to awaken Peter Bart, who was quietly sleeping on a bench, soaked through as he was by the waves which swept over him. He had given orders that he should be awoke when it was high tide, as it now was. Our commander asked him if he knew any way to enter the port without being lost. "Yes," said he ; "I will bring you in just in the same way as I enter with my boat when I return from fishing—at full sail." "What," said the commander, "enter at full sail ! we shall perish undoubtedly;" for a galley never enters a port at full sail because of the difficulty of managing it by helm, for it is by the oars that it is steered. "But," said Peter, "you cannot steer because of the heavy sea." "It is that which puzzles me," said the commander. "Leave me to act," said Peter ; "all will be well."

Meanwhile we were all more dead than alive, wet to the bones, having neither eaten nor drank for two days, because we could have neither bread, wine, brandy, or anything, in short, not daring to open the hatchway lest the galley should fill with water. Besides this, the apprehension of the approaching peril took away the little courage that remained to us, for we knew that we must enter by that narrow mouth between those two pier-heads, and that if, unfortunately, the galley touched them, however little, she would be dashed into a thousand pieces and not a soul would be saved. Peter Bart was the only one who showed that he had no fear, and who laughed at the panic which had seized us all, officers as well as the rest. He told the commander, however, that he could not prevent the galley from breaking her prow against the Quai de la Poisonnerie, where the harbour entered, because entering at full sail with such a strong wind they would not be able to stop her. "What matters that?" said M. de Langeron; "it is only wood; the carpenter will repair the damage."

Peter then quickly prepared for his operations. He veered the cables, arranged the sails, and, ordering a perfect silence, he kept quite close to the southern shore as far as the mouth of the harbour, and steered so skilfully, that he turned sharp round into the entrance between the two jetties. He then lowered his sails, but the galley was impelled with such force inwards, that two or three thousand sailors and other seafaring people whom the mayor of the town had sent on to the jetties to help us, and who every minute threw ropes to stop us, could not succeed, the thickest ropes breaking like thread; and at last the galley broke her nose against the quay, as Peter had foretold. M. de Fontête's galley observed and made the same manœuvre as we had done, and entered the port successfully. Peter Bart at once took leave of the commander, who wished by all means to retain him in his vessel, promising him double wages. "No, no," said Peter, "not if you would give me a housand francs a month; I have had enough of it; you will never catch me again;" and then he went off. We scarcely left Dunkirk harbour again all the year, and we dismantled early for the winter.

In the month of April, 1708, we rearmed, and during the whole campaign we merely cruised about the English coast, only alarming the enemy sufficiently to make him keep his troops on the alert; but as soon as any large coastguard ship appeared, we escaped as quickly as possible to the French coast. This lasted till the 5th of September, a day which I shall never forget by reason of the event which then occurred, and of which I bear the marks of the three great wounds I then received. I must now relate this story, which may interest the reader, for it is a very curious one, and, like all which is contained in these memoirs, perfectly true.*

At the beginning of the summer of 1708, Queen Anne of England, among a large number of men-of-war which she sent to sea to cruise along the coasts, possessed a guard-ship of seventy guns, which was commanded by a concealed Papist, whose intentions towards his country were very hostile, as experience afterwards proved. This captain was

---

* Some doubt has been expressed as to the following statement respecting Captain Smith. It is, however, fully confirmed by authentic documents. See Charnock's *Naval Biography*, etc.—ED.

named Smith. Not belonging to any squadron, but being alone and at liberty to execute his treason, he sailed to Gottenburg in Sweden. There he sold his ship, whether to the King of Sweden or to private individuals, I know not ; however that may be, he sold it and received money for it, and having dismissed the crew, he went in person to the court of France to offer his services to the king against England. The king gave him a warm reception, and promised him the first vacant captainship, advising him, however, to go to Dunkirk and wait for it, serving meanwhile as a volunteer in M. de Langeron's galley, where he would give orders that he should be treated with honour and respect. Captain Smith saw that this *advice* was really his majesty's *command.* He obeyed, and was received very politely by the Chevalier de Langeron, and entertained at his expense.

Captain Smith took part in all the expeditions which we made to the English coast. He much wished to make a descent there that he might distinguish himself by burning a few villages, but it was dangerous to attempt it. There were coast-guards all along the shore, and at short intervals bodies of land troops, which our sailors feared like fire. Captain Smith, burning with hatred against his country, always had his head full of projects to injure the English. Among other schemes he sent to the court, one was proposed to burn and pillage the little town of Harwich, situated at the mouth of the Thames, provided the six galleys at Dunkirk were placed under his command. The king approved of

this project, and gave orders to M. de Langeron to
follow Captain Smith's commands for this expedition, and ordered the master of the admiralty to
provide him with everything that he might require.
M. de Langeron, though with repugnance at finding
himself obliged to submit to the orders of a foreigner,
obeyed apparently with a good grace, and told
Smith that he had only to command the preparation and departure of the galleys for this expedition.
Smith took on board all that was needed from the
master of the admiralty—combustible materials,
and everything that was necessary for the sack
of Harwich, with a division of soldiers to assist.

All being ready, one fine morning, the 5th of
September, we put to sea with the best weather
possible for the galleys. A soft breeze from the
north-east favoured us so well that with very
little sail we arrived at the mouth of the Thames
about five o'clock in the evening, without rowing
at all. But Smith, thinking that it was too early,
and that they might be able to discover us
from the shore, which would spoil everything, ordered us to retire farther out to sea to await the
night, before making the descent, which we did.
We had not been lying-to more than a quarter of
an hour when the sentinel on the watch at the top
of our mainmast called out, "Ships." "Where
from?" they asked. "From the north." "In what
direction?" "Towards the west," said he. "How
many sail?" "Thirty-six," said he. "Of what
sort?" "Thirty-five merchant vessels, and a frigate
of about thirty-six guns serving as an escort," re-

plied the sentinel. It was, in truth, a merchant fleet, sailing from the Texel to the Thames.

Our commander at once held a council of war, at which it was decided that, instead of undertaking the Harwich expedition, we should try and make ourselves master of this fleet, which would be more to the king's interest than burning Harwich; for the opportunity of seizing so rich a booty did not present itself every day, while the expedition to Harwich could be undertaken at any time. The commander alleged all these reasons to Captain Smith, who protested against the conclusion of the council of war, asserting that he must follow the orders of the king, and not turn aside to any other enterprise, and also that we should have to steer towards the south to allow this fleet to enter the Thames without perceiving us. But the council of war kept firm to their resolution, being secretly glad that they had an opportunity of causing the failure of the Harwich expedition, on account of the jealousy they felt at being obliged to obey the commands of Smith.

After the decision of the council, at which each captain received the commander's orders to attack the fleet, we hoisted fresh sail and rowed with all our might to meet it; as it was coming towards us, and we hastening towards it, we were very soon near each other.

Our commander's orders were, that four galleys should invest and take possession, if possible, of the merchant ships, which are generally without means of defence, while our galley, which was the

1

head of the squadron, was to join with that of the Chevalier de Mauviliers, in attacking and overcoming the frigate which served as an escort.

Following these directions, the four galleys sailed to surround the merchant vessels and cut them off from the mouth of the Thames, and we with our consort made straight for the frigate. She, seeing our manœuvre, perceived that her fleet, or at all events the greater part of it, was in imminent danger. She was an English frigate, and the captain in command one of the bravest and most skilful of the age, as he proved himself to be on this occasion. Having given orders to the merchantmen to force on all sail, and gain as quickly as possible the mouth of the Thames, to avoid falling into the hands of the French, he added that, as to himself, he reckoned on giving so much work to the six galleys that he hoped to save them all, and that, in a word, he was going to sacrifice himself for them. He thereupon spread all his sails to the wind and turned at our two galleys which were about to attack, as if he were coming to attack them himself.

The galley which was to serve as our consort was half a league behind ours ; either she did not sail so fast, or her captain designed that we should bear the first brunt of the attack.

Our commander was not much disturbed by the approach of the frigate, as he thought with his galley he was strong enough to master it. The result, however, proved, as will be seen, that he was wrong in his conjectures.

The frigate coming, as I have said, towards us and we towards it, it will easily be perceived that we were soon within range. We fired at the frigate, which did not reply by a single shot, which made our commander say in a joke, that the captain of this frigate was evidently tired of being an Englishman, and was going to surrender to us without fighting, but he soon changed his tone. We advanced so rapidly towards each other, that our galley was soon within musket shot, and our musketeers already began to play upon the frigate, when all of a sudden she veered round as if she were about to flee from us. The flight of an enemy generally increases courage, and it had this effect upon our crew, who began to cry out to the men on board the frigate that they were cowards in trying to avoid the battle, but that it was now too late, and if they did not strike their flag and surrender at once, they would sink the ship. The Englishmen took no notice of this, but they were preparing to enact, as will be seen, a bloody tragedy.

The frigate, which was feigning flight, turned her back upon us, and now gave us a chance of boarding her, for the manœuvre of a galley which is about to attack and board a ship is to bring her bows to bear against the stern (which is the weakest part of the ship). The whole strength of a galley is in her bows, and here she has the greater part of her artillery ; she therefore endeavours to force her bows into the enemy's stern, firing her five guns, and her crew then scramble on board. The commander of the galley at once ordered this attack, bidding the pilot to steer straight at the frigate, that we might force our bowsprit into her. All the soldiers and sailors appointed to jump on board, were standing ready with naked swords and axes in their hands, when the frigate, anticipating our manœuvre, evaded, by a clever stroke of the helm, our prow, just as it was about to strike into her stern, and we suddenly found ourselves with her broadside upon us, against which we shaved so closely that our oars were broken to pieces.

The coolness and courage of the English captain were admirable ; he had foreseen what would occur, and was all ready with his grappling-irons, by means of which he seized our galley and hooked her on to his broadside. Then he gave us a taste of his artillery. All his guns were charged with grape-shot. Every man on board the galley was as exposed as if upon an open bridge or raft. So close were the frigate's guns to us, that not a single shot was without effect, and a frightful carnage ensued. Moreover, the captain had placed in the rigging a number of his men, with barrels full of hand-grenades, which they rained down upon us like hail, with such good aim that all our crew were disabled, not only from attacking, but even from making any defence; those who were neither killed nor wounded, lay flat down to pretend that they were so, and the terror was as great among the officers as among the crew. The enemy perceiving this, added to our discomfiture by sending forty or fifty men on board our galley, sword in hand, who cut to pieces any of the crew they could lay their hands upon, only sparing the convicts, who made no attempt at defence. After they had hacked about like butchers, they returned to their frigate, continuing to pelt us with their guns and grenades.

M. de Langeron seeing himself reduced to this condition, and that not a person on board except himself seemed able to stand, hoisted with his own hands the flag of distress, thus calling all the galleys of the squadron to our aid.

Our consort was soon with us, and the four galleys which had already attacked and forced the greater number of the merchantmen to strike their sails, seeing this signal, and the peril of their commander, quitted their prizes to come to his assistance, and turned away from the Thames, so that the fleet, hoisting their sails again, escaped up the river. All the galleys now rowed with such speed, that in less than a quarter of an hour all six surrounded the frigate, which was soon no longer in a condition to fire either cannon or musket-shot, and not a man of the crew appeared upon the deck. Twenty-five grenadiers out of each galley received orders to board the frigate. They had not much trouble in mounting, as there was no one to dispute their way, but once on the deck they found some one to speak to. The officers were entrenched under the quarter-deck, and poured such a murderous fire on these grenadiers that they soon discovered that the enemy had not yet surrendered. But the worst of all was that this deck was composed of a grating of iron; the greater part of the crew were between decks, under this grating, through the apertures of which they struck at the legs of the grenadiers with pikes and swords, so that they soon obliged them to jump back into their galleys. Another detachment was now ordered to board, but they too came down much quicker than they had gone up. This grating had at last to be broken through with axes and other strong instruments, in order that the crew might be forced from between decks; this was done, notwithstanding the heavy fire from the officers, and the blows of the pikes, which killed and wounded very many. By force of numbers the crew were at last obliged to leave the middle-deck, and were made prisoners. But the officers were still entrenched under the quarter-deck, and poured forth their shot unceasingly. They, too, had to be overcome, which was not done without loss.

The whole crew of the frigate had now surrendered, with the exception of the captain, who had shut himself up in his cabin on the quarter-deck, firing different guns and pistols which he had with him, and swearing that he would not surrender so long as a breath of life remained in him. The officers, who had already descended into our commander's galley as prisoners of war, gave a terrible report of their captain, who, they said, made every one tremble. He was, they said, determined to set fire to his frigate rather than surrender; this was a danger more terrible than any which we had yet undergone, for at any moment we expected to be blown up in the air with the frigate. The captain was master of the stern-cabin, from whence is the entrance to the powder-magazine ; he could, consequently, set fire to it in a twinkling, and, the frigate exploding, the six galleys would share her fate. There were more than three thousand men in the six galleys, and all were shuddering for fear of instant death, in so great danger were we. In this extremity it was resolved to summons the captain with civility and politeness to surrender, promising him the best treatment possible, but he only replied by firing his guns.

An extreme remedy was now resorted to, which was to capture him dead or alive. A sergeant, with twelve grenadiers, was ordered with fixed bayonets to go and break through the door of the cabin and force him to surrender. The sergeant at the head of his detachment soon broke through the door, but the captain who was waiting for him, pistol in hand, at once blew out his brains, so that he fell down dead. The twelve grenadiers, seeing this, and fearing the same fate, fled, and it was not possible for the officers to make any other soldier advance, for they said in their defence, that only being able to enter one by one into the cabin, the captain would kill them all one after the other. Gentle means must, then, again be employed to take him. The captain, who had only been re-sisting so long in order to give his fleet time to enter the Thames, and perceiving by the lights of these ships that they had all entered, no longer turned a deaf ear to the summons that he should surrender. But to give still more time to a few laggards in the fleet to escape, and that the night might completely hide them from the pursuit of the French, he still feigned a delay, saying that he would only surrender his sword into the hands of the commander of the galleys, who must come on board the frigate to take it. A truce was arranged, while this message was taken to the commander, who sent his second in command to the English captain, representing to him that it was not the duty of a commander to quit his post.

The captain, who had nothing more to do to place the fleet in safety, now gave up his sword. They brought him down into the galley to our commander, who was surprised to see a very little man, quite deformed, and hump-backed. Our commander complimented him, telling him that it was the fortune of war, and that he might console himself for the loss of his ship by the kind treatment which he would show him. "I have no regret," replied he, "for the loss of my frigate, since I have succeeded in my design, which was to save the fleet entrusted to my care. Moreover, I had resolved from the moment I saw you to sacrifice my ship and my own person for the preservation of the property which I had undertaken to defend. You will still find," added he, speaking to the commander, "a small quantity of lead and powder, which I had neither time nor opportunity to give you; it is the most valuable thing you will find in the frigate. As for myself, if you treat me as a man of honour, I, or some other of my nation, will some day perhaps have the opportunity of acting in the same way towards you."

This noble independence quite pleased M. de Langeron, who, returning him his sword, said very civilly, "Take back this sword, sir, you deserve only too well to wear it, and you are my prisoner only in name." Soon after our commander had occasion to repent that he had returned his sword to him, for the captain being introduced into the cabin of the galley, and seeing there the traitor Smith, whom he immediately recognised, and upon whose head the price of £1,000 sterling was set in England, "Traitor," said he, "you shall receive death from my hand, since the executioners in London cannot give it you," and at the same time he rushed upon him, sword in hand, and would have thrust it through his body, but the commander seized him by the arm and prevented the blow, to the great regret of the captain, who protested that he would rather have taken Smith than the six galleys. Captain Smith, who was greatly offended at this occurrence, represented that the captain and himself ought not to be in the same galley, and begged the commander to place his prisoner on another vessel; but the commander replied that this captain being his prisoner, Captain Smith must go to another galley, and his prisoner remain with him, which was done. We manned our prize, which was called the *Nightingale.* The name of this brave captain has escaped me.

We at once left the mouth of the Thames with

our prize, but we had to go out of our way and profit as much as possible by the darkness of the night to evade four light-decked ships which came out of the Thames to give us chase. They could not overtake us, and we arrived at Dunkirk three days after, without any accident.

I said that I should never forget the date, 5th of September, 1708, when these events occurred, and when I received three great wounds and escaped death, as by a kind of miracle. It happened thus :—

The frigate, having seized us with her grappling-irons, we were exposed to the fire of her artillery, and our bench, on which were five convicts and a Turkish slave, happened to be just opposite to one of the guns of the frigate, which I perceived to be loaded. Our broadsides were touching, consequently this gun was so near to us that by raising myself a little I could have touched it with my hand. This unpleasant neighbour made us all tremble ; my companions lay down quite flat, thus thinking to escape its fire. On examining this cannon, I perceived, from the manner in which it was pointed, that its discharge would bear directly upon our bench, and that, lying down, we must receive it upon our bodies. Having made this observation, I determined to stand straight up on my bench. I could not get away, I was chained to it ; what else could I do ? I must resign myself to pass under the fire of this cannon ! As I was attentive to all that was passing on board the frigate, I saw the gunner, with his lighted match in his hand, begin to touch the gun at the bows of the frigate with the fire, and then go from gun to gun till he came to the one which pointed upon our vessel ; I then lifted up my heart to God, and uttered a short but fervent prayer, as a man who expects the stroke of death. I could not take my eyes off this gunner, who kept gradually approaching our gun, as he applied his match in succession to the others. Now he came to this fatal gun ; I had the courage to watch him put the portfire to the gun, still standing straight up, and commending my soul to my Saviour. The cannon fired ; I was suddenly stunned and thrown prostrate, not upon the bench, but in the centre of the galley, as far off as my chain could extend. Here I lay, stunned and unconscious, stretched across the body of the lieutenant, who was killed, for I know not how long, but I imagine it must have been a considerable time. At last, however, I regained my senses. Raising myself from the lieutenant's body, I returned to my bench. It was night, and I saw neither the blood nor the carnage which was upon the bench, by reason of the darkness. I first thought that my comrades were still lying down, for fear of the cannon. I did not know that I was wounded, feeling no pain, and I said to my comrades, "Get up, lads, the danger is over." But I received no answer. The Turk on the bench, who had been a janissary, and who boasted that he was never afraid, remaining prostrate like the others, I said, jokingly, "What, Isouf, this is the first time you have been afraid ; come, get up,"

and at the same time I took him by the arm to
help him.   But oh! horror! which makes me
still shudder when I think of it, his arm, separated
from his body, remained in my hand.   With terror
I let fall the arm of this unhappy fellow, and
perceived that he, as well as the four others, were
literally hewn in pieces, for all the shot from the gun
had fallen upon them.   I sat down upon the bench.

I had not been long in that attitude when
I felt something cold and damp streaming down
upon my body, which was naked.   I put my hand
to it and felt directly that it was wet, but could not
in the darkness distinguish if it was blood.   But I
soon found that it was, and streaming from a large
wound which went quite through my left shoulder.
I felt another on my left leg, below the knee, as
deep as the one in my shoulder, and a third, nearly
a foot long and four inches broad, in my stomach.
I was losing an immense quantity of blood, without
being able to get assistance from any one, all
around me being dead, as well in my bench as in
the two adjoining ones, so that of the eighteen men
who were in those three benches, I alone had
escaped with my three wounds; and all this
slaughter had been caused by one cannon!   This
will easily be understood when I mention that
these guns were charged up to the muzzle, first
with cartridge-powder, then a long tin box, in size
varying according to the calibre of the gun, filled
with large musket-balls and old pieces of iron.
When they fired these guns the box broke, the
balls and grape-shot spread in an incomprehensible

manner, and caused a fearful carnage. I was then obliged to wait for assistance till the combat was over and order could be restored, for everything on board the galley was in a frightful state of disorder. No one knew who was dead, wounded, or alive ; we heard only the piercing cries of the wounded, of whom there were a large number.

The *coursier*, which is the deck or gangway passing down the middle of the galley from one end to the other, and is about four feet broad, was so encumbered with dead bodies that we could not pass over it. The rowers' benches were for the most part equally full of the bodies, not only of convicts, but of sailors, soldiers, and officers, either dead or wounded, so that the living and unhurt could scarcely move, either to throw the dead into the sea, or to help the wounded. Add to this the darkness of the night, and that we dared not light either torches or lanterns, fearing to be seen from the coast, and lest the ships of war which were in the Thames should pursue us, our galley was in a terrible state of chaos and confusion, which lasted far into the night, when the combat being ended by the surrender of the frigate, things were arranged as best they could be. The other five galleys helped us, replacing our dead and wounded, as well as the oars and equipments which we had lost, for they had not endured nearly so much loss or injury as we had done. They worked diligently, but as silently as possible, to put us into order.

I say silently, and without light, for we saw lights proceeding from the Thames, and heard several signal guns which we thought proceeded from ships of war which were coming to look after us.

The first thing done on board our galley was to throw the dead into the sea, and carry the wounded into the hold. But God knows how many wretches were thrown into the sea as dead who were not really so, for in this darkness and confusion they took for dead those who had only fainted, either through fear or loss of blood from their wounds. I found myself in this extremity, for when the *argousins* came to my bench to unchain the dead and wounded, I had fallen down in a fainting-fit, and lay motionless and unconscious among the others, bathed in their blood and my own. These *argousins* at once concluded that all belonging to this bench were dead. They only unchained them and threw them into the sea, without further examining whether they were dead or alive; it was quite enough if they did not hear them cry out or speak. These obsequies were so hastily performed that a bench was emptied in a moment. All my four comrades who were slain were frightfully mangled. I was the only one who was whole, but buried and prostrate in this carnage, making no movement nor sound. They unchained me to throw me into the sea, judging me to be dead. Now it must be remembered that I was chained by the left leg, and that it was in this leg I was wounded. One *argousin* seized me by this leg, to drag me up, while another was unfastening the bolt of the iron ring which held my chain. The latter, happily for me, put his hand upon my wound, which caused me so great pain that I raised a great cry, and I heard the *argousin* say, " This man is not dead;" and imagining at once that they were going to throw me into the sea, I exclaimed (for this pain had brought back my consciousness), " No, no ; I am not dead." They took me down to the bottom of the hold among the other wounded, and threw me down upon a cable. What a strange place of repose for a wounded man, agonised with pain !

We who were wounded were all cast pell-mell into the hold, sailors, soldiers, officers, and convicts, without any distinction, laid down upon the hard boards, and receiving no help or relief, for, on account of there being so many wounded, the surgeons could attend to but few. As to myself, I was three days in this terrible place without having my wounds dressed, only a little camphored brandy being applied to stop the bleeding, without any bandage or further treatment. The wounded died like flies in this horrible hold, where there was a stifling heat and dreadful stench, so that gangrene set in on most of our wounds. In this state we arrived, three days after the battle, in the roadstead of Dunkirk. The wounded were at once landed and carried to the naval hospital. We were hauled up out of the hold with ropes and pulleys, like cattle, and taken to the hospital, more dead than alive. The galley slaves were separated from the free men and placed in two large wards containing forty beds each, and we were all neck-chained to the foot of our beds. At one o'clock in the afternoon the head surgeon

of the hospital came to examine and dress our
wounds, accompanied by all the surgeons of the
ships and galleys which were in the harbour. I
had just been strongly recommended to the head
surgeon, and this is how it came about.

Since the year 1702, when I was taken to the
galleys at Dunkirk, I had been recommended by
my relations at Bordeaux, at Bergerac, and at
Amsterdam, to a rich and celebrated banker, named
M. Piecourt, who had a house at Dunkirk, and
frequently resided there. He was a native of
Bordeaux, a Protestant by birth and at heart, but
outwardly a Papist. He was quite a man of the
world, generous as a friend, and his purse was
always open to please and oblige the great nobles,
by whom he was much caressed and flattered. M.
Piecourt, then, perceiving that he was solicited
from so many different quarters in my favour, and
by people whom he highly valued, thought that
I was worth the trouble of any service he might
render me, and that if he could obtain my release
he would, at all events, greatly oblige some of his
best friends. He spoke in my favour to the
Chevalier de Langeron, my captain, who, out of
consideration to him, as he was his great friend,
granted me several indulgences. But wishing to
carry his good offices still further, he one day
begged my captain to have the kindness to order
that I should be brought to him the next day,
which was Christmas day, at eight o'clock in the
morning. He chose this time that his wife might
not know of it, for she was a bigoted Papist, and

that morning she would remain in church till noon. In the course of the evening M. de Langeron came to his galley (in winter these gentlemen do not live on board) to order the *argousin* to take me himself, without a chain, to M. Piecourt's, and to wait at the street-door, or in the hall, till I had finished my business with him. This was done.

M. Piecourt made me enter his room, telling his servants that he could see no one while I was there. He began by exaggerating the desire which he had to render me any service in his power, adding that he had devised a scheme for my release which would certainly succeed if I would leave it in his hands. I thanked him for his kindness, and told him that I would do all that he directed me, provided it could be reconciled to my conscience. "Conscience," said he, "will have a little to do with it, but so little that you will not feel it ; and what you think is wrong you can atone for when you get to Holland. Listen," said he. "I am a Protestant, like you. I have good reason, on account of my fortune, to play the hypocrite before the world. I don't believe there is any great harm in it when one does not apostatise at heart. This, then, is the scheme I have devised to set you at liberty. M. de Pontchartrain, the Minister of Marine, is a friend of mine, and will refuse me nothing. You will only have to sign a declaration which I will send to him, and in which you will promise, when you are set at liberty, and in whatever country you may be, to live and die a good Roman Catholic ; you will have no ceremony to perform, no one will even know what

K

you have promised, and you will not become a scandal to your brethren in the faith. If you will do this, I can assure you that within a fortnight you shall be released, and I will take care to send you safely over to Holland without the least danger. What do you think of it?" said he. "I think, sir," replied I, "that I was deceived in believing you to be a good Protestant. You are a Protestant, but we must take away the word *good*. I am very sorry, and I pray you to pardon me, when I venture to take the liberty to tell you that you are nothing at all, though you may believe yourself to be a Protestant. What, sir! do you think that God is deaf and blind, and that the promise which you propose that I should make, concealed from the eye of man, would not greatly offend him, as much and even more than if I made it to a simple curé? For I have only to do it before the chaplain of my galley, and he would at once procure me my release. Do not deceive yourself, sir," I continued, "the light which you possess concerning the truth condemns you, for you know as well as I do, and even better, that if the confession which we make to God in our hearts is not confirmed by that of our lips, instead of being a virtue it becomes a crime."

He then urged several reasons for relaxing the strictness which the Gospel prescribes. I refuted them all as my faith and my conscience dictated to me. I then told him that I did not think that my relations, who had commended me to his kindness, had petitioned him to procure me my release at the

expense of my conscience. "Certainly not," said
he; "very far from that; and I would not for a
great deal that they should know of it." He
embraced me, with tears in his eyes, desiring and
praying God that he would grant me grace to persevere in sentiments so worthy of a confessor of the
truth. "I do not love you so much," said he, "on
account of the recommendation I have received
regarding you, but out of pure respect for those
excellent sentiments which you profess; and you
may reckon that I shall watch for opportunities to
render you services." He then offered me as much
money as I needed. I thanked him as well as I
could, and then took leave of him, and returned to
my galley. Since then M. Piecourt frequently came
to see me on the galley, always offering me his
services.

It happened, then, that having heard how our
galley had lost many men at the capture of the
English frigate, he ran at once to the harbour to
inquire about me. He learned that I was severely
wounded, and had already been taken to the hospital. He went immediately to the head surgeon
of this hospital, who was his friend, and commended
me to his care as warmly as if I had been his own
son. I can indeed say that, after God, I owe my
life to this surgeon, who undertook, contrary to his
usual custom (for he never did anything but give
orders), to dress my wounds himself. At the first
visit which he made to our ward, he took his tablets
from his pocket, and asked who was called Jean
Marteilhe. I replied that it was I. He approached

my bed, and asked me if I knew M. Piecourt.   I
said that I did, and that he had had the kindness
to procure me all the indulgence possible during the
six or seven years that I had been at the galleys.
"The manner," said he, "in which he has commended you to my care proves the truth of what
you say. I shall with pleasure attend to his request.
Let us see your wounds."   The principal was that
in the shoulder, very dangerous on account of its
situation.   He at once took off the only bandage
which the surgeon of the galley had applied, and
whose negligence had caused my wounds to gangrene.   He summoned this surgeon, and reproached
him for being such a butcher as to have treated me
thus, and that if I died, as he feared I should do,
he would be my murderer.

The galley surgeon made the best excuse that he
could, and begged the head surgeon to allow him
to dress me.   This he refused, and declared to all
the others that I was his patient, and that he would
not allow any one to dress me except himself.   He
took, indeed, so great care of me, and used so many
remedies, that, humanly speaking, I may say he
saved my life.   Quite three-fourths of our wounded
died, the majority of whom were not wounded so
dangerously as I was.   The large number of men
who died at the hospital, both of the crews of the
galleys and of the convicts, made some think that
the English frigate used poisoned balls.   But I
believe, with all reasonable people, that it was a
calumny caused by the hatred which the French
bear to this nation.   The opinion of the head

surgeon, who was the most skilful in all France in his profession, was that this great mortality arose from the shot of these guns being dirty and rusty, and tearing the wounds which they made, added to the carelessness of the galley surgeons in their manner of dressing the wounds.

In less than two months my wounds were healed, but the surgeon made me remain a month longer in the hospital to regain my strength ; and as the director of the hospital, to whom I was also recommended, ordered the brethren of the order of St. Francis, who served this hospital, to give me all that I asked for which was not injurious to my health and to the healing of my wounds, I was fed and cared for like a prince.

At the end of three months I was sleek and fat as a monk, and the head surgeon having written out and given me a certificate that, owing to my wounds, I was rendered incapable of rowing or of doing other hard work in the galleys, I was sent back to the galley to my usual bench.

In the ensuing campaign, in 1709, the galleys armed in the month of April. There are six convicts to each oar ; the strongest and most vigorous is always strokesman, and has the hardest work. He is of the first class, the next is second class, and so on till the sixth class. This last has scarcely any work, so the weakest and feeblest on the bench is placed there. Now before I was wounded I was of the first class, and the *comite*, whether by inadvertence or otherwise, had left me in his list in this class, the work of which I could not perform, by reason of the weakness of my arm, which was almost useless, as I was scarcely able to put my hand to my mouth. I placed myself then, of my own accord, in the sixth class, waiting to pass through the test. This test is terrible, for the first time the galley puts to sea, to discover whether the convict is not feigning to be maimed, and thus endeavouring to exempt himself from the hard work of the oar, the *comite* overwhelms the poor wretch with strokes of the lash till he is very nearly dead.

We sailed out of the harbour, then, for the first time that year, and after the *comite* (who always stands on the prow of the galley till she is out in the open sea) had directed the starting of the galley, he visited each bench to see if the rowers were well classed. He held a thick cord in his hand, lashing those who were not rowing according to his fancy. I was in the sixth bench from the stern, and as he had begun his inspection from the bow, and was much excited, striking on all sides, before he came to my bench, I expected, in the greatest state of anxiety in the world, that he would treat me pitilessly. He arrived at last before our bench, and stopping with a ferocious air he ordered the strokesmen to cease rowing. Then addressing me, "Dog of a Huguenot," said he, "come here." I dragged my chain to approach the *coursier* upon which he was standing, my heart trembling with fear, and firmly believing that he had ordered me to come near to him that he might flog me the better. I approached him, cap in hand, in a suppliant posture. "Who ordered you," said he, "to row?" I replied that, being maimed as he could see by my scars (for I was naked to the waist, as one always is at the oar), and having only the use of one arm, I was employing it as well as I could to help my comrade on the bench. "That was not what I asked you," replied he; "I ask you who ordered you to row?" "My duty," replied I. "And I," said he, "command you not to row, nor any other of my crew who is in a similar condition, for if those who are wounded in battle are not released according to the law, I will not have them to row in my galley." Mark that he said this so that the other galley slaves might approve of it, and that they should not think that he favoured the Reformed. After having spoken these words, which I listened to as if an angel of heaven had appeared to me, so delighted was I, he called the *argousin*, and said to him, "Unchain that incapable dog, and put him down in the store-room." This is the place in the hold where all the victuals are kept. The *argousin* then unchained me from that fatal bench, where for seven long years I had suffered so much, and made me descend to this store-cabin. The steward of this cabin was a convict, with whom I had contracted a friendship for the last two or three years, although he was a Papist. He was about twenty-three years of age, a good-looking fellow, and the son of a gentleman of Limousin; he was at the galleys rather on account of a youthful misdemeanour than for gross crimes. His name was Goujon. When poor Goujon saw me introduced into the store-room, he threw himself on my neck. "My dear friend," said he, "is it, indeed, true that we shall add to the title of friend that of companion?" We congratulated each other, whilst the galley proceeded on her way, without the aid of our arms; and, as we had plenty of time for conversation, he told me his history, which till then I only knew imperfectly.

The galleys, during that day and the following night, cruised about in the Channel, after which they returned to the roadstead of Dunkirk. As soon as we had anchored there, the *comite*, seated on the table of his bench, called me to him. "You have seen," said he, "what I have done to relieve you. I am delighted to have found this opportunity to show you how I esteem you, and all those of your religion, for you have done no harm to any one; and I consider that if you are damned on account of your religion, you will be punished enough in the other world." I thanked him as well as I could for his kindness. "I am somewhat perplexed," continued he, "as to how I shall manage this affair so as not to make an enemy of the chaplain, who will never suffer me with impunity to favour a Huguenot. However, I have thought of an expedient which will, I hope, succeed. M. de Langeron's secretary is dead, and he is anxious to find another. I will propose to him that you should take the office, and will do it in such a way that I am sure he will accept you; you will then not only be exempt from work, but even respected by every one, and I shall be protected from the censure of the chaplain. Go away," said he, "to the store-cabin ; you will soon be called." I did so. The *comite* went immediately to speak to M. de Lan-geron. He described to him how he had a man on the sixth bench, but that he would rather have a sheep there, for this convict was maimed of one arm ; he had put him to the test by severe blows of the lash, but as he really was incapable of rowing he had removed him from the bench because he embarrassed and prevented his comrades from row-ing. Upon this M. de Langeron asked him how I had been maimed. " By the wounds," replied the *comite*, "which he received at the capture of the *Nightingale* at the mouth of the Thames." " How comes it, then," said the commander, "that he has not been released like the others ? " " Because," said the *comite*, " he is a Huguenot." Mark that it is the law to release all those who are wounded in a battle, however heinous the crime for which they have been condemned to the galleys, *except th. Reformed.* " But," added the *comite*, "this fellow knows how to write, and is very well behaved, and I think if you want a secretary he would be just the man for you." " Call him," said the commander. I was summoned at once. Directly he saw me he asked me if I was not M. Piecourt's friend ; I told him that I was. " Well, you shall be my secre-tary," said he ; " send him to the store-cabin, and remember that no one is to give him orders but myself."

Here I was, then, installed as the commander's secretary. I knew that he liked neatness. I had a little red coat made (a convict is obliged to wear that colour); I got also some finer linen; I had permission to let my hair grow; I bought a scarlet cap; and, thus polished up, I presented myself to the commander, who was charmed to see me in this costume, which I had purchased at my own expense. He ordered his steward to give me at every meal a plate from his table, and a bottle of wine a day, which was done throughout the campaign of 1709, and I can in truth say that I wanted nothing except liberty. I was night and day without a chain, having only a ring round my ankle. I had a good bed and perfect rest, while all the others were working at the oars. I was well fed, honoured and respected by the officers and the crew, and especially loved and esteemed by the commander and his nephew, the major of the six galleys, whose secretary I also became. I had, indeed, at certain times, very much to write, but I was so exact about it that I sometimes passed whole nights writing that I might complete my work sooner even than the commander expected.

In this happy state I continued till the year 1712, when it pleased God to submit me to a trial, great in itself, and all the more bitter because nearly four years of ease had accustomed me to prosperity. I shall say nothing here about the years 1710, 1711, and the greater part of 1712, except that the galleys remained unarmed in the port of Dunkirk, France being so denuded of everything connected with her navy that she could not even arm a boat, so that no event worthy of notice occurred till October, 1712, when our great tribulations, and those of our suffering community, took place. But before I proceed to this, I must relate the history of my friend, Goujon.

Goujon was a native of Serche, in Limousin, the son of rich and noble parents. He was the youngest of three brothers. One was a captain in the regiment of Picardy, and the other an ensign in the king's musketeers; Goujon himself had also an inclination for a military life. They were just levying a new regiment in his province, called the regiment of Aubesson, which was joined by the majority of the youth of the district, nearly all the officers belonging to Limousin nobility. M. de Labourlie, an uncle of Goujon's, was lieutenant-colonel of the regiment; Goujon joined it as a cadet; he was magnificently equipped by his father, who provided him with all the money necessary to cut a good figure.

The regiment being complete, was quartered at Gravelines, a small town four leagues from Dunkirk. Goujon had been well-educated; he had studied and learned all those accomplishments which befit a young nobleman, and he well-sustained the honour of his family. Being magnificently equipped, young, and well-made, and having plenty of wit, he soon gained the friendship and consideration of all; and as he frequented all the society of Gravelines, it was not long before he loved and was loved by a young lady, who quite merited his attachment. This lady was the only daughter of an old officer, a pensioner of the king,

and who was immensely rich.   These young lovers
were passionately attached to each other.   Goujon
flattered himself that the lady's father would joyfully give her to him in marriage.   In this hope
he made his request, but was much surprised, not
only to be flatly refused, but to be ordered by the
old officer never to see nor to hold any communi-
cation with his daughter again.   He most strictly
forbade his daughter from ever seeing her lover
again, on pain of being shut up in a convent.

This misfortune so greatly afflicted the two
lovers, that not seeing any means of bending the
old man, they formed a project of escaping to some
place where they could be married without obstacle,
and which having been decided upon, Goujon made
all his preparations for the elopement.   A post-
chaise was to be ready outside the town, on a day
fixed, when the young lady was to escape from her
father's house and go to a certain spot on the
ramparts.   The difficulty was how to get out of the
town, which could only be done under cover of the
darkness, and the gates of the town were always
closed at night-fall.   But Goujon thought of an
expedient, which proved less successful than he had
hoped.   There was an old breach in one part of
the ramparts which they had neglected to repair;
Goujon was well acquainted with it, as he had
often ascended by it when he was too late to enter
by the town gate.   There was, indeed, always a
sentinel at this breach, who was forbidden, under
pain of death, to allow any one, whoever it might
be, to pass.   But as there were no troops in

Gravelines except the regiment of Aubesson, all the soldiers of which knew and loved Goujon, who besides always gave money to the sentinel when he passed through this breach, he persuaded himself that whatever soldier was stationed there he would find the same facility and be able to pass through with his lady. He went then to the rendezvous; the young lady had kept her appointment; he led her straight to the breach, when a rough sort of a sentinel who was on duty there, a new recruit, who had even been the servant of Goujon's father, hearing some one approach, cried out, "Who goes there?" "A friend," replied Goujon. The sentinel, who recognised his voice, cried out to him not to approach any nearer unless he wanted a bullet through his heart. Goujon, calling him by name, spoke kindly to him, and promised him money to drink his health if he would let him descend by the breach. The sentinel, who kept to the letter of his orders, replied, that for all the money in the world, he would not risk being hanged. Goujon continued to advance, but the sentinel having again warned him to retire, took aim, but his gun having missed fire, Goujon, furious with rage, sprang upon the soldier, seized him in his arms, and threw him from the top of the rampart into the moat below.

The sentinel, though he was not hurt by the fall, yelled and screamed. Close by was one of the town gates, and beside it an office of the custom-house, in which a dozen clerks, all citizens of the town, were amusing themselves. Directly they heard the sentinel in the ditch cry out, they sprang to arms, and hastened to the place where Goujon was, some armed with pistols and others with swords, crying out, " Help, for the king's sake." Goujon, seeing this storm approach, and not being able to save himself without exposing his mistress, who would have been dishonoured for her whole life if he had abandoned her, took the most generous course. " Escape quickly, mademoiselle," he said to her, " and regain your home, whilst I favour your retreat by holding these people at bay. She at once escaped without being perceived. Goujon, however, was surrounded and attacked by these twelve clerks ; he drew his sword and used it too well for four of these unfortunate fellows, whom he slew, and wounded several others, not without receiving several wounds himself.

Not far off stood a little public-house, where a sergeant of Goujon's company happened just then to be, who, hearing the cries and the sound of arms, went out and asked what was the matter. Goujon, recognising his voice, cried out, " It is I, my friend La Motte, whom they are assassinating." La Motte, sword in hand, ran at one of the clerks who had a pistol in his hand which he discharged at La Motte, who at the same moment plunged his sword into the clerk's body, and both fell down quite dead. During this massacre the nearest guard hearing the cry, " Help, for the king's sake," had given the alarm to the whole garrison, which was at once under arms and hastened to the scene of the combat. Goujon had fallen down through weakness caused by loss of blood, which was flowing from four wounds. The major, who had come up with the nearest guards, had all the dead and wounded, as well as those who were unhurt, taken to the hospital. All the officers of the regiment, and especially the lieutenant-colonel, in order to save Goujon, warmly espoused his side of the affair against the clerks ; accusing them of rebellion and wishing to assassinate the king's soldiers. They even suppressed the fact of the sentinel having been thrown down from the rampart by Goujon, which was the real cause of all this slaughter. Besides, twelve citizens against two soldiers was an unfavourable sign for these clerks, and one by which they profited to save Goujon ; and notwithstanding the injustice towards the seven clerks who remained, they proceeded against them with extreme rigour.

The council of war undertook this affair, and gave sentence very precipitately. It justified Goujon, and praised him as a man of honour, for having, in the king's service, slain four citizens out of twelve who had attacked him ; and sentenced the seven clerks who remained—three to be hanged, and four condemned to the galleys for life ; for which fate they were to draw lots. The whole town exclaimed against this sentence of the council of war. The magistracy took the affair to heart, and went in a body to the governor to protest against the injustice of this sentence. A delay of thirty days before the sentence should be carried into execution was granted, and meanwhile, the whole affair was to be referred to the king, and Goujon confined in the town prison till the decision of the court was known.

The magistracy drew out a *procès verbal*, in which the whole affair was truthfully and minutely represented. They did not forget to insert Goujon's crime in assaulting the sentinel, and throwing him off the rampart. It was moreover proved that the clerks taking the king's side, and being peaceably disposed, had, before using any act of hostility, implored Goujon, in the king's name, to lay down his arms, but that Goujon had replied very disrespectfully, "that the king and all his family might go about their business." This imprudence cost Goujon very dearly, for the king, who was fully informed of it, would never pardon him. The court, after due examination, ordered that the sentence of the council of war should be annulled, and that the magistracy should pronounce the final sentence, which acquitted the clerks, and condemned Goujon to be hanged, leaving him the option, if he preferred it, on account of his rank, to be shot at the foot of the gallows.

The consternation which this sentence caused throughout the regiment, may well be imagined. The lieutenant-colonel, Goujon's uncle, was in despair. He at once hastened to the governor, imploring him not to carry out the execution of this sentence, and to grant him at least a delay of twelve days. The governor granted it to him, and the lieutenant-colonel immediately travelled post to solicit the pardon of his nephew at court. He threw himself at the king's feet, beseeching him with clasped hands to pardon Goujon, trying to touch his majesty on his most sensitive points. But the king, offended at Goujon's insolent disrespect towards himself and the royal family, remained inflexible. The lieutenant-colonel was not disheartened, he moved heaven and earth, and petitioned Madame de Maintenon, who every one knew had immense power over the king. She took the affair to heart, and notwithstanding the monarch's repugnance to pardon Goujon, she obtained his forgiveness so far, that Goujon's sentence was remitted to servitude for life on board the galleys at Dunkirk; the king added his command that he should never more be spoken to about him.

The lieutenant-colonel returned with all diligence to Gravelines, bringing with him this commutation of the sentence of death. He went to the governor, to whom he delivered Goujon's sentence, with the king's orders that he should be conducted to the galleys, well guarded, and that if he escaped, his head and that of the commander of the garrison would have to answer for it.

Fearing lest the garrison should form a design to rescue Goujon, either in the town or on the road, they pretended that Goujon had received a full pardon from the king on the sole condition of serving as a soldier in the Chevalier de Langeron's company at Dunkirk. The lieutenant-colonel accordingly went to the prison, where he found Goujon with two Capuchins, who were exhorting him to prepare for death on the morrow. The lieutenant-colonel immediately exclaimed, "Courage, my nephew, you shall not die. I have obtained your complete pardon, and the king has ordered you to serve as a soldier in M. de Langeron's company. This punishment is nothing, as we shall soon obtain you an officer's commission. To-morrow two archers, merely for form's sake, will come to take you to Dunkirk, and there you will be free, but as a common soldier."

The next day two archers, who had orders how to act, came to the prison. With much civility to Goujon, they told him that they were all three going to ride to Dunkirk, not as if they were conducting a prisoner, for in fact he was not one, but as if they were going on a party of pleasure. Goujon, who believed all this, was quite content with his fate ; the officers of the regiment, equally deceived, came in a crowd to the prison to congratulate Goujon, and to wish him a pleasant journey. Then he mounted his horse with the two archers, and they set out. At some distance from the town, in a deep and narrow road, one of the archers turned suddenly on Goujon, pistol in hand, telling him he would blow out his brains if he made the least resistance, the other archer meanwhile tied his legs under the horse's belly, and put irons on his hands. The distress of the young man may easily be imagined, for he thought they were going to kill him. Having asked the archers his destination, they brutally ·replied that he would know when he arrived there. In this condition they arrived at Dunkirk, conducted Goujon to the galleys, and delivered him to the *argousin*, who made him take off his laced clothes, and put on a red jacket. Then they cut off his hair, the most beautiful I ever saw in my life, and chained him to a bench. However, the recommendations in his favour which came to our captain from all quarters soon mitigated his sufferings. The captain ordered that he should be placed in the store-cabin, to distribute the victuals to the band of galley slaves and to the crew, and exempted him from every other kind of labour. He was unchained also night and day, and had only a ring round his ankle as a mark of servitude. I soon made his acquaintance; he was a young man of great talent, and most agreeable in conversation.

Goujon and I remained friends and comrades in the store-cabin till the year 1712, in the month of July, when he escaped from the galleys. The manner in which he succeeded is curious enough. I have already said that Goujon had influential relations and friends who were interested in his misfortunes, and unceasingly endeavoured to procure his deliverance. His father, a venerable old man, threw himself at the king's feet with his two other sons, imploring his majesty's clemency for his son at the galleys. He expressed, with much force, the affection of a father for his children, promising the monarch that, old as he was, he would cheerfully go at the head of his three sons to shed his blood in his service. He spoke in such a touching and pathetic manner, that all those who were present were melted to tears. He could not, however, move the king, who constantly refused Goujon's pardon, which shows that injuries done to the great are spots of the deepest dye, which

cannot easily be effaced. Notwithstanding the
ill-success of this last step, they made yet a new
attempt to obtain Goujon's liberty. They gained
over Marshal de Noailles to their cause; he had
just returned from the siege of Gironne, which he
had taken with much glory.

The king, to whom he came to render an account
of his conduct, received him most graciously. The
opportunity was favourable to ask and obtain some
favour from his majesty. But M. de Noailles confined himself to asking for the pardon of Goujon.
The king told him that he was sorry to refuse him,
but that he had sworn never to grant it. Goujon,
who was informed of this, saw very well that he
could not obtain his release as long as the king
lived, and consoled himself with the hope that his
own death, or that of the king, would deliver him,
some time, from this slavery. Notwithstanding
his pitiable condition, he enjoyed some pleasures.
His father sent him everything he needed, and his
friends in the regiment, officers as well as soldiers,
often came to visit him—for everybody is allowed
to enter the galleys.

In May, 1712, a sergeant of grenadiers of the
regiment of Aubesson, then in garrison at Nieuport,
came to see Goujon, to whom he was greatly attached. After several complaints on the subject of
his slavery, and on his little hope of ever being released from it, the sergeant said to him, "I come
here, sir, expressly on the part of your friends in
the regiment, to inform you that if four grenadiers
and myself, all men of courage and experience, can

procure your liberty, either by open force or otherwise, you have only to tell us the means by
which we can serve you, and you know that we are
all five at your disposal, at the risk of our lives.
We are aware in the regiment that you often have
occasion to go into the town. If you think that we
might carry you off then, I protest to you that no
danger would hinder us from doing so. Reflect
upon what I have the honour to tell you, and reckon
upon our discretion and courage. It would be '
useless for you to ask me who those are who will
undertake the work, you can guess without my
telling you. I shall come, from time to time, to
talk over and consult with you on the resolutions
which you may think fit to take."

I was present at this conversation; Goujon and I
were so intimate that we had no secrets from each
other. Charmed with the proposal, he thanked the
sergeant for his kindness, but said that such a
perilous enterprise demanded time and reflection;
that he would well consider it, so as not to undertake anything which was not certain of success; and
that as soon as he saw any opportunity of escape
he would let him know, so that they might devise
together all necessary measures. The sergeant
then took leave of us, and from that moment Goujon thought of nothing else than of planning some
means of escape. The thing was not easy. It is
true that he often had occasion to go into the town
on account of his business, which was to distribute
the victuals to the galley slaves; but he never
went alone, the *argousin* always chained him to a

Turk, and gave him as a guard a man named Guillaume, who was very strict, and to no other guard would the *argousin* intrust Goujon. I must mention that it was strictly forbidden to allow any couple of convicts, who went into the town on business, to enter the public-houses, either to buy or sell, under the penalty of three years to the galleys for the guard, and a thousand crowns fine to those who allowed them to enter their houses. The privilege, therefore, which Goujon enjoyed of going into the town could not serve him in the execution of his design. It was impossible to carry him off in the street in broad daylight, and in sight of a large number of soldiers, and of the crews of the galleys. Besides, the town was filled with a numerous garrison, which had guards and sentinels everywhere ; in short, the thing did not appear practicable. There was only one way to succeed, which was to bribe the guard largely, and so obtain permission from him to enter a public-house. This Goujon determined to try, persuaded that if he could obtain this favour from his guard, for only once, he should easily attain his object. Having formed this project, he wrote to his father to beg him to send him a large sum of money which he required for a matter of importance. The good man did not fail to send it to him, and he had no sooner received it than he began to take measures to carry out his daring plan.

One day, in the month of June, when it was very hot weather, Goujon was in the town with Guillaume, his usual guard. After having performed several errands connected with his business, while they were passing through a narrow bye-street, and opposite to a public-house, Goujon seeing that his guard was faint with thirst, and being also very thirsty himself, he begged to ask for a pot of beer to be brought to the door that they might refresh themselves. Guillaume, who saw in this nothing contrary to his orders, willingly accepted it. The landlady brought them a pot of beer into the street, and seeing that fatigue made them look for something to sit down upon, she said to them, "There is a bench in my hall, make use of it, and come under the doorway if you like, where, being as visible as in the street, I shall not be compromised." They did not want much asking. Goujon treated his guard and the Turk very liberally, and after having passed two or three hours, he asked the landlady what he owed. She told him that it was thirty sous. "Here, my good woman," said he, "is a crown of five francs, I will make you a present of the rest." This woman, who was not very rich, felt so much obliged by this generosity that she offered to let him enter her house whenever he liked. "No," said Goujon to her, "I do not wish to expose either you or my guard, it is a duty which I shall always observe." Upon this they went out to return to the galley. But before they reached it Goujon put a crown into Guillaume's hand, out of gratitude, he said, for the permission which he had given him to refresh himself at this public-house. Guillaume was so delighted with this present that he was quite beside himself.

These guards have very small wages, and for the last three years they had not been paid, nor had any of the crew, so that this crown was a treasure for him. He at once told Goujon that in future he would give him more liberty, for that by taking certain precautions there could be no danger for any one.

Goujon was much pleased at this adventure, which he related to me in all its particulars, and which greatly raised his hopes. It was not long before he went to the town again. He felt how necessary it was for him to conciliate these people more and more, and not to allow their good-will to cool down. After having performed his pretended business they went to breakfast at this public-house. The landlady made them enter her vestibule, and gave them what they wanted, while the servant stood as sentinel at the street-door to observe if any suspicious persons made their appearance. After breakfast the landlady, probably in her own interest, said to them, " Gentlemen, we shall always be under apprehension lest any one should discover you in this vestibule. There is a way by which we can avoid this ; I have a room quite at the end of the house. You can remain there in quiet ; and when you come here you will only have to be careful as you go in, and as you come out, to see if any one in the street is watching you." Goujon, not wishing to show the joy which this proposal gave him, did not reply ; but Guillaume, who, besides the hope that he would come oftener and enjoy the more good cheer, was still reckoning on Goujon's generosity, said at once that it was a very good idea of the landlady, and that they must see the room. It was found to be very convenient. Guillaume, for his own security, Goujon, for the execution of his design, readily agreed to accept it. " I do not wish," said the latter to the landlady, " that in order to oblige us, you should ruin yourself. Your room might be occupied by others, who come here to spend their money, when we arrive, and it would not be just that you should be deprived of such profit. Let us arrange in a manner fair to both parties ; let me this room by the month, so that it may be always at our disposal when we come to your house." " Ah ! Monsieur Goujon," said Guillaume, " how clever you are ; nothing in the world could be better." Goujon, always liberal, gave the landlady twenty francs a month for the room, which he paid in advance ; and gave the same sum to Guillaume, telling him that as he ran the same risks as this woman, it was but fair that he should have the same profit. He also gave a piece of money to the Turk, lest he should tell tales to the *argousin*. After which they returned to the galley, all well content with the events of the day. Guillaume and Goujon arranged to go next day and take possession of this room. So Guillaume went by Goujon's request to order a good dinner, and the next day they went and enjoyed themselves perfectly. They continued to go there frequently till towards the end of July, when Goujon's project was carried into execution.

The sergeant of grenadiers, whose name was La Rose, did not fail to come from time to time to see Goujon, who told him all that had taken place. " What most embarrasses me," said La Rose to him one day, " is, that I do not see any means by which I and my four grenadiers can get into the room of which you have spoken. For the landlady will never allow any one to enter while you are there, for fear of being betrayed ; and, besides, your guard for the same reason would strongly oppose it." " Do not trouble yourself about that," said Goujon ; " I have thought of this difficulty before you, and have provided for it. When the right time comes I will communicate to you the plan which I have formed, and the measures it will be necessary to take in order to succeed. Leave to me the care of making all arrangements. I only ask from you and your four faithful grenadiers constancy in your resolutions, and firmness and courage in their execution."

The sergeant assured him anew that he might rely upon them. After which he returned to his garrison. Guillaume and Goujon often went to regale themselves at their mother's (thus they called the landlady), and they became so much at home in this public-house, that the hostess regarded them as if they belonged to her family. At last Goujon, thinking that it was time to carry his project into execution, gave his last orders to La Rose, who had come to see him. After telling him that the time had come to put his courage to the proof, he gave him the plan of the enterprise in writing, so that he might forget nothing, and fixed the day and hour that he was to be at Dunkirk with his four grenadiers. This plan, which he showed me, charmed me as much by its ingenuity as by the means which he had taken to prevent the shedding of any blood, as will be seen. The day fixed for Goujon's abduction having arrived, the sergeant and the four grenadiers did not fail to come to Dunkirk, after having each learned by heart the part they had to play. Goujon being ready to set out for the town, embraced me with tears in his eyes. " Pray God for me, my dear friend," said he ; "to-day will be an epoch of happiness to me, or the end of my life, for if anything arrests my flight, and I have a sword in my hand, I will die in the defence of my liberty." This farewell alarmed me. I entreated him, by our warm friendship, to abandon his enterprise, and patiently to await his release till a less dangerous opportunity should present itself. "No," said he, "the die is cast. I have a presentiment that the issue will be favourable, which decides me to wait no longer." He embraced me again, wiped away his tears, and then went to be chained to his Turk, that he might go to the town under the guardianship of Guillaume.

The signal which Goujon had given to the sergeant was that he would pass about nine o'clock in the morning before the town-hall, and that if everything was favourable for the execution of his project he would take his handkerchief out of his pocket, and then the sergeant was to follow in due order the directions which he had given him.

Accordingly he passed by the appointed place, pretended not to see the sergeant who was there watching for him, gave him the signal agreed upon, and went to breakfast at the public-house with his usual escort. About ten o'clock, whilst they were at breakfast, two of the grenadiers passing before the public-house with their knapsacks on their backs, one said to the other, " Comrade, we must drink a glass of brandy here." They entered the bar, and after the landlady had poured them out a glass and they had sat down, one asked the other if he had not seen their other two comrades and the sergeant; he replied he had not. " What a bother they are with their plague of a Goujon," said the first, " it will be their fault if we cannot get back to our garrison to-day." The woman, who had heard Goujon named, curious to know if they were speaking of him who was then in her house, asked them if they knew this Goujon whom they had just mentioned. " Know him ! I should think we did !" said they. " He was a cadet in our regiment, and had the misfortune some years ago to be condemned to the galleys for an affair of honour. But, thank God, he is just going to be released. Our lieutenant-colonel has so long petitioned the court for his deliverance, that at last he has been pardoned and received a lieutenant's commission. It is about this affair that our sergeant has come to Dunkirk ; the lieutenant-colonel has sent him to carry this act of pardon to the master of the galleys, that he may at once release this M. Goujon, and we other four grenadiers have profited by this opportunity to come into the town to buy provisions for our mess. The sergeant, in the execution of his commission, went to the galley where Goujon is to obtain his release, but not finding him there, as he had been sent to the commissariat in the town to purchase provisions, our sergeant, who in vain searched for him there also, separated from us that he might go and seek for him to tell him this good news." "What!" said the landlady, "is Goujon going to be released?" "Yes, indeed," said they, "and he would be free now, if we had found him in his galley."

The woman fell into the trap, and ran to tell Goujon all that had passed. The story had so much appearance of truth, that Guillaume also believed that Goujon was about to be set at liberty. Goujon, pretending to be in transports of joy, asked if these two grenadiers had gone out. "No," said the landlady, "they are still at the bar." Guillaume, firmly believing all he had heard, and no longer seeing any danger in being found at a public-house, was the first to exclaim that they should be asked to come in. The landlady at once went to ask them. These two fellows, who had learned their part very well, threw themselves at once on Goujon's neck and congratulated him upon his happy release, telling him all the particulars of it, as well as the search which the sergeant was making to find him. They drank several glasses to Goujon's health, and all testified to the joy they felt. Meanwhile, the other two grenadiers were preparing to come upon the scene

of action. They, in their turn, passed before the
public-house, and, as if they had come there quite
by chance, one said to the other, " Just look into that
public-house, comrade, and see if our people are
perchance in there." Looking in at the door he
called out, " No, they are not in there." " I don't
care where they are, then," said the other ; " don't
let us trouble ourselves any longer looking for
them." The landlady, who saw by their uniforms
that they belonged to the same regiment as the
others who were within, asked them who they were
looking for. " For two of our comrades," replied
they. "You shall see them in a moment, gentlemen," said she, "they are in my house ; have the
kindness to come in and follow me " Having introduced them into the room where Goujon was,
the embraces and congratulations recommenced.
" To make our joy complete, we only want the
sergeant," said Goujon. " If one of you would go
and look for him, it would give me much pleasure."
The grenadier who undertook this commission, and
who knew well enough where he was, was not long
before he returned with him. As yet the plan had
succeeded very well, the greatest difficulty was
over ; it only remained to complete the undertaking
with the same success, and to remove every obstacle
out of the way.

The hostess was a widow, and had only one
servant, who might have cried out, spread the
alarm, and rendered the adventure perilous and
sanguinary. Goujon, who had foreseen this incon-
venience, in order to avoid it, said to the grena-

diers that as they had come too late for breakfast he would treat them to some oysters. They declined in order to look less suspicious, and said that they must go back to Nieuport, and that if they enjoyed themselves any longer here, they would be too late to reach it that evening. But Goujon at last persuaded them, telling them it would not take long, and at the same time calling the servant, to whom he gave some money, told her to go and buy some oysters at the fish market, which was quite at the other end of the town.

Soon after she was gone, they called the hostess to bring some wine. When she had brought it, Goujon said to her, " Mother, you must drink to my happy release." " With all my heart, my son," said she ; and just as she had the glass at her mouth, and the others, too, were raising their full bumpers, Goujon gave his signal. At the same instant the sergeant, with fixed bayonet, sprang upon the landlady, threatening to strangle her if she cried or made the least resistance. From the other side a grenadier rushed upon Guillaume, threatening him in the same way, and another upon the Turk, who laid down under the table. They placed the landlady, who had fainted with fright, upon a bed, and commanded Guillaume to lie down without making the least resistance ; this he did, after imploring for quarter upon his knees, and remained as. still as if he were dead. Each one having his appointed duty, the two second grenadiers quickly emptied their knapsacks. In them was a complete costume, everything that was

necessary to dress Goujon from head to foot.
Having provided themselves also with a small
anvil, a hammer, and a driving bolt, they had soon
unchained him and dressed him like an officer,
with a sword at his side, for the sergeant had
brought one under his arm, saying that it was for
an officer of the regiment who had commissioned
him to buy it for him at Dunkirk. This being
done, Goujon, with the sergeant and two grenadiers,
went out and quickly reached the Nieuport gate.
The other two remained a few minutes after them
to watch their three patients, the hostess, the guard,
and the Turk, and then, one saying to the other
that they would take a little more brandy, they
went to the bar, swearing that if either of them
made the least movement, they would come back
and stab them all three. In this way these two
grenadiers got out at the door and hastened on the
road to Nieuport, where they joined their comrades. Their three victims had no desire to move.
Fear made them think that the three grenadiers
were still in the house. They remained in this
attitude till the servant came in with the oysters.
Finding them all lying on the ground, and pale as
death, she inquired what had happened to them,
and told them that there was no one at the bar or
in the house. Then they began to breathe freely
and to take courage. Guillaume, getting up
quickly, fled to Nieuport, where there was the
right oi sanctuary in the churches as there is everywhere in Brabant and Flanders. When he arrived,
he took reiuge with the Capuchins, where he found

Goujon, the sergeant, and the four grenadiers, who had also sought safety there.

Meanwhile, I was very anxious and curious to know how it had fared with my friend Goujon, for whom I feared greatly, knowing that in enterprises of this nature, in which there are so many dangers to guard against, the least thing often causes them to fail. In this perplexity I sat upon the prow of the galley, always looking towards the quay, when I saw Goujon's Turk coming, carrying his chain upon his shoulder. This was quite enough to make me certain that Goujon was already far away, which greatly relieved the anxiety which I felt on his behalf. The *argousin* who was standing on the quay, seeing the Turk coming with the chain upon his shoulder, eagerly asked him where Goujon was. "Well," said the Turk, "he is far off—more than five hundred grenadiers, with bombs, cannons, and other arms, came to carry him off from us." Fear had so disturbed the brain of this poor Turk that he had become quite foolish, and continued so all the rest of his life. The *argousin*, not being able to get anything reasonable out of the Turk, saw that he had lost his senses, and that Goujon had escaped. Upon which, fearing to be summoned before a council of war, he too fled to Nieuport, and took refuge also with the Capuchins. The commander of the regiment of Aubesson wrote to the court to obtain the pardon of the sergeant, the four grenadiers, and of Goujon. The commander of the galleys, likewise, wrote for the pardon of his *argousin* and of the guard. As

M

in these cases of sanctuary it is not generally refused, the pardon of all was granted, with the exception of Goujon, whom the king would never hear mentioned, much less pardon. He was obliged to escape secretly and in disguise from the town of Nieuport, and some days after he wrote to me from Bruges, telling me that he should remain in that town till his father had settled his destination; but of this I never heard. I was suspected of having connived at his escape. They insinuated this to M. de Langeron, but he liked me too well to listen to such accusations. Any one else would have received the bastinado, for it is a law of the galleys that if any one knows of the intended escape of his comrade or any other convict, and does not inform the *argousin*, he is to be bastinadoed without mercy. Moreover, if a convict escapes from a bench, the five others on that bench, and the twelve on the two adjoining benches, all receive the bastinado. This is a politic law, and makes each watch to prevent the escape of another, but it is very unjust, as a man can escape without any of his neighbours knowing it. But there is no justice for a galley slave, at least very little.

After the flight of Goujon they added to my secretaryship the office of distributor of the victuals to the band of galley slaves, which I exercised till the 1st of October, 1712, when they took us away from Dunkirk to conduct us to Marseilles. Before I come to this removal, I must relate an event which placed me and others of our brethren in extreme peril of dying under the bastinado. It must be known that our brethren of the French churches in the United Provinces sent from time to time a remittance of money to the Reformed who suffered in the galleys of France. This money generally passed through Amsterdam, whence a banker sent it to one of his correspondents in the places where the galleys were. One of my relations at Amsterdam, an elder of the Walloon Church, charged me with the commission of receiving it. This office is a very perilous one, for if it is found out, you risk being bastinadoed to death, unless you reveal the name of the banker who has received the money, and in such case the banker would be utterly ruined.

The missionaries from Marseilles, who have always persecuted us to the utmost, never found any opportunity of renewing and increasing our suffering which they did not embrace with ardour. Knowing that our brethren in foreign lands sent us money from time to time, to prevent us from dying of hunger, and persuading themselves that if this resource was taken from us they would overcome us by famine, proposed to the court to give orders to the galley-masters at Marseilles and Dunkirk, and to the majors and other officers of the galleys, to watch if any merchant or banker remitted money or letters of exchange to any of the Reformed galley slaves. The court did not fail to send these orders, and commanded that they should be rigorously carried out, and proceedings taken against the merchants or others convicted of acting contrary to them. The missionaries, of course, narrowly watched that no help reached us. Their greatest attention was given to find out what bankers or merchants furnished us with money through correspondence with foreign countries, that they might so severely punish them that no other would afterwards dare to expose himself to a like fate. But by the grace of God they never succeeded in making this discovery, although these remittances came to us very often. I ought to add, also, thanks to the fidelity of the Turkish slaves, who served us wonderfully well, out of pure charity and kindness.

In speaking of the fidelity and affection which the Turks bore to us, I must mention the example of the Turk who served me on these occasions at Dunkirk. I have said that I was commissioned to receive these remittances, and to distribute them to our brethren. I was chained to my bench, without having the liberty to go into the town. This was through the malice of the chaplain of the galleys, who prevented us from having this privilege, which the other convicts, condemned for their crimes, could have at any time by paying a sous to the *argousin* and a sous to the guard who went with them. How, then, was this money to be received ? M. Piecourt sent it me once or twice by his clerk. But the orders of the court having been renewed with great threats towards the master and the officers who neglected to watch, M. Piecourt's clerk no longer dared thus to expose himself. His master having told me this, begged me to find some one of great fidelity whom I could send to him to take the money at each remittance. I knew nothing then of the affection and faithfulness which the Turks bore us. Nevertheless, I opened my heart to the Turk on my bench, who joyfully undertook to render me this service, putting his hand upon his turban, which is with them the sign of the outpouring of the heart to God, and thanking him with all his soul for the favour which he had shown him in giving him the opportunity to exercise charity at the peril of his blood, for this Turk knew well enough that if he had been taken in the act of rendering us any service, he would have been bastinadoed to death, to make him confess what banker had paid us the money. This Turk, then, whose name was Isouf, served me in this way very faithfully for several years, without ever accepting the smallest reward from me, alleging that if he did so he would cancel all his good deeds, and that God would punish him for it. This good Turk was killed at the battle in the Thames. It was he whose arm I took up in my hand, as I have already narrated. I was much grieved at his death, and did not know to whom to apply to serve me in such a perilous employment. But I had not the trouble of seeking, for ten or twelve Turks came to petition me just as one petitions for a lucrative office in the world. It must be known that when the Turks have an opportunity of exercising charity or other good works, they communicate this joy to their *papas*, as their theologians are called (whose whole learning consists in being able to read the Koran), asking them their advice about the good works which they have undertaken to perform; and though I had urgently begged Isouf not to tell any one about the service he was rendering me, he could not, on account of the principles of his religion, help telling the affair to his *papas*, as I heard after his death.

These good people, seeing that I did not know whom to trust, came one after the other to beg me to make use of them, showing so much good feeling, and professing so much affection for those of our religion, whom they called their brethren in God, that I was moved to tears. I accepted one named Aly, who danced for joy at obtaining an employment so perilous for him. He served me for four years, till the time when we were removed from Dunkirk, and he behaved with indescribable zeal and disinterestedness. This Turk was poor, and several times I tried to make him accept one or two crowns, assuring him that they who sent us this money desired that those who so kindly served us should have some share in it. He always firmly refused, saying, in his figurative style, that this money would burn his hands; and when I said once that if he did not take it I should employ another, the poor Turk was like one in despair, beseeching me with clasped hands not to shut him out from the road to heaven. These people are called barbarians by Christians, but in their conduct they often put to shame those who give them this name. We must distinguish these Turks from those who, although of the same religion, have not the same manners. These latter, the Turks of Africa, from Morocco, Algiers, Tripoli, etc., are cruel, traitorous murderers and assassins; but the Turks of Asia and Europe, especially those from Bosnia and the frontiers of Hungary and Transylvania, and also from Constantinople, of whom there are a great many in the galleys of France, who have been made slaves by the Imperialists, and sold to the French to man their galleys,—these Turks are generally well-made, fair in feature, wise in their conduct, zealous in the observance of their religion, honourable and charitable in the highest degree. I have seen them give away all the money they possessed to buy a bird in a cage, that they might have the pleasure of giving it its liberty. When they are taking their meals, all those who pass by, whether Christians or Turks, friends or enemies, are invited to partake, or, at least, to taste their food, and if they refuse it is the greatest affront they can offer to them.

They never drink wine nor spirits, nor eat pork, because their religion forbids it. As to the African Turks, who are generally called Moors, they get drunk like brutes, and commit, when they can, the most horrible crimes. The Asiatic Turks detest these Africans, and never associate with them. Thanks to God's mercy, and the fidelity of Isouf and Aly, nothing unpleasant happened to me in the reception and distribution of the remittances with which I was charged during several years. But at Marseilles it happened very differently to one of our brethren who had a similar office.

The missionaries, not content with watching till they could catch some one in the act of paying money to the Reformed in the galleys, often came to examine and search these poor confessors of the faith, and took from them, without ever returning them, all their money, books of devotion, and letters.   These examinations were performed with great strictness, and the missionaries having perceived, or fancied, that the Reformed, expecting these visits, gave their property to the Romish convicts, or to the Turks on their bench, to take care of, determined, in order to surprise them better, to keep the day and the hour of this search quite secret.   At the time appointed a gun was fired, which was the signal for the under officers of the galleys to throw themselves upon the poor Reformed, each having his man in view, and to search them most severely, not without strokes of the lash.   In this way they often surprised us also at Dunkirk.   But since Bancilhon had become M. de Langeron's waiter and attendant, our commander showed good-will to us all, and when he received, as was frequently the case, orders from the court to have us searched, he warned Bancilhon beforehand, saying to him, " Bancilhon, my friend, the cock has crowed."   We were then at once on our guard, and when we were searched they found nothing.

But to return to Marseilles, one of our brethren, named Sabatier, who had the charge of receiving and distributing the remittances, received them without any obstacle by the help of his faithful Turk ; but he had also to distribute the money to the other brethren in their separate galleys, which the good Turk was obliged to do with great pru-

dence and discretion. Sabatier folded the portion
of money which was to go to each galley in the list
of those who were to share it, which he sent by the
Turk to a brother in each galley. As the Turk was
necessarily obliged to go often to Sabatier's bench
to receive these commissions, the *argousin* or the
comite perceiving it, suspected what was going on,
and having acquainted the major of the galleys with
the fact, he gave orders that the Turk should be
watched when he came from Sabatier, and that
when he left his galley he should be seized and
examined, which did not fail to take place ; for the
Turk having received the little packet to take to
one of the galleys, he was seized, the money was
found on him, with the list of those among whom
it was to be divided. The Turk was asked from
whom he had received this money. He would not
tell, but there was no need of his deposition. It
had been seen that it had come from Sabatier, who
openly confessed that he had given the packet to
the Turk. The master of the galleys was delighted
when he heard of this discovery, hoping that they
would at last discover the banker who paid the
money to the Reformed. As the master had the
gout, he could not go to Sabatier's galley that he
might make him confess by the torture of the bastinado what he so passionately desired to know,
so he ordered Sabatier to be chained to a Turk, and
brought by a guard into his presence, which was
done. He first spoke amiably enough to Sabatier,
telling him that as he made so great a profession of
telling the truth, he hoped he would do so now.

Sabatier replied that he would boldly speak the truth about everything which concerned himself, at the risk of enduring the most cruel tortures, and even at the peril of his own life. " Very well," said the master, " if you confess the truth, you will not be harmed."

He asked him first if this packet and the writing in which it was wrapped up came from him. " Yes, sir," replied Sabatier. Then to whom he was sending the packet. Sabatier replied that he was sending it to one of his brethren in the faith to distribute the money to several others who were in this list.

" For what purpose is this money ? " the master inquired.

Sabatier replied that it was sent out of charity to help them in their miserable slavery.

" From whence does this money come to you ? " asked the master.

" From Geneva, sir," replied Sabatier.

" Do you often receive it in this way ? "

" From time to time, when our friends think that we are in want of it."

" In what manner do you receive it ? "

" Through a banker of Geneva, who remits it to a banker at Marseilles."

" Who is the banker who pays it to you ? " asked the master.

" So far, sir," said Sabatier firmly, " I have been able to tell you the real truth. I have promised to tell you all that concerns myself, and if you find what I have said and done criminal, punish me for it as you think proper; but to denounce a man who has only acted out of kindness and to do us a favour, and whose ruin I know my deposition would cause, is what I will never do."

"What! wretch, you dare to refuse to tell me what you confess to know yourself? You will either expire under the lash or tell me," said the master.

"Make me die," said Sabatier, "by the most horrible tortures, I shall never tell it."

The master, transported with rage, ordered the guard who had brought Sabatier, to beat him with a stick in his presence. The guard, who had known Sabatier for several years, deeply touched by his unhappy fate, replied, "Sir, he is a brave man; I cannot strike him." "Rascal!" said the master, "give me your stick;" which the guard having done, this cruel man made Sabatier approach his own chair, and then broke the stick upon his body, Sabatier not making the least complaint in the world, nor changing his position to avoid the blows of this furious master. Then, not being able to beat him any longer, as his strength failed him, he ordered Sabatier to be led back to the galley, and commanded the major to give him the bastinado till he died or confessed the name of the banker who had paid him the money, which took place immediately without any form of trial. Sabatier endured with constancy this more than barbarous treatment, and as long as the power of speech remained to him during this punishment he continued to call upon God, praying him to grant him grace to resist even unto the death, which he was momentarily expecting, and to receive his soul in His divine mercy.　Speech and motion having failed him, they still continued to strike to the utmost his poor mangled body.　The surgeon of the galleys, watching if he still breathed, said to the major that if they continued to strike him now ever so little, he would certainly die, and his secret with him, but if they tried to make him revive, they might begin again to force him to confess what they wished to know.　To this the major assented.　They rubbed his mangled back with strong vinegar and salt. The pain which this application caused made him revive, but so weak was he that they could not recommence his punishment without killing him at the first blow.　They thought it best therefore to take him to the hospital, that he might regain sufficient strength to undergo a second punishment. But he was so long hovering between life and death, that either the lapse of time made them forget him, or that even his executioners dreaded exercising such a punishment for a cause which did them no honour, and he was not again exposed to this torture.　He recovered, but was always so sickly and weak in the head, that during the few years he lived afterwards, he could not carry on the simplest conversation, and his voice was so low that he could scarcely be heard.　Such is an instance of the unparalleled cruelty of these missionaries of Marseilles !*

Through the mercy of divine Providence I had been, without any danger, the distributor of the money which M. Piecourt remitted to me.　To aid

* See Note at end of volume.

me in this anxious duty I had the help of my honest and faithful Turk, Aly. I generally knew pretty exactly the time when this remittance would be sent, and despatched Aly alone (for the Turks are allowed to go anywhere without guards) to M. Piecourt, who gave him the money to remit to me, with a receipt which I had to sign, and which Aly took back with my letters for Holland. But it happened that M. Piecourt had the misfortune to be embarrassed in his affairs, so that our remittance was intrusted to another Dunkirk banker, a M. Penetrau. This gentleman two or three times paid me the money with similar punctuality and precaution, and, as my Turk was so well acquainted with his commission, with equal safety and facility. Moreover, the chaplain who belonged to our galley was very reasonable with regard to us. Speaking of the chaplain reminds me that I must relate some particulars with regard to those who exercise this office in the galleys.

These chaplains are secular priests of the society commonly called "of the Mission," or "of St. Lazarus." It was founded by Vincent de Paul, a simple priest, who by his pious reputation became the confessor of the queen, the mother of Louis XIV. He was then charged to hold missions in the country for the instruction of the peasants and common people. This gave rise to the establishment of this society, which, small at first, increased in time, had branches in the most important towns in France, and acquired divers privileges and prerogatives, among them the nomination of the village curés, and of the military, naval, and galley chaplains. They had insinuated themselves so well at court, that the ministry regarded them as oracles, and the Jesuits only with envy and jealousy. Notwithstanding their cunning, the Jesuits had never foreseen the future greatness of the Lazarists, of which they had themselves been the principal instruments. In supporting this society they had thought only to increase the number of their own partisans. But abandoning the instructions of their founder, the Lazarists concealed their ambitious views under a cloak of humility. They knew how well a humble exterior and an air of mortification had served the Jesuits ; they, therefore, imitated them in their dress and behaviour, and even surpassed them in the coarseness of their robes and in their negligent and almost dirty appearance. This so imposed upon the public and upon the court, that they obtained the care of the chapels and royal palaces, the administration of a number of seminaries, and the possession of immense wealth, which they now enjoy. So powerful and formidable were they in my time at Marseilles, that if any of the king's officers displeased them they soon obtained a warrant to have them disgraced. In this way they were so feared and apparently so respected that all submitted to their tyranny.

These fathers, then, having the spiritual direction of the galleys, placed chaplains in them, men like themselves — cruel persecutors of any of the reformed religion they might meet with there. But our chaplain having just died when the six galleys passed from the Mediterranean to the Channel, M. de Langeron, on account of the distance, which acquitted him from the necessity of waiting for the nomination of the missionaries, and who, moreover, would not be without a chaplain on board his galley, took at Rochefort a monk of the Dominican order. This chaplain at first treated us as badly as he could, but in time he relented and conformed to our captain's way of acting, which had much changed to our favour. To the ill-treatment which at first we had endured, succeeded obliging acts towards us all, and especially towards me, since I had become M. de Langeron's secretary, an employment which often gave me the opportunity of conversing with this chaplain. During the three last years that I remained at Dunkirk, where the galleys were always disarmed, scarcely a day passed that he did not come to the galley, when we passed an hour or two together, without speaking of religion, or at least very little about it. He was a learned man and a good preacher, and as I often, by means of my friends, received religious books from Holland, among others several volumes of the late M. Saurin's sermons, he asked me one day if I had not some sermons of our authors to lend him. Though this request appeared to me suspicious, I nevertheless hazarded lending them to him, and offered him a volume of M. Saurin's works, which he punctually returned to me. It was so much to his taste, that I then lent him all the books I had, even the " Legitimate Preiudices against Popery," by M. Jurieu, which, as well as the others, he carefully returned to me.   One day, in conversation, he asked me if we Reformed did not receive money from Holland.   I thought it best to reply negatively on this subject, for fear of the consequences which might ensue.   It will be seen by the sequel that it is not without a motive that I have written so much about this chaplain.

I now come to the danger which I incurred myself in the distribution of the remittances.   I have said that M. Penetrau, the banker of Dunkirk, now conducted the business.   This gentleman one day planned to ruin me.   He received an order from Amsterdam to pay me one hundred crowns.   But he happened to be embarrassed in his affairs, and in order that his Amsterdam correspondent should not discover this, he wished to find a plausible pretext to excuse himself from paying me this sum. Although he knew he was about to sacrifice me that he might maintain his credit, he went to our chaplain and declared to him that he had an order from Holland to pay me one hundred crowns, but as the prohibition of the court made him afraid to meddle in such affairs, he wished first to ask his permission.   He thought that the chaplain, far from granting it, would at once forbid it.   By this means he would have got out of his embarrassment, and I should have been exposed to an examination, which would not have taken place without a furious bastinado to make me confess who the bankers were who had paid me the money before.   The chaplain understood the consequence which this affair might have been, and looking fixedly at M. Penetrau, he said to him, "I am sure, sir, this is not the first time that you have made similar payments without asking permission, and that your correspondents in Holland are not so imprudent as to intrust you with such a commission at random, and without being certain by experience that you will well perform it. But, however that may be, as it seems to depend on my permission, I willingly grant it to you." Penetrau was much disconcerted by this reply, which he had not expected. He replied to the chaplain that his permission would not secure him from danger, and that he should see the master of the galleys and ask him for his. The chaplain was annoyed at this reply, and said sharply, "What, sir ! after you have given me to understand that my consent would decide you, you dare to tell me that you will apply to the master ? You can do as you please. But remember that if you mention a word of it to the master, or to any one else, I have a very long arm, and I shall know how to reach you and make you repent of it."

Penetrau, utterly vanquished, and not knowing what to do, confessed that he was a little out at elbows, and that although one hundred crowns would not bring him to extremities, he did not possess them at the moment ; but that if I would wait a fortnight, and meanwhile not write to Holland to say I had not received this sum, he would pay me without fail at the end of that time. The chaplain told him that he had done well to confess the matter to him, and that he would forgive the

N

expressions he had previously used. " But," continued he, " I wil. not run the risk of being your
dupe ; to ensure your punctuality, make me out a
bill for the one hundred crowns, payable in fifteen
days, which money I will remit to the person to
whom you have to pay it, and I will procure you a
receipt. You can make yourself quite easy about
this convict, I will pledge you my word that he
will not write to Amsterdam before the bill is due."
Penetrau, quite pleased that the matter had taken
this turn, readily drew out the bill, and at the same
time gave the chaplain the letter which he had for
me. That same day the chaplain came to the
galley, and called me into the stern-cabin. He at
once said to me, with a serious air, " I am surprised
that a confessor of the truth dares to lie to a man
of my character."

I was taken quite aback by this speech, and told
him that I did not know what he meant. " Have
you not told me," said he, " that you do not receive
money from Holland, nor from any other place?
I hold in my hand that which convicts you of this
falsehood," and at the same time he showed me the
bill which M. Penetrau had made out for him.
" Do you know that?" said he. " Yes, sir," I said,
" I see that it is some money which belongs to
you." " It does not belong to me," said the chaplain, "but to you." And then he related to me
all that had passed between Penetrau and himself,
and giving me the letter of advice, again reproached me for having lied. I took the liberty to
tell him that he was no less guilty than I was, for

knowing very well that it was not a thing which I could confess, he had obliged me to deny it by asking me. He agreed to this, and told me to make myself quite easy, and that in a fortnight he would bring me the one hundred crowns. This he did punctually to the day, and in counting them out to me offered me his services. " Write to your friends in Holland," said he, " that they can address their remittances to me, and be assured that I will pay them punctually to you, by which means you will avoid all risk." I thanked him for his kindness, which, however, I did not think I ought to make use of. This reserve on my part did not prevent our always remaining good friends.

There were five of the reformed faith in the galley ; the chaplain never molested one of us ; on the contrary, he showed us a thousand kindnesses. The Jesuits and the chaplains of the other galleys determined to punish him for having dared to show more humane and Christian sentiments than they did. So, to revenge themselves, they addressed a memorial to the Bishop of Ypres, in which they accused the chaplain of being a heretic, of loving and favouring the pretended Reformed, and of leaving them in peace instead of forcing them to enter the pale of the Roman Church. The bishop cited our chaplain to appear before him to give an account of his conduct. In consequence of this command, he went to Ypres and presented himself to the bishop, who told him that he had been accused of favouring the Reformed in his galley, and that he left them in a quiet security without trying to convert them. " My lord," said the chaplain with firmness, "if your highness orders me to exhort them, to press them to listen, and to conform to the Roman Church, that is what I do every day, and no one can prove the contrary ; but if you enjoin me to imitate the other chaplains, who cruelly persecute these poor wretches, I shall tomorrow set out for my convent." The bishop replied that he was content with his conduct, and encouraged him to persevere in it, and then censured the other chaplains for their method of conversion.

I have now reached the end of the residence at Dunkirk of myself and my brethren in suffering, and must begin the description of a new kind of pain, fatigue, and fearful torture, which we were made to suffer from the 1st October, 1712, when they removed, or rather smuggled us off, from Dunkirk, till the 17th January, 1713, when we were placed on board the galleys of Marseilles.

Every one knows that in that year, 1712, the Queen of England made peace with France, and among other articles it was stipulated that the English should occupy the town, fortifications, and port of Dunkirk, till they had demolished the fortifications and filled up the harbour. Consequently the English came to Dunkirk in the month of September, with about 5,000 men, and took possession of the town, forts, and citadel, which the French garrison evacuated. But the French navy was reduced to such a deplorable condition that they could not even fit out the galleys to put to sea. Thus France agreed with the Queen of England that the galleys, with their crews and gangs of slaves, should remain in the harbour till they began to fill it up, which could not be done till after the winter. It was also stipulated that nothing should leave the harbour, neither boats, ships, sailors, nor galley slaves, without the permission of her majesty the Queen of England.

The English had no sooner taken possession of this port, and established their garrison in the town and citadel, than they ran in crowds to the galleys to gaze on those vessels, which the majority of them had never seen before. Several of the officers, who were French refugees, having heard that Protestants were confined in the galleys for the sake of their religion, immediately inquired if there were any in these galleys, and learned that there were twenty-two in number. These officers testified their zeal for their religion by coming to embrace us, pitying and weeping with us on our benches ; and they could not restrain their indignation when they saw our chains, and the miseries which accompanied this hard and degrading slavery. They remained a great part of the day with their dear suffering brethren, seated very uncomfortably, neither fearing the vermin nor the stench which this misery engendered, and taking pleasure in the presence of the officers of the galleys, who saw their actions in caressing us, consoling us, and exhorting us to perseverance. Their example attracted a large number of distinguished English officers, who testified to their piety by actions worthy of true Protestants.   The soldiers also crowded down to the galleys, and, according to their manner of expressing their zeal, swore that if the court did not release us willingly they would do so by force, sword in hand. The chaplains begged M. de Langeron to give orders that no one should be allowed to enter the galleys, seeing the scandal, as they said, which all this caused to the Roman Catholic religion. This was tried, but the English soldiers still pressed eagerly to come on board, and when begged very civilly to retire, they only replied by placing their hands upon their swords, saying that, being masters of the town and the harbour, they were also masters of the galleys, and that they would go on board, if not with their consent, by force.   So they were obliged to leave the plank free for any one who wished to go on board.

An English colonel, whose name I have forgotten, came one day to speak to me, and told me that Lord Hill, the Governor of Dunkirk for the Queen of England, was probably ignorant of our detention, and of the cause of our slavery, and advised me to draw up a petition to him to inform him of it, and to implore his good offices for our release.   I wrote out this petition as well as I could, and the colonel took charge of it, and gave it to Lord Hill. The next day his lordship sent his secretary to tell me that he would use every effort to obtain our deliverance ; that he was about to write to the queen on the subject, and that her orders, which he was sure would be favourable towards us, would determine his actions, and he begged us to wait patiently for another fortnight. This secretary added that Lord Hill offered us his purse if we had need of money. I replied that we only needed his lordship's protection, and that I was very grateful for his answer to my petition, and for the zeal which he had shown in rendering us his services. I made known his reply to our brethren in the six galleys, exhorting them to be circumspect with the English soldiers, and to avoid all conversation which might excite them to use violence in order to procure us our liberty, but to tell them on the contrary to wait patiently for the queen's orders, for which their governor had written. Henceforth all was quiet, and each of us eagerly awaited the news from England. During the fortnight which the governor had told us to wait (it seemed doubtful whether he had really written to the queen), he became great friends with M. de Langeron, our commander.

One day his lordship told him that he could not understand how the French court could have made such a blunder as not to make us leave Dunkirk before they entered, for the court surely could not be ignorant of the horror with which the English nation regarded the cruelties practised upon the Protestants on account of their religion, and how in all the churches of England they prayed God every day for the deliverance of the Reformed who were suffering in the galleys of France ; that, in a word, the French court might have foreseen that the English, being masters of Dunkirk, and those twenty-two Protestants who groaned in irons for

their religion being under their standards, and in
sight of the English garrison, the queen could not
fail to deliver them, if only to avoid a riot among
the soldiers, who already threatened violence if
these unhappy slaves were not delivered. M. de
Langeron could not help agreeing that his court
had made a great mistake in this matter, and begged
Lord Hill to advise him what to do so as to prevent
accidents, adding that he knew that the king his
master would never consent to the release of those
Reformed. Lord Hill said that he knew of an
expedient by which all trouble and collision might
be avoided. " Write," said he, " to the minister
of your court, and request him to order you to
leave Dunkirk secretly by sea ; I will provide
hands for you, and the thing will be easy and
without danger." M. de Langeron did not fail to
follow this counsel, and he soon received orders
to act in concert with Lord Hill for our secret
removal, which took place in the following manner.

On the 1st of October, the feast of St. Rémy, we
perceived a fishing-bark chained to our galley. It
was reported that this bark was confiscated for
smuggling, and that the English had taken possession of her. That evening the rappel was beaten
as usual, and every one went to bed. I was in my
store-cabin, sleeping tranquilly, when I was suddenly awakened by our major, armed with a pistol,
and accompanied by two soldiers of the galley,
who placed their bayonets at my throat, threatening
that if I uttered the least cry or noise all would be
over with me. The major, who was one of my

friends, exhorted me in a friendly manner not to make any resistance, or he must execute the orders which he had to kill me. " Alas ! " said I, " what have I done, major, and what is going to be done to me ? " " You have done nothing," said he, " and no harm will be done to you if you are only quiet." He then made me descend quickly into the fishing-bark of which I have already spoken, and this without either fire or light, and with great silence, for fear of being perceived by the English sentinel of the citadel, from which we were not very far distant.

On entering the boat I found in it my twenty-one brethren, whom they had taken from their benches in the same manner as they had taken me. They chained us all down in the hold, observing the strictest silence ; and though they made us lie down upon our backs like cattle about to be slain, each of us had a soldier of the galley, who held his bayonet to our throats to prevent us from crying out, or even from uttering a word. The boat was now unmoored to leave the harbour. It was obliged to pass by an English ship, which was always stationed in the middle of the port to prevent anything from going out. The ship summoned the bark to her side, and inquired whither she was going. The master of the bark, who was an Englishman, replied that he was going to fish for Lord Hill, from whom he showed a note. The captain of the vessel took the note and read it ; it was written and signed by Lord Hill's own hand : "Allow this boat, which is going to fish for my household, to leave the har-

bour." The captain at once allowed the boat to
depart. All those who commanded the forts in the
harbour, as well as on the jetties, did the same ;
and at last we found ourselves in the open sea.
Then the soldiers left us, went on deck, and shut
down the hatchways upon us, so that we were at
liberty to arrange ourselves more comfortably upon
the sand, which served as ballast, in the bottom of
the boat. We knew that they never put to sea
without provisions, if only bread and water, and as
we had seen none on coming on board, we strongly
imagined that they were going to sink us, and that
the soldiers would escape to land in the small boat
which was attached to the bark. The anguish into
which this idea plunged us, and the terrible situation in which we found ourselves, can well be imagined. Being without light in the hold, neither
seeing nor hearing any one, our imagination, in-
flamed by terror, only pictured to us, the more
vividly, the danger in which we thought ourselves
to be. In this cruel perplexity we passed the
night, not ceasing to address our prayers to the
Saviour, as those who are awaiting the stroke of
death. Some of us, seized with sudden fear, increased the alarm by crying out from time to time,
"Brothers, we are perishing, the water is coming
into the bark!" At these exclamations each of us
redoubled his prayers, thinking that it was the last
moment of his life. It happened, however, that an
old man of seventy did not believe it as firmly as
the rest of us, and indeed he would have made us
laugh had we been in less distressing circumstances.

He was seated on his knapsack, and hearing them cry out that the water was entering the bark, he stood up holding his knapsack in one hand, eagerly feeling with the other to find a nail to hang it on. As he was near me, and his moving interrupted my devotions, I asked him what he was doing. " I am trying to hang up my knapsack as high as I can," said he, "lest my clothes should get wet." " Think of your soul, my good man," said I ; " if you are drowned, you will not want your clothes any more." " Alas ! " said he, "that is only too true ; " and then he left off seeking for the nail.

We felt that our bark was sailing, but did not know which way the wind was taking us. When it was day they opened the hatchway, and as I was just under it, by standing up I could see on to the deck. I did so at once, and the first person I saw was our master-at-arms, who is generally the first sergeant of the four which there are in the companies of marines. He was one of my friends; and not long before I had spoken a good word for him to our commander. " What, you here, M. Praire ? " I said to him. " Yes, my friend," said he, with a smiling air. " I don't think you slept too well last night." " But where are you taking us to ? " " Look," said he, " there is Calais," pointing to the town off which we were ; "we are going to land you there ; " adding, that we should not make a long stay there, and should have to get our legs ready. " But, sir," said I, "you are not able— neither are all the men in the world—to make men, decrepit through age, or maimed, or sick, as I am

(I was then suffering from a fever) to walk." " In that case the king, who never asks what is impossible, will provide waggons for the infirm ; and I am sure that, with the order of your route, there are directions to provide them for you. There," said he, showing it to me, " see if there is not a waggon ordered for such like and for the baggage." As I wished to see our destination, which he had not told me, instead of looking at the beginning I looked at the end, and read these lines :—" To Havre-de-Grâce, where they shall be given over to the governor until fresh orders."

I had seen enough to satisfy the curiosity of our brethren, to whom I told our destination in a whisper, lest the master-at-arms should hear me. They landed us at Calais. We were taken to prison loaded with our chains. The next morning the *argousin*—for one had followed us—fettered us two and two, each by a leg, and then passed a long chain through the rings of the chains which coupled us, so that the eleven couples were all chained together. Now, it must be remembered, that amongst us there were old people, who, by the feebleness of their age or by their infirmities, could not walk a quarter of a league, even if they had not been laden with chains. We had also several who were sick, and others worn out with misery and fatigue ; and, moreover, we had none of us walked at all for a very long time. It was, therefore, impossible for us to perform four or five leagues a day, as our orders directed. After they had chained us I called our master-at-arms and said to him,

" See, sir, if it is possible for us to walk in our present condition ; I entreat you to provide us with one or two waggons to carry the infirm. You have a right to exact them wherever you pass." " I know my orders," said he, "and I shall observe them." I was silent ; and we started. We had not gone a quarter of a league when a small hill had to be ascended ; it was impossible for us to do it, for three or four of our old and sick men fell on the ground, not being able to take a single step ; and as we were all held by one chain, we could not advance, unless we had been strong enough to drag them on. The master-at-arms, and the soldiers of our escort which he commanded, exhorted us in kind words to take courage and to redouble our efforts ; but against the impossible nothing can be done.

The captain was much embarrassed, and did not know what to do. We all sat on the ground to give time to those who had fallen down to rest and to resume the march if they were able. But this did not help us out of our difficulty. I told the captain that, in the extremity in which we were, of two pieces of advice which I would give him, he must take one. " Either shoot us," said I, " or, as I have already said, provide us with waggons to carry us. You will permit me to observe that, having never served except at sea, you cannot know what the king's orders are on an expedition by land. In the orders which he gives for a march, whether of soldiers, recruits, or criminals, it is understood that when those who are to be conducted are quite unable to walk, their conductors ought to find them conveyances, which they take in the king's name, in the towns and villages where they are to be found. You, sir, are in this case. Send a detachment of your soldiers to the nearest village to take as many waggons as you require to carry the infirm ; and, to show our submission to his majesty's orders, we will give you six francs a day for the hire of a waggon, which will be a clear profit to you, for in the king's service waggons can always be had gratis, so these six francs will be yours." Some of the soldiers, who knew more than the captain, confirmed what I said, which decided him to take my advice. The peasants provided two waggons as far as the first resting-place for the night, and so from place to place as far as Havre-de-Grâce.

The master-at-arms was a good sort of man, but not particularly clever. They had made him take an oath at Dunkirk neither to tell us, nor any one else, the place to which he had orders to take us. The fear lest some of the garrison of Aire, which made expeditions between Calais and Boulogne, should carry us off, had made them take this precaution. One day, on the road, this captain, who always rode on horseback, came up to the waggon in which I was, and engaged in conversation with me. While speaking on indifferent subjects, I asked him the place of our destination. Seeing that he evaded the question, I said it was useless his doing so, since I knew it as well as he did. He defied me to tell him, which I did immediately, repeating to him what I had seen in the directions for our route, which he had shown me before we landed at Calais. The good man not having remarked that I had looked at the last article in the document when he had shown it to me, was so astonished to find that I knew as much as he did on this subject—as not one of his company knew the secret—that he asked me, with great simplicity, whether I was a sorcerer or a prophet. I replied, that I was too honest to be a sorcerer, and too great a sinner to be a prophet. " Besides," said I, " there is not one of us who does not know as much as I do ; and you are making a great secret of a thing which is quite public among us." I laughed at him a little for his pretended circumspection. We had, however, no reason to complain of him during our journey ; he was very particular in giving us our rations at every lodging ; but not being able to act beyond his orders, he could only lodge us in prisons, or in stables in those places where there were no prisons.

At last we reached Havre-de-Grâce, where we had a better and more comfortable lodging than any we had had on the road. It happened that there were in the town a great many new converts to Romanism, who, notwithstanding their apostacy, were still zealous in favour of the reformed religion. These gentlemen anticipating our arrival, and knowing that we were to be given into the charge of the Master of the Marine, went to beg him to show us some compassion, reminding him that these poor chained prisoners had formerly been their brethren in the faith, who had by their firm-

ness and constancy borne testimony to the religion
of their fathers, adding, that if he would have the
kindness to treat them well, they would be greatly
obliged to him, and would be responsible that they
did not abuse the relief he granted them by
endeavouring to escape.   As those who had undertaken this deputation were the richest merchants
in the town, the governor replied to them very
graciously, adding that out of consideration to them
he would treat us as well as he possibly could.   " I
have the orders of the court," said he, " to confine
them in a place of security, but as these orders do
not specify that it must be a prison, I shall try and
give them a more comfortable lodging ; and as the
court simply directs me to give them bread and
beans, you can rely upon their having the same
food as is served up to my table.   You will have
perfect liberty also to see them and assist them."
Matters were thus happily arranged when we
arrived at Havre.   They made us alight before the
royal arsenal, where the governor had prepared a
large room for us, belonging to the ropery, with
mattresses, pillows, and counterpanes for us to
sleep upon.   On entering this room, which was on
the ground floor, we found there the governor and
our protectors.   These gentlemen embraced us
with tears in their eyes without fearing to commit
themselves in the presence of the governor, who
appeared quite affected by it.   Whilst this was
going on the officials of the custom-house arrived
and asked the governor's permission to search us.
He granted it, and they examined us at once, but,

of course without finding anything. But perceiving among our clothes a small box with a lock and key, in which we kept all our books of devotion, they asked to examine that. I had the key of this box, and I would not give it to them, fearing the fire for our small library. But the governor said to me, "Give them the key, my friend, and fear nothing ; these gentlemen must do their duty." I gave it them with trembling ; one of the officials opened the box, and only seeing books, he exclaimed, "Here is Calvin's library ; to the flames ! to the flames !" Seeing this, the governor said to him, "Rascal, what are you meddling with ? Do your duty and nothing else, or I will teach you what to search for." The official said no more, shut up the box, and went out.

As soon as we were installed in our new abode, they took away the great chain which held us all together, leaving us only bound in couples. The governor was so greatly prepossessed in our favour, that he was kind enough to ask us if we were content with our guards. We told him that we had received from them during the journey as good treatment as they were able to give us. "Very well," said he, "then I shall leave them with you." He quartered them in a room opposite to ours. Every day he sent us bread from his own table. Our protectors told him that, with his permission, they would take care to supply us with food, and requested to be allowed to come and see us from time to time. Thereupon the governor called the master-at-arms, and told him to allow

O

any one who wished to come into our room to visit us, between nine o'clock in the morning and eight o'clock in the evening, and never to interfere with any of our religious exercises.   The master-at-arms conformed to these orders, and henceforth our room was never free from persons of both sexes and all ages.   We had prayers morning and evening, and after having read the good sermons which we had with us, we sang psalms, so that our prison was something like a little church.   The tears and sobs of these good people who came to see us, and scarcely ever left us, were mingled with our songs. Seeing the chains which we wore, and the resignation with which we bore them, they reproached themselves for their weakness, and lamented that they had not resisted unto death in face of the persecutions they had suffered, and the allurements that had been employed to make them renounce the true religion.   Alas! I must say, that it was rather the sight of our misery that softened them, or still more strictly speaking, the rebuke of their own consciences, than our exhortations and sermons, for we were not called to so worthy a ministry, and were in no respect capable of exercising it.   The conduct of these new converts showed very plainly that the Romish Church, instead of converting, only makes hypocrites.   The zeal of our weak brethren in coming to visit us was, however, the cause that, from the day after our arrival at Havre-de-Grâce, all the churches of the town were emptied of the new converts, notwithstanding the prayers and menaces of the curé, who complained to the gover-

nor. But the latter contented himself with replying that he could not force people's consciences,
and that an open heretic was worth more than a
concealed hypocrite; moreover, that this occurrence
had done much good, as now one could distinguish the good Catholics at Havre from those who
were not so. These reasons, weighty as they were,
did not satisfy the curé, who sometimes came to
see us, and always found our room full of new
proselytes, who did not fear to say to him, " Here,
Monsieur le Curé, are brave people (pointing to us)
and good Christians, who have had more firmness
than we." One can judge whether such words
were pleasing to the curé.

No one was able to fathom the policy of the
court in having us removed to Havre-de-Grâce.
Some thought that we were to be sent to America;
and I have always believed that this was the
original design of the ministry, for if their first resolution had been to send us to Paris to join the
chain of galley slaves there, what was the use of
sending us to Havre, which is nearly as far from the
capital as Dunkirk? Moreover, it doubled our
journey, as the distance from Dunkirk to Havre
is about the same as from Dunkirk to Paris. Probably, the scandal which we caused to the Roman
Catholics at Havre was the cause which induced
the court to change its intentions concerning us.
The curé left no means untried to get us out of the
town. We knew that he had written and informed
the court that our residence there had had an evil
influence on the new converts, who, since our arrival,

had deserted his church.   This alone, was quite enough to induce the ministers to send an order to the governor to send us away as secretly as possible, for fear of exciting any commotion ; these precautions, however, were quite unnecessary.   The Reformed at Havre had no intention of carrying us off by force, and, as for ourselves, we were led as easily as sheep to the slaughter-house.   But the curé had described us in such black colours, that the court could not fail to take umbrage.   Before our departure, a singular incident occurred which confirmed the master-at-arms in his idea that we were prophets.

On the fifteenth day of our residence at Havre, about nine o'clock in the evening, just as we were beginning our supper and our guards were doing the same, I felt myself touched upon the shoulder ; turning round to see who it was, I recognised a young lady of good position in society, the daughter of one of the first bankers of the town, to whom I had lent a volume of sermons a few days before.   She was wrapped up in a shawl which she hurriedly drew aside, and said to me hastily and in tears, " Here, my brother, is your book, which I return to you.   May God be with you in all your trials !   They are going to carry you off to-night at twelve o'clock ; four waggons are ordered for the purpose, and the White Gate will remain open for your departure from the town."   I thanked her for the trouble which she had taken in coming at such an hour to give me this information herself, and asked her how she had been able to gain access

to our room. "That," said she, "does not affect
you ; it is more expedient to tell you, dear confessors of the faith, that you are going to be taken
to the frightful prison of the Tournelle, at Paris, to
be joined to the great chain which leaves that city
every year for Marseilles. I wished to announce
these sad tidings to you, that you might not
remain in anxious uncertainty about your destination, and that you might prepare yourselves to
suffer, with constancy, this new trial." Having said
this, she departed as invisibly as she had entered,
without any of our guards perceiving her. This
young lady evidently obtained permission from the
guard of the arsenal to enter by his house, which
communicated with the ropery where we were confined. We continued our supper very quietly ; after
which, instead of lying down upon our mattresses
to go to sleep as usual, we began to pack up our
little luggage. Whilst we were thus employed, our
captain, according to his custom, came into our
room to chat with us for an hour while he smoked
his pipe, and seeing us arranging our baggage
instead of preparing our beds, he asked us what we
were doing. "We are getting ready to start at
midnight, sir," said I ; "and you had better do the
same." "You are mad," said he. "I tell you,"
I replied, "that precisely at midnight there will be
four waggons at the gate of the arsenal to take us
out by the White Gate, which will remain open on
purpose, and you will continue to conduct us as far
as Paris, and deliver us up there at the prisons of
the Tournelle, to join the great chain for Mar-

seilles." "I tell you," answered he, "that you are mad, and that there is not a word of truth in what you have just said. I took the governor's orders at eight o'clock, as I always do, and he told me that there was nothing new." "Very well, sir," said I, "you will see." As we were finishing this conversation the governor's servant came in, to tell the captain that his master wished, at once, to speak to him. It was not long before he came back, making great exclamations; clasping his hands, he said to me, "In God's name, tell me whether you are sorcerers or prophets ! still, I cannot help thinking that God favours you, for you are too devout and too honest to ask the help of the devil." "No, sir," said I, "we are neither the one nor the other, and there is nothing but what is quite natural in that which surprises you so much." "I cannot understand it at all," said the master-at-arms, "for I have heard from the governor's own lips, that no one in the town knows anything about your departure, except himself; and whatever you may say, you won't take away my firm belief that God is with you." "I hope he is," said I, and we continued to prepare for our departure.

How the young lady became acquainted with this secret, we learned afterwards from her father, whom we saw in the prison at Rouen, to which town he came expressly to give us the amount of a collection which had been made for us at Havre, to procure us some alleviations on our painful journey to Paris and Marseilles. He told us that his daughter was engaged to be married to the governor's secretary. The governor having received the letter from the court the evening before our departure, his secretary saw the order which concerned us, and knowing the affection which his daughter bore us, he ran at once to tell her the news.

At midnight the four waggons came to take us. We smiled at the mysterious secrecy they observed in our removal. The iron was taken from the wheels of the waggons, and the shoes from the horses which drew them, so that we might not be heard passing through the street. Each waggon was covered up as if it contained bales of merchandise; and with neither lanterns nor torches, we left the town. Nothing remarkable happened to us as far as Rouen. On arriving there, we were conducted before the town-hall to receive the magistrates' orders as to our lodging, which was, as usual, in prison. But we were much surprised to be refused admittance, by the gaoler, to that to which we were taken. The master-at-arms showed the magistrates' order commanding him to receive us, which the gaoler persistently refused to do, saying that he would rather give up his office than take us under his charge. We were sent to another prison, where the same thing happened, and finally they sent us to a tower destined for the most infamous criminals. The gaoler here, who only received us under the strongest protest, cast us into a fearful dungeon, and, by the help of five or six turnkeys with swords in their hands, fastened our feet to huge beams of wood, so that we could not move, and without giving us either light or bread, or anything else, he shut up the dungeon, and went away with his turn-keys. We were both hungry and thirsty, and called out as loudly as we could for nearly two hours that they should bring us some food for our money. At last some one came to the door, and we heard them say, "Those people speak very good French." This made us think that there was some misunderstanding and some mystery in their conduct with regard to us. We still continued to cry out, and to implore them to help us for our money, and that we were ready to pay in advance. Upon this the gaoler opened the door, and came in with his six turnkeys, and, after having examined us one after the other, he asked us if we were Frenchmen. We said that we were. "But how is it then that you are not Christians?" said he, "and that you worship the devil, who makes you more wicked than he is himself?" We replied, that apparently he wished to joke with us, but that he would please us better if he would give us something to eat and drink ; at the same time I gave him a louis d'or, begging him to give us immediately what we required for that money, and adding if that was not enough, I would give him more. "Truly," said the gaoler, "you do not appear to be such as you have been described to me; for during the last week that you have been expected, they have spoken of you as people who come from the north, quite sorcerers, and so wicked and violent, that they could never tame you in the Dunkirk galleys, and so are sending you to Marseilles to bring you to reason; and this is the reason why I have received you with such repugnance in this prison." I easily recognised that this piece of malicious calumny came from the Jesuits, who had spread the report that we might be regarded with horror and execration in the town of Rouen, where there were a great many good Reformed. With this idea, I began to converse with the gaoler. I told him our history, and the reason why we were going from Dunkirk to Marseilles.

Just then, our master-at-arms arrived in our dungeon to give us our rations. The gaoler took him aside, and asked him if we were as docile as we appeared to be. "Yes, certainly," said the captain. "I would undertake to conduct them alone through the whole of France; and their only crime is that they are Huguenots." "Is that all?" said the gaoler; "the most honest people in Rouen belong to that religion. I don't like it," added he, "but I like the people who belong to it; they are a brave set." And, addressing us, he said, "You are to stay here to-morrow; I shall take care to tell some of your own people, who will not fail to come and see you, and my doors will always be open to them." He then ordered his turnkeys to unfetter us, and to leave us only our usual chains, while he went to procure us refreshments. Next day he kept his word, and brought several persons of the reformed religion to see us, who soon made the news of our arrival public; so that during the whole day our dungeon, which was tolerably large, was never empty. I have never seen such zealous people as these gentlemen of Rouen. They made us quite abashed by their excessive praises of the constancy of our faith. They exhorted us in so pathetic a manner to perseverance, that we could not restrain our tears. Their ardour was so great, that several of them actually wished (after asking the permission of the master-at-arms) publicly to accompany us, on our departure, for about a league from the town, and help us by carrying our chains upon their shoulders. This we would never suffer, both on account of the humility which we professed, and to save them the trouble into which it certainly would have brought them. We left Rouen in the waggons as before. I cannot sufficiently express the many acts of kindness which our captain showed us during this journey; for besides the gratuities which he received from our friends at Rouen, he was firmly persuaded that we were saints favoured by God, and that we had the gift of prophecy. When the *argousin* was taking his usual precautions, such as examining our chains, etc., he told him that he was taking useless trouble, for that we would go anywhere voluntarily if the king wished it; that otherwise neither all his precautions, nor those of all mankind, would be able to keep us. We wished much to disabuse him on this subject, but we could not dissuade him from his opinion that we possessed supernatural powers.

On the 17th November, 1712, about three o'clock in the afternoon, we arrived at Paris. We alighted at the Chateau de la Tournelle, which was formerly a pleasure-house of our kings, but which then

served as a depôt for all the unfortunate wretches
condemned to the galleys for every sort of crime.
They made us enter the vast but gloomy dungeon
appropriated to the great chain. The dreadful
spectacle which here presented itself to our eyes,
made us shudder, and all the more so, as they
were about to join us to the actors who were
playing such a prominent part in it. I confess
that, accustomed as I was to dungeons, fetters,
chains, and other instruments of torture which
tyranny or crime have invented, I had not strength
to resist the fit of trembling which seized me, and
the horror with which I was struck on beholding
this fearful place.

Not being able to describe all its horrors, I must
content myself with giving a faint idea of it. It is
a large dungeon, or rather a spacious cellar, furnished with huge beams of oak, placed at the distance of about three feet apart. These beams are
about two feet and a-half in thickness, and are so
arranged and fixed in some way to the floor, that
at first sight one would take them for benches, but
their use is a much more uncomfortable one. To
these beams thick iron chains are attached, one and
a-half feet in length, and two feet apart, and at the
ends of these chains is an iron collar. When the
wretched galley slaves arrive in this dungeon, they
are made to lie half down, so that their heads may
rest upon the beam ; then this collar is put round
their necks, closed, and riveted on an anvil with
heavy blows of a hammer. As these chains with
collars are about two feet apart, and as the beams

are generally forty feet long, twenty men are chained to them in file. This cellar, which is round, is so large, that in this way they can chain up as many as five hundred men. There is nothing so dreadful as to behold the attitudes and postures of these wretches there chained. For a man so bound cannot lie down at full length, the beam upon which his head is fixed being too high ; neither can he sit, nor stand upright, the beam being too low ; I cannot better describe the posture of such a man than by saying he is half lying, half sitting, part of his body being upon the stones or flooring, the other part upon this beam.

It was in this manner that they chained us ; and thoroughly inured as we were to pains, fatigues, and sorrows, the three days and three nights which we were obliged to pass in this cruel situation, so racked our bodies and all our limbs, that we could not longer have survived it, especially our poor old men, who cried out every moment that they were dying, and that they had no more strength to endure this terrible torture. I may perhaps be asked, "How can all those other poor wretches who are brought from the four corners of France, and who sometimes are obliged to wait three, four, or even five and six months before the great chain starts for Marseilles, endure such torture for so long?" To this I reply, that an immense number of these unfortunates succumb under the weight of their misery, and that those who escape death through strength of constitution, suffer pains of which it is impossible to give any adequate idea. One hears in this horrible cavern only groans and mournful lamentations, capable of softening any other hearts than those of the ferocious officials of this terrible place. The scanty relief of uttering these lamentations is even denied to the pitiable slaves, for every night five or six brutes of turnkeys form the guard in the dungeon, and they fall without mercy upon those who speak, cry, groan, or lament, barbarously striking them with huge ox bones. With regard to food, that is tolerably good. The "Grey Sisters" bring every day at twelve o'clock, soup, meat, and good bread, in abundance. The duty of these sisters is to attend to the poor in Paris, to whom they take food every day, and even medicine if they require it. They also have the direction of several hospitals, especially of those for soldiers, and by their rules they are obliged to visit the prisoners and relieve them. In some places they are also charged with instructing the young of both sexes; whether they are capable of this, my readers may judge from what I am now about to relate.

The mother-superior, who came every day to our dungeon to serve out the soup to the galley slaves, always stayed a quarter of an hour with me, and gave me more to eat than I required. The other galley slaves often laughed at me for this, calling me the favourite of the mother-abbess. One day, after giving me my portion, she said to me, among other things, that it was a pity that we were not Christians. "Who has told you that, my good mother?" said I; "we are Christians, by God's mercy." "What!" said she, "you are? but you believe in Moses ?" "Do you not believe," asked I, "that Moses was a great prophet?" "I," said she, "believe in that impostor! in that false prophet who seduced so many Jews as Mohammed seduced the Turks! Oh, no, thanks to the Lord, I am not guilty of such a heresy." I shrugged my shoulders at this ridiculous speech, and contented myself with telling her that it was neither the time nor the place to discuss this matter, but I only begged her to confess what she had just said, and she would see that her confessor (if perchance he knew more than she did) would certainly tell her that what she had said about Moses was a very great sin. One can judge from this whether these good women were capable of instructing the young.

I mentioned that for three days and three nights we were chained to the beams. The cause of our being so soon delivered was as follows :—A good Protestant of Paris, M. Girardot de Chancourt, a rich merchant, having heard of our arrival at the Tournelle, went to beg the governor to allow him to see us, and to assist us in our necessities. The governor, though he was his great friend, would never allow him to enter the dungeon to speak to us, for no one was permitted admission except the ecclesiastics. M. Girardot then could not see us nearer than from the courtyard of the castle, through a double grating of iron, with which the windows of the dungeon were furnished. He could not even speak to us, as the distance between us was too great, and it was with difficulty that he could see any of us, as we could only be distinguished by our red jackets. But seeing us in the frightful attitude in which we were placed, our heads nailed down to these beams, he asked the governor if there was no means of chaining us by the leg, as were others of the galley slaves whom he saw much nearer the windows inside the dungeon. The governor told him that those whom he saw there paid a certain price a month. "If you will, sir," said M. Girardot, "give those poor fellows the same liberty, and arrange the price with them, I will pay you if they cannot." The governor told him that he would see if there was any room near the grating, and if there was he would do as he requested. Next morning the governor came to the dungeon, and from the first of us that he saw asked who had charge of our expenses. They pointed to me. The governor came and asked me if we should like to be at the grating, chained by the foot. I told him that we could ask for nothing better, and then we agreed to pay him fifty crowns for the time that the chain remained at the Tournelle. I paid it at once out of the common purse of which I was the treasurer. The governor at once had us unbound from these frightful beams, and placed us as near as possible to the grating, chained by the foot.

As, for several years, we had been accustomed to this kind of chaining, we found ourselves quite relieved. Our chain, which was fastened into the floor, and which held us by one foot, was two yards long, so that we could either stand upright, sit, or lie down, and considering the condition in which

we had been upon those cruel beams, we now found
our situation a very tolerable one.   M. Girardot
often came to see us, and spoke easily to us through
the grating, but with prudence and circumspection,
on account of the other galley slaves who surrounded
us.   This rest we only enjoyed for a month, at the
end of which we set out with the chain on the
17th December.

The Jesuits have the spiritual direction of the
Chateau de la Tournelle.   A week before the departure of the chain, one of their novices, who, by
his sermons, appeared to us to be a great igno-
ramus, came to preach every day in the dungeon
to prepare these miserable galley slaves to confess
and receive the Holy Sacrament.   This preacher
always took the same text,—that precept of the
Gospel, "Come unto me, all ye who are weary and
heavy laden, and I will give you rest."   He maintained, and tried to prove by divers passages from
the fathers, that the Saviour, in the words of this
text, taught that one could only come to him by
auricular confession.   We heard his sermons, and
were shocked at his absurdities, but we never had
the opportunity of being able to speak to him, for
he feared our conversation as he would the fire,
believing that we were all very dangerous Huguenot ministers, quite capable of entrapping good
Catholics, as report said in Paris.   This poor
novice, therefore, both in coming in and going out
of the dungeon, always made a great *détour* to
avoid us.   Several Jesuit fathers, soon after, came
to confess all these unfortunate wretches, and

brought them the Holy Sacrament, which they made them take in that frightful attitude, with their heads nailed down upon the beams, a proceeding which appeared most irreverent, even to us, who had not such superstitious faith in this mystery as the Romanists have, and which filled us with horror. I remarked that, after they had given them the host, they made them drink some wine out of a chalice. I asked one of them if they received the Communion in both kinds. He replied that they did not, and that the wine which they gave them in this chalice was not consecrated—that it was only a precaution which they took at the Tournelle to make them swallow the host, as a profane story was told, which the Jesuits pretended to believe, of a wicked galley slave who had made a compact with the devil that, if he would release them all, he would give him a consecrated wafer, which he therefore kept in his mouth for the purpose. The galley slave gave it to him, and on the journey the whole chain was set at liberty by the evil one.

On the 17th December, at nine o'clock in the morning, they took us all out of the dungeons, and brought us into a spacious courtyard before the castle. They chained us by the neck, in couples, with a thick chain three feet long, in the middle of which was a round ring. After having thus chained us, they placed us all in file, couple behind couple, and then they passed a long and thick chain through all these rings, so that we were thus all chained together. Our chain made a very

P

long file, for we were about four hundred. Then they made us all sit down on the ground to wait till the procureur-général of the parliament came to dispatch us, and give us into the charge of the captain of the chain. His name was Langlade, an officer under M. d'Argenson, lieutenant of the Paris police. About noon the procureur-général, and three councillors of the parliament, came to the Tournelle, called us all by name, read out the copy of our sentence to each of us, and then gave them all into the hands of the captain of the chain. This formality detained us three good hours in the courtyard, during which M. Girardot, who was not idle in our cause, went to beseech M. d'Argenson to recommend us to the captain of the chain, which he did very strongly, ordering him to distinguish us above all the others, to procure us all the relief in his power, and to bring back to him, after his return from Marseilles, a certificate, in which we attested that we were contented with him. He also directed him to arrange with M. Girardot for our comfort during the journey.

The procureur-général, having kindly granted permission to M. Girardot to come into the courtyard, he came and embraced us all with an affection worthy of the principles of that Christianity which influenced him. Then he talked to the captain, who told him that it was necessary that the money we had with us should be given over to him, because at the first lodging where the chain stopped we should be searched, and then the galley slaves forfeit all the money which is found on them.

M. Girardot asked us if we would intrust our money
to the captain ; we replied in the affirmative ; and,
as our money was in a common purse which I kept,
I at once put it into M. Girardot's hands, who at
once counted it out to the captain. It amounted to
about eight hundred francs. The captain then
told M. Girardot that, as we had sick and infirm
people among us, it would be quite necessary that
we should be provided with one or two waggons.
He added that he could not do this at the government's expense without having first severely lashed
those who could not walk, to be certain that they
were not feigning weakness. M. Girardot at once
understood what these words signified, and agreed
that we should pay the captain one hundred
crowns, so that, when we complained of not being
able to walk, they might put us into waggons
without striking us, and otherwise ill-treating us ;
thus, strictly speaking, these one hundred crowns
which he took from our common purse were to buy
us off from blows during the journey.

For our security, M. Girardot made the captain
sign a receipt, with the promise that, in giving us
back our money and our box of books (the carriage
of which to Marseilles was included in our one hundred crowns), he would render up an account of what
had been spent, and receive our attestation that we
were satisfied with him. This done, and the captain having received his orders for the departure of
the chain, we left the Tournelle about three o'clock
in the afternoon, and traversed a great part of
Paris, that we might arrive at Charenton to sleep.

A great number of people belonging to the reformed religion stood in the streets through which the chain passed, and, notwithstanding the cuffs and blows which our brutal archers gave them to prevent them from coming near us, they threw themselves upon us to embrace us, for we were distinguished by our red jackets. Moreover, we twenty-two were all together at the end of the chain.

These good people, among whom were many of distinction, cried aloud to us, " Courage, dear confessors of the truth ; suffer with constancy for so good a cause, while we will never cease praying to God that he may give you grace to endure your severe trials," and other similar words of encouragement, very consoling to us. Four gentlemen, rich merchants of Paris, accompanied us as far as Charenton, with the captain's permission, who was a great friend of one of them. They made the captain promise to let them entertain us to supper at Charenton, and to detach us from the great chain, that we might be with them in private in a room of the inn where the chain was to lodge. We arrived at Charenton about six in the evening, by moonlight. It froze terribly hard. The difficulty which we had in walking, and the excessive weight of our chains (which was 150 lbs. for each, as our captain himself said), had warmed us after the great cold which we had suffered in the courtyard of the Tournelle, so that on arriving at Charenton we were as wet with perspiration as if we had been plunged into water. Here they lodged us in the stable of an inn ; but, alas ! what a lodging ! and what a rest they prepared for us to refresh us after this great fatigue. We were chained up to this stable in such a way that we could with difficulty sit down, and then only on a dung-heap; for as the captain conducts the chain at his own expense as far as Marseilles, receiving there twenty crowns a head for each man, he spares even straw, and we had none during the whole journey. Here, then, they left us to rest (though such a rest was almost worse than the fatigues we had endured) till nine o'clock in the evening, to prepare another scene for us, the most cruel that can be imagined, as I am going to describe. However, our four gentlemen from Paris, who had followed us to Charenton, and were lodging in the same inn, had engaged the largest apartment there, and ordered a supper for thirty persons, reckoning that the captain would keep his word with them. But how different an entertainment from that which they expected was the one we had to take part in, and they to behold ! It makes me shudder every time I think of it.

At nine o'clock, when it was bright moonlight, with a very hard frost and a north wind, they unfastened our chains, and turned us all out of the stable into a spacious courtyard, enclosed by a wall, before the inn. They arranged the chain on one side of this courtyard ; then they ordered us, huge whips in their hands, blows from which fell like hail upon the slothful ones, to strip off all our clothes and to put them down at our feet. We were forced to obey, and we twenty-two, as well as the whole chain, submitted to this cruel treatment. After we had stripped perfectly naked, the chain was ordered to march across to the other end of the court, where we were exposed to the north wind for two long hours, during which time the archers searched and examined all our clothes, under the pretext of looking for knives, files, and other tools, which might be used for cutting or breaking the chains. One may judge if the money that was found escaped the hands of these harpies. They took anything that they fancied—handkerchiefs, linen (if it was at all good), snuff-boxes, scissors, etc., and kept everything, returning nothing ; and when the poor wretches asked for what had been taken from them, they were overwhelmed with cuffs and blows from their muskets and sticks. The examination of our clothes being made, the chain was ordered to march back to the place where they had left them. But oh, cruel spectacle ! the greater part of these unfortunates, ourselves included, were so stiffened by the piercing cold to which we had been exposed, that it was impossible to walk, even that short distance, across to our clothes. Then blows from the cudgels and the whips rained down on all sides ; and this horrible treatment not succeeding in reviving the poor frozen bodies, which were heaped one upon another, some dead, others dying, the barbarous archers dragged them by the chains round their necks like carrion, their bodies streaming with blood from the blows they received. That evening, or the next morning, eighteen died. We twenty-two were neither beaten nor dragged along, thanks to God and our hundred crowns, which on this occasion we experienced to have been well employed. The archers helped us to walk, and even carried some of us in their arms to the place where we had left our clothes ; and, by a sort of miracle, not one of us perished, neither there nor during the whole route. For three times more this barbarous examination took place in the open air, with a cold as great and even more intense than it was at Charenton. Whilst we were receiving this cruel treatment at Charenton, the four gentlemen from Paris saw from the window of their room what was taking place in the courtyard. They cried and lamented, entreating the captain with clasped hands to spare us, but he did not heed them ; and all that these good gentlemen could do was to call out to us to commend ourselves to God, as they do to victims who are about to undergo the punishment of death. Since then we have never seen those gentlemen, for they chained us down again in the stable as before. They could not have had much appetite for the supper which they had prepared for us. The captain would not even allow them to go into the stable to see us and assist us in our sad condition, nor to bring us the least refreshment ; so we had to content ourselves with a piece of bread, an ounce of cheese, and a very small quantity of bad wine, which our captain distributed among us.

Next morning we started from Charenton. Some

of us twenty-two, who required it, were placed in the waggons without being in the least ill-used, but the other poor wretches, overcome with the suffer-- ings of the preceding evening, and some at the brink of death, could only obtain this favour after having passed under the ordeal of the whips. In order to put them into the waggons, they detached them from the great chain, dragged them by that which they had round their necks, like dead cattle, and threw them upon the waggon like dogs, their naked legs hanging out, so that they froze in a short time, which caused indescribable torture ; and worse still, those who complained and lamented at the pains they were suffering, were frequently killed by repeated blows of the stick.   It may well be asked, why the captain did not take more care to spare their lives, as he was to receive twenty crowns a head for those whom he delivered up alive at Marseilles, and nothing for those who died on the road.   The reason is clear.   The captain had to provide conveyances for them at his own expense, and the waggons being dear, he found it did not pay to hire them.   For example, to take a man in a waggon as far as Marseilles, would have cost him more than forty crowns, without his board, which shows that it was more profitable to kill them than to convey them in waggons.   He left to the curé of the first village he came to, the care of interring these dead bodies, and received from him an attestation of their burial.

Thus we traversed the Ile de France, Burgundy, and Maconnais, as far as Lyons, performing three or four leagues a day, which is a great deal, considering how we were laden with our chains, sleeping every night in stables upon dunghills, badly fed, and, when it thawed, always up to our knees in mud, soaked through with rain, and afflicted with vermin and the itch, the consequences of this wretchedness. As to the latter, not one of us twenty-two had it, though several of us were coupled with those who were suffering from this disease. I was chained to a man who had been condemned for desertion. He was a good sort of fellow. They coupled him with me at Dijon, because the Reformed who had been chained to me had hurt his foot, and therefore was put in a waggon. He was suffering frightfully from this loathsome disorder, but notwithstanding its infectious nature, I did not catch it.

On arriving at Lyons, the whole chain was placed in large flat-bottomed boats, to descend the Rhône as far as Pont St. Esprit, from thence by land to Avignon, and from Avignon to Marseilles, where we arrived on the 17th January, 1713, all twenty-two of us, thanks to God, in good health. Of the others, many had died on the road, and there were very few who were not sick; many of these died in the hospital at Marseilles. Thus ended our journey from Dunkirk to Marseilles, a journey during which I suffered more, especially after leaving Paris, than I had done during the twelve previous years of my imprisonment and servitude at the galleys. God be praised that henceforth I shall only have to relate the events which preceded and finally resulted in our precious liberty: events which have, thank God, nothing tragical in them, but which may perhaps interest the reader, who will see in them the deep malice and inveterate hatred of the missionaries of Marseilles, and the grace of God towards his children, which made them triumph over their implacable enemies.

They placed us twenty-two Protestants in a galley named the *Grande Réale*, which served as a depôt for the new comers, and for the infirm of the thirty-five galleys which were then in the port of Marseilles. These new comers did not remain there long; they soon divided them among the other galleys, but we twenty-two were not divided, because they expected that the six bands of galley slaves from Dunkirk would return to Marseilles, and that we should all then be replaced in the galleys which we had left. We increased the number of our brethren who were on board the *Grande Réale*, so that we were now more than forty Reformed. These dear brethren received us with embraces and with mingled tears of joy and grief,—of joy at seeing us all safe and well, constant, and resigned to the will of God; and of grief at the sufferings which we had endured, praising Divine Providence for having sustained us in such long and painful trials.

The superior of the missionaries of Marseilles, named Father Garcin, happened to be in Paris at the same time we were. He came to see us in the dungeon of the Tournelle, and exhorted us strongly, by worldly promises, to change our religion, for such is almost always the text of their mission. "I could obtain your release in twenty-four hours," said he, "if you would only recant. Think of what you are about to expose yourselves to. There is every probability that three-fourths of you will perish between here and Marseilles at this inclement season ; and then when those who survive arrive at Marseilles, they will, as all the other Protestants have done, make their abjuration in my presence." Father Garcin reached Marseilles before we did, and the day after our arrival came to see us in the *Grande Réale*, and having summoned us all to the stern of the galley, he counted us, and finding the same number as he had seen at Paris—"It is wonderful," said he, "how you have all escaped! Are you not weary of suffering?" "You greatly deceive yourself, sir," said I, "if you think that sufferings weaken our faith. On the contrary, we experience what the psalmist says, that the more we suffer afflictions, the more we remember God." "Nonsense!" said he. "It is not so much nonsense," I replied, "as that which you told us at Paris, that all our brethren in the galleys at Marseilles had abjured in your presence. Not one has done so ; and were I in your place I should be ashamed all my life at being convicted of such a gross imposture." "You are a reasoner," he replied rudely, and departed.

Two or three months passed after our arrival at Marseilles without anything particular happening, but about the beginning of April, the missionaries made a general exhortation to us all, to persuade us to change our religion, employing for this purpose rather worldly promises than demonstrative arguments. They flattered themselves that they would gain at least a few, if it were only one or two, in order that they might carry into execution a diabolical design which they had formed, as will presently be seen. I must go back a little in order to make this intelligible.

During the congress at Utrecht for a general peace, we lived in hopes that the treaty would procure our deliverance. We knew that the Protestant powers were interesting themselves warmly on our behalf; but France would not hear of it, and peace was concluded without any mention of us, so that all hope from man being taken away, we turned entirely to God, and resigned ourselves to his holy will. We were in this state of mind when the missionaries began their exhortation. They persuaded themselves that, having lost all human hope, it would be easy for them to tempt us by their fine promises, and to seduce some one of us to play that part which they had so artfully designed,—but by God's grace they did not succeed.

We knew nothing of what was taking place in England in our favour, but the missionaries, who knew everything, had information that Queen Anne was being strongly solicited to employ her good offices for us with the King of France; and, as good politicians, they were certain that if the queen demanded our release, the king, for reasons known to every one, would not refuse it. These gentlemen were resolved to oppose in every possible way our regaining our liberty, so they made the king, who was always ready to listen to them, believe that the heretics at the galleys were about to return into the pale of the Roman Church, that the king might thus have something to oppose to the solicitations which Queen Anne might make for our release. But not having been able to persuade any of us to recant, and requiring some one to do so in order to execute their project, what did these deceivers do? They persuaded two wretched convicts, who were condemned—the one for theft, the other for desertion, both Roman Catholics by birth, and who for several years that they had been at the galleys had always professed that religion—to pretend that they belonged to the reformed faith, and then to turn Roman Catholics, after which, they promised them their release. These conditions were very acceptable to these two poor wretches; so they lent a willing ear, and readily acquiesced in the proposal. We were in perfect ignorance of this crafty proceeding, and were much surprised one Sunday, when mass was being said on the galleys, to see these two pretended Reformed roll themselves up in their cloaks and lie down upon their benches, as the real Reformed were accustomed to do; this manner of acting being allowed to those who professed to have no faith in the mass.

The reason of this toleration, which may surprise my readers, was as follows :—After the peace of Ryswick, the missionaries undertook to force the

Protestants in the galleys, when mass was said, to fall on their knees, bare-headed, and in the same posture of devotion which the Roman Catholics observed. To effect this object they had not much difficulty in gaining on their side M. de Bonbelle, major-general of the galleys, one of the greatest and most inveterate of persecutors. They arranged with him that the bastinado should be given to all the Reformed, till they consented to observe the required posture during mass. And to make this punishment the more fearful, by lasting all the longer, it was agreed that the major should begin at one end of the galleys (there were forty of them) and give the bastinado to one or two galleys a day, and thus to the other end; and then begin again with those who remained obstinate, and continue till they either submitted or died under the lash. Bonbelle carried out this abominable scheme, and his favourite words, in exhorting these poor martyrs to obey, were these, which makes one shudder with horror : " Dog," said he, "down on your knees when mass is being said, and if you won't pray to God in such a posture, pray to the devil if you like, what does it matter to us ? "

All those who were exposed to this punishment, endured it in a holy and courageous manner, praising God in the midst of their sufferings. Some kind souls, however, informed the ambassadors of the Protestant powers at the French court, who, struck with such an atrocious piece of injustice, presented a memorial to the king, in which they alleged, among other things, that it was disgracefully unjust that men who were suffering the cruel hardships of the galleys for refusing to conform to the Romish Church, should be assailed by new tortures to make them submit to it. The king confessed that it was very unjust, and declared that this violence had been committed without his orders ; he immediately sent orders to Marseilles to cease these excesses, and that reparation should be made to the Reformed on the galleys, which was done feebly enough, by saying that it was a misunderstanding which should not occur again. Since that period the Reformed have been allowed to sit or lie on their benches during mass, as I mentioned above.

I must now return to the two false Reformed, the tools of the missionaries. These wretches having lain down on their benches during mass, the *comité*, who was in the plot, and whose duty it is to observe that each does his duty, seeing them thus out of their usual posture, asked them the reason. They replied by swearing that they were Huguenots, because their parents had been so. The *comités* told the chaplains, for this scene took place on two different galleys. The chaplains exhorted them to return into the pale of the church. They pretended to resist at first, but finally yielded. We fancied that this was a trick of the missionaries, but we did not penetrate the real object of it till a few days after, when the missionaries made it known themselves, as will be seen.

These two false Huguenots having made their

public and solemn abjuration, to render this grand conversion more important and attractive, received, a few days after, their pardon from the court, and were at once set at liberty. The day of their release Father Garcin and another missionary went from galley to galley to announce this favour, which they said the king had granted to two of our brethren. They came at last to the *Grand Réale*, where there were, as I have said, forty of the Reformed. They ordered the *argousin* to unchain us all, that we might go and speak to them in the stern-cabin. We went thither, and after the most flattering civilities, which these fathers had always ready at hand, they began their harangues in these terms :—

"Gentlemen, you know the pains and the cares which we have always given ourselves for your conversion, especially of late, when we delivered a general exhortation to you all, without, however, reaping all the fruits which we had hoped from it. But as God dispenses his favours as it pleases him, two from among you, to whom the Saviour has given grace to listen to us more fairly, have embraced the truths which we have taught them, and with great zeal have made their abjuration in our presence ; and as we know that nothing can give his majesty greater pleasure than the conversion of his erring subjects, we have not failed to tell him the good news, and this is what he has ordered his minister, M. de Pontchartrain, to write to us." Then they read the minister's letter, the substance of which was, that his majesty had been glad to learn that two of the principal Calvinist heretics in the galleys had abjured their errors, and that his majesty hoped, from the information that had been given him, that all the others on board the galleys would soon follow their good example, in which case his majesty promised them not only their release, but also his royal favour as to good subjects. We easily judged from this letter that the missionaries had played this trick in order to make his majesty believe that these two new converts were, as it were, the buttresses which sustained the others, and that, having this idea, his majesty would not listen to any solicitation in our favour, supposing that we were all converted, or on the point of being so. By such infamous deceit did these missionaries endeavour to impose upon the king. How great, too, was the impiety of these impostors, who thus recklessly played with religion, and who sacrificed the truth to their execrable lies. But these gentlemen care for nothing, provided they can effect their pernicious designs. Impiety, falsehood, hypocrisy, cruelty, and all the most atrocious crimes, are merely peccadilloes to them, if they are only used for the destruction of that which they call heresy, and to satiate their hatred and vengeance against their enemies, who are only such because they do not think as they do.

After Father Garcin had read M. Pontchartrain's letter to us, he harangued us very pathetically, exalting the king's fatherly kindness for his subjects, which was not content with procuring them merely temporal good, but which also extended to

Q

the salvation of their souls ; that this letter which he had ordered his minister to write, was more than a sufficient proof of this. He then dilated on the goodness and gentleness of the Romish Church, which, following the example of the Saviour of the world, only drew men by persuasion to embrace the truths of the gospel. "And do not allege," exclaimed this father, "that we persecute you to make you return into the pale of the church ; far from us is that system of persecuting which you so often raise as an objection to us. We declare to you that we detest it, and we agree with you that, according to the precepts of the gospel, it is not right for any to persecute others on account of their religion. Reflect, then, for a time," continued the father, "and yield yourselves to the royal and pious solicitation of his majesty—to the gentle persuasion of the truths which we announce to you with all our heart, and with a real zeal for your salvation."

Having finished his discourse, one of our number then spoke. He testified that we were very sensible of the offers so full of kindness which his majesty had made to us, through his ministers ; that we should continue all our lives good and faithful subjects of his majesty; and as to our holy faith, that we were all resolved, with God's grace, to profess it with heart and lips, even to our lives' end. Here Father Garcin interrupted him, saying that he could not answer for us all ; that, besides, he did not ask us for an immediate answer, wishing each to reflect in private upon what he had just said to us.

Not being able to say anything more to these

fathers (there were two of them), we left the cabin, where they remained a little longer, apparently to see if some few among us, at least, would not come and declare that they were convinced. The *argousin* began to chain us each to our several benches, but as we were forty, a good hour passed before that was done. Meanwhile, I conversed with three of our brethren, waiting till our turn to be chained arrived. I told them that I could not keep back what was passing in my heart ; that I was anxious to answer Father Garcin's imposture, who dared to assert that we were not persecuted. These brethren represented to me that, knowing as we did the harsh and cruel character of these fathers, we could only expect that our replies, however humble, would result in nothing but further ill-usage. "Gentlemen," said I, " we have suffered so much bad treatment, which God has given us grace to bear with joy for his cause, that anything more of the kind will not astonish us, and with the continuance of the divine grace we shall still know how to suffer if it be necessary. I beg you, therefore, that we four return to the room where these fathers still are, that in your presence I may give vent to what I feel in my heart. I will speak, and I promise you that no invective or impertinence on my part shall furnish them with a pretext for ill-treating us."

They consented, and we entered the cabin where these fathers still were. Directly they saw us coming they put on a cheerful air, which persuaded us that they believed we had seriously reflected upon their harangue, and had come to confess ourselves vanquished. They saluted us in the most amiable manner, offering us seats. I had promised our three brethren that I would speak, which I did after Father Garcin had asked us if we had reflected upon what he had said, and upon the king's promise in case we abjured our errors. I replied that we were fully persuaded of the kindness and sincerity of his majesty, but that we had several scruples which must be removed, and that we came to them to ask them to give us some explanations upon that which we were about to propose to them.

I must confess that the manner I was obliged to assume, in making this début, was rather hypocritical, and made them think that we were coming to capitulate, and finally to recant. I had the pleasure of seeing how easily they fell into the snare which I had laid for them. I wished to make them tacitly confess that we were persecuted for the sake of our faith, and this is how I managed it. I told this father, then, that we had seriously reflected on what had taken place, but, among others, there was one great obstacle to what they called our conversion, which we were now going to mention to him, and to ask him to remove. " That is just what you ought to do," cried Father Garcin, quite joyfully. " Speak, sir," said he to me, "and you will be quite satisfied as to all your scruples."

Thereupon I continued in the same tone, and said to him, " I can certify to you, sir, that, thanks to God and to my parents, I have been brought up and very well instructed in the principles of the reformed religion ; but I must confess to you, that nothing strengthens me more in it than to see myself persecuted for its sake ; for when I consider that Jesus Christ, his apostles, and so many faithful Christians have been persecuted, according to the prophecy of their divine Saviour, I cannot but believe myself to be in the right road to salvation, since I am persecuted as they were. Thus, sir, if you can prove to me that we are not persecuted, as you asserted just now, I confess that you will gain considerable advantage over me." " I am delighted," replied Father Garcin, " that you have so clearly made known your scruples to me, and equally delighted that there is nothing so easy as to remove it by proving to you that you are not persecuted for the sake of your religion, and it is in this way : Do you know," he asked me, " what persecution is ?" "Alas! sir," said I, "my condition and that of my suffering brethren has made us only too well acquainted with it." " Pshaw !" said he, "there is the mistake you make : you take *chastisement* for persecution, and I am now going to convince you of this. Why are you at the galleys, and what is the motive of your sentence ?"

I replied that, finding myself persecuted in my own country, I had wished to leave the kingdom to profess my religion in liberty, and that I had been arrested on the frontiers, and for this condemned to the galleys. " Do you not see," exclaimed Father Garcin, " what I have just told you, that you do not know what persecution is ? I will explain it by telling you that persecution consists in being badly treated to oblige you to renounce the religion which you profess. Now, in your case, religion has nothing to do with it, and here is the proof. The king has forbidden all his subjects to leave the kingdom without his permission. You attempted to do this, therefore you are being chastised for having disobeyed the king's orders. This is connected with the police of the kingdom, and not with the church, nor with religion."

He then addressed another of our brethren present, to ask him why he was at the galleys. "For having prayed to God at a religious meeting," replied this brother. "Another act of disobedience to the king's orders," said Father Garcin. "The king has forbidden his subjects to meet in any place to pray to God, except in the parish and other churches of the kingdom. You have done the contrary, and you are punished for having disobeyed the king's orders."

Another of our brethren told him that, being very ill, the curé had come to his bedside to receive his declaration, whether he would live and die in the reformed religion or in the Roman Catholic; that he had replied in the reformed; and that, having recovered from his sickness, he had been arrested and condemned to the galleys. "Again another act of disobedience to the orders of the king," said Father Garcin. "His majesty wishes that all his subjects should live and die in the Roman religion. You declared that you would not do so; that is disobeying the king's orders. Thus, gentlemen, all of you have disobeyed the king's commands; the church has no part in it. She has neither taken part in nor presided at your trial; in a word, all has happened independently of her and of her knowledge."

I well saw that I should have some trouble to make him grant that we were persecuted for the sake of our religion if I continued in this somewhat hypocritical strain. I told him with a simple air that I was content with his explanation as to what persecution was, and that now I wanted to know whether, if my other doubts could be cleared up, I might be released before making my abjuration. " Certainly not," replied Father Garcin; "you will never leave the galleys till you have made it in its complete form." " And if I do make this abjuration, can I then hope to be released soon?" "A fortnight afterwards," said Father Garcin, "on the faith of a priest; for you see that in such a case the king promises it to you." I then resumed my natural air to tell him with the greatest seriousness how I had to-day experienced the force of truth, which penetrates the most cunning falsehood. "You have endeavoured, sir," said I, "by all your sophistical reasons to prove to us that we are not persecuted on account of our religion; and I, without either philosophy or rhetoric, by two simple and plain questions, have made you confess that it is our religion which keeps my brethren and myself in the galleys; for you have asserted that if we made our formal abjuration, we should be set free at once; and, on the contrary, that there will never be any liberty for us if we do not abjure it." I should have pushed still further my reflections upon his avowal, to show him the absurdity of his sophisms, but this father saw himself so thoroughly entrapped by his own mouth, that, fury overpowering his senses, he broke off the conversation with brutality and precipitation, calling us wicked and obstinate fellows, and cried to the *argousin* to come and chain us to our benches, forbidding him to give us the slightest alleviation from our chains.

This incident shows the diabolical character of these cunning and cruel missionaries. I now pass on to the events which gained us our liberty.

The peace of Utrecht being concluded without anything having been done for us, the Marquis de Rochegude, a French refugee in the Swiss cantons, who had been sent by Switzerland to Utrecht, to petition in favour of the poor confessors in the French galleys, determined to strike a last blow on our behalf, which he did with an amount of trouble and fatigue surprising at his great age. He left Utrecht for the North, obtained from Charles XII., King of Sweden, a letter of recommendation to the Queen of England, others from the Kings of Denmark, Prussia, and from several German Protestant princes, from the States-General of the United Provinces, from the Swiss Protestant cantons, and from all the powers of the same religion, recommending us to the powerful intercession of her Britannic majesty for our deliverance. The marquis crossed the sea, and requested Lord Oxford (then prime minister of England) to procure him an audience of her majesty. The minister asked him what was the object of his mission. " I have all these letters," said the marquis, " to present to her majesty," and he named them all. " Give them to me," said his lordship ; " I will warmly back them up." " I cannot," said the marquis, "for I have strict orders from these powers to place them myself in her majesty's own hand ; and if not, to bring them back immediately." Upon this, Lord Oxford procured him the requested audience. He presented all these letters to her majesty, telling her from whom they came. The queen promised to examine them, and give him an answer. Thereupon the marquis retired. For a fortnight he heard nothing. At the end of that period, hearing that the queen was going to walk in St. James's Park, he went thither that her majesty might see him. In this he succeeded, for the queen having perceived him, ordered him to be called to her side, and said, " Monsieur de Rochegude, I beg you to let all those poor fellows on board the galleys of France know that they will be released immediately." This pious and favourable answer had nothing doubtful in it. The marquis at once informed us of it by the way of Geneva. Thus our hope of help from man, which we had entirely lost, revived again, and we praised God for this happy event. Soon after an order came from the court to the governor at Marseilles to send up a list of all the Protestants at the galleys, which was done ; and a few days after, at the end of May, the order came to the governor to release one hundred and thirty-six of the Protestants ; a list of whose names was also sent. We did not understand what was the policy of the court, which did not release all, as there were altogether more than three hundred suffering for the same cause. The others were not released for a year after.

The governor having received this order, communicated it to the missionaries, who were furious, saying that the king had been surprised and overreached, and that to release us would be an eternal blot upon the Romish Church. At the same time, they prayed the governor to suspend the execution of his orders for a fortnight, that they might send an express to the court to get them reversed, and to keep them secret till they received the answer they expected. The governor, who could refuse nothing to these fathers without drawing down their hatred upon him, granted their request, keeping the order to release the one hundred and thirty-six Protestants secret. But, from the day after, we were secretly informed, by degrees, of the names of those in the list. I was kept in great suspense, as I was the last mentioned, and did not hear for three days that my name was there at all. Imagine the affliction of our poor brethren whose names were not in the list. They comforted themselves, however, with the hope that their turn would come, since the Queen of England had asked and obtained the release of us all. But what does not one suffer between fear and hope! For three weeks one hundred and thirty-six of us were in this state of suspense; for we had learned that the missionaries had written to the court to obtain the reversal of these orders, and to prevent our release. We knew by sad experience the power of these gentlemen, and that they were scarcely ever refused. Our fear, therefore, was not without foundation. We could not sleep either by day or by night. The missionaries' express arrived at last at Marseilles; but, to their great astonishment, it brought no answer, neither good nor bad, which made the governor judge that the king wished his orders to be carried out. However, the missionaries, not losing all hope, petitioned for a week longer, to wait for another express, which they had despatched after the first. This express arrived with the same silence.

Meanwhile we had not been able to keep secret that we knew about this order, though the missionaries constantly came to the galleys and told us that we were quite out of our reckoning, and that we should certainly not be released. After the arrival of the last express they were quite confounded; still they did not the less employ their malice to oppose our deliverance. They asked the governor in what manner he was going to release us. The governor replied his orders were, "Perfect liberty to go where they liked." They strongly exclaimed against this article, and warmly maintained that heretics like us, spreading themselves all over the kingdom, would pervert not only the new converts, but even good Catholics: so that they persuaded the governor to declare that it was a condition that we left the kingdom immediately by sea, never to return to it on pain of being sent back to the galleys for life. This was another instance of their cunning and malignant policy, for how could we leave by sea? There was not a ship in the harbour to take us to Holland or England. We had not the means to engage one large enough to carry so many people, for that would have cost a considerable sum, which we did not possess. This the missionaries foresaw, and were delighted that it seemed to leave us without any resource.

It is the custom when galley slaves are to be released, to announce it to them some days before. One day, then, the *argousin* of the galleys received an order from the governor to conduct us, one hundred and thirty-six, to the arsenal at Marseilles. The governor having called us each by our name, declared that the king granted us our liberty, at the solicitation of the Queen of England, on condition that we left the kingdom by sea at our own expense. We represented to the governor that this condition was very burdensome to us, and almost impossible to effect. "That is your affair," said he; "the king is not going to spend a sous for you." "That being the case," said we, "order, sir, if you please, that we may be allowed to seek for some way of leaving by sea." "That is quite fair," said he, "and immediately gave orders to the *argousins* to allow us to go along the harbour with a guard, to look for a passage, as often and whenever we liked. Still the missionaries, to place more obstacles in the way of our deliverance, invented another project. This was to make us all declare where we wished to go. Their design was this: they knew that we all had

our relations or acquaintances out of the king
—some in Holland, others in England, othel
Switzerland, or elsewhere. They thought he who
says to Holland, will be told to wait till there are
Dutch ships in the harbour to take him ; the same
to him who will go to England ; and as to those
who say they want to go to Switzerland, they will
be told that they must be taken to Italy, but they
expected that these latter would be quite the mino-
rity. According to this plan it would have been
almost impossible to have got out of their clutches ;
but by God's gracious permission, who had determined on our deliverance, these malicious missionaries were foiled in their attempt, for having
made us all come to the arsenal to exact this declaration from each of us, which we knew nothing
about, they made us ascend a gallery, at the end of
which was the office of the commissary of the navy,
who was sitting there with two of these reverend
fathers. This gallery being very narrow, we were
obliged to stand there in file, one behind the other,
waiting to hear what they had to announce to us.
Fortunately, he whose name was at the head of the
list of the one hundred and thirty-six, had his relations at Geneva. He was called for, and being asked
where he wished to go, he said, "To Geneva."
He who stood behind him thought that all of us were
to say the same, "To Geneva," and turning round
he said to the next, "Pass on the word, and let all
say To Geneva." This was done, for the commissary
having called out to several and hearing them all
answer "To Geneva," he said, "I think they all

want to go to Geneva." "Yes, sir," we said all at once, "to Geneva." The commissary told us we had now only to provide ourselves with vessels to take us to Italy, for, as every one knows, we could not go from Marseilles to Geneva by sea, and not being allowed to pass through France, we could take no other route than that by Italy, which is a very great détour. However, the fact of our all saying "To Geneva," facilitated our deliverance, as will be seen.

We now employed ourselves in seeking for a vessel to take us to Italy. One day, when we were much disheartened at our fruitless search, a pilot of the galley *La Favorite*, named Jovas, told one of our brethren that he had a tartane, a kind of bark much used in the Mediterranean, and that he would willingly undertake to convey us from Marseilles to Villafranca, a seaport in the county of Nice, belonging to the King of Sardinia, and consequently out of France, and that from there we might go to Geneva through Piedmont. We made a bargain with this captain to pay six francs a-head for the passage, for which he was also to provide us with food. We were delighted to have found this opportunity; and Captain Jovas was also much pleased, as it was a profitable freight for so short a passage, Villafranca being only twenty or twenty-five leagues from Marseilles. One of our brethren went with the captain to inform the governor that we had arranged for our departure. He was content, and said he would at once prepare our passports. We expected to be released on the morrow, but these miserable missionaries placed an obstacle in the way. Having been informed that we had arranged for Villafranca, they went to the governor and represented to him that that town was too near the frontiers of France; that we should all return thence; and that we must be transported to Genoa, Leghorn, or Oneglia. This was pure malice and animosity on the part of these cruel missionaries, who wished to persecute us when afar off as they had done when near, for they knew that the journey from Villafranca to Geneva was much shorter than from Genoa or Leghorn, besides the great difficulty on the roads from these latter places, as we should have to cross the Alps, an impossibility for us with our decrepit old men, paralytics, and cripples. These heartless men knew too, well enough, that, once out of France, nothing could make us wish to return to it, and that we had every reason to flee far away, bleeding as we were with the wounds we had received in it. The governor, as well as every one else, saw that it was only a cunning pretext of the missionaries to torment us. But everything was obliged to bend to their will. The governor therefore told us that the agreement we had made with Captain Jovas could not be carried out, on account of the proximity of Villafranca.

Thus we were again disappointed, and seemed as far from our departure as on the first day. We told this sad news to Captain Jovas, who was furious with the missionaries, for indeed they are hated and feared by everybody, as well by the common people as by the great. However, Jovas consoled us, for either out of spite against the missionaries, or out of kindness to us, or for his own profit, he told us that our bargain with him still held good, and that he would take us for the stipulated price of six francs a-head, even if it were to the Archipelago. He asked one of us to go with him to the governor to make this declaration, which was done. The governor still appeared quite content and delighted to get rid of this affair, for he had told the missionaries that he was risking his head in not executing the king's precise orders, and that if the Queen of England complained of it it might fare very ill with him. He told us then that we should be immediately released. But the barbarous missionaries, inveterate in persecuting us, and still hoping for some counter orders from the court, invented a new trick. They told the governor that Jovas's tartane was too small to carry one hundred and thirty-six men in its hold, and that he would be obliged to allow the greater number to be on deck; that we should then make ourselves masters of this bark, throw the captain and his crew into the sea, and sail whither we pleased ; and that they could not give their consent to the souls and bodies of the captain and his men being exposed to such an evident danger; that, in a word, we must be put on board vessels large enough to confine us in their holds. The governor saw the absurdity of this pretext, but he dared not resist it ; so new orders were issued by him to provide ourselves with vessels capable of confining us all in the hold. Jovas, informed of this fresh obstacle, was furious and indignant against the missionaries, pouring forth against them a thousand imprecations in secret. All the more determined to get us over to Italy, he protested that if he gained nothing by it, and even if he lost, he would not be prevented. Next day he brought us the good news that he had so arranged that he thought the missionaries could not raise any more opposition. At his own risk and expense he had hired two larger barks than his own, each of which could easily take fifty men in the hold, while his own would carry thirty-six.

Again we had to go to the governor, who, to remove all pretext for any delay on the part of the missionaries, sent his secretary to examine these three tartanes, to assure him that they could take us all in their holds. We greased, as they say, the paw of this official, that he might give a favourable report, which in fact he did, and it was agreed with the governor that the thirty-six which Captain Jovas was to take in his tartane should be released in the course of two days, 17th June, 1713, and that the other two barks should be dispatched at intervals of three days, each containing fifty men. This being settled, the missionaries, quite at the end of their stratagems, no longer opposed our departure, except by endeavouring to intimidate the captains of the barks. They obliged them to sign a declaration, making them promise not to land us at Villafranca, but at Oneglia, Leghorn, or Genoa, under penalty of a fine of four hundred francs,

R

and the confiscation of their barks. The missionaries then entirely abandoned their persecution,
and Father Garcin was so filled with spite and
disappointment, that he left Marseilles for a time,
that he might not behold the sad and afflicting
sight of our deliverance.

On the 17th of June, then, that happy day, in
which the grace of God was so visibly manifested
in us by the triumph which it obtained over our
implacable enemies, the thirty-six men, of whom I
was one, who were appointed to go in Jovas's bark,
were brought up to the arsenal. The commissary
of the navy read to us the king's orders, inserted
and printed in each of our passports. The agreement which Jovas had signed was also read to him.
This done, the commissary ordered an *argousin* to
unchain us completely, and then, giving all our
passports to Captain Jovas, the commissary told
him that he gave our persons into his charge, that
he might take us to his bark, and start as soon as
possible. We left the arsenal then, freed from all
our bonds, and, like a flock of lambs, followed our
captain, who led us to the place on the quay where
his bark was. We were about to go on board, and
to descend into the hold, which contained nothing
except the sand used for ballast, but the wind was
contrary for leaving the harbour, and the sea very
stormy, so that it was impossible to set sail. Captain
Jovas, seeing that we were resolutely about to enter
his boat, to be shut up there according to the will of
the missionaries, said to us, " Do you think, gentlemen, that I am as cruel as those fellows, and wish

to shut you up like prisoners in my bark while you are free? We cannot leave the harbour till the wind changes, and God only knows when it will change. Go all of you into the town to lodge and sleep in good beds, instead of in my boat, where there is nothing but sand. I have no fear that you will try to escape; on the contrary, I know that you will come and entreat me to take you away from hence out of the hands of your enemies. I can answer for you; and, provided I take you when I am ordered, I have nothing to fear. Go wherever you like in the town; it is useless for me to know where you lodge. Only observe the weather, and when you see the wind change come down to my bark to set out."

We followed the advice which our kind captain gave us, and all went to lodge in different inns in the town. We were not, however, without anxiety, seeing that we could not leave till the wind changed, and always feared some new obstacle from the missionaries. For this reason we went next morning to the commissary, to beg him that he would not impute our delay to any other cause than that of the weather, which prevented our punctually obeying the king's orders. He received us very graciously, was pleased with the step we had taken, and added, very kindly, "The king has not released you that you might perish at sea; remain in the town as long as the weather prevents you from starting, but I advise you not to go outside the gates; and as soon as the weather permits, put to sea. May God give you a prosperous and happy voyage!" This commissary, it must be known, was a Reformed by birth.

The weather continued contrary for three days, at the end of which it changed, and became favourable for leaving the harbour, but still very stormy, and the sea very rough. However, we went to our bark in the port. There we found Captain Jovas, who said that we could indeed leave the harbour, but that we should find very coarse weather at sea. We told him that, if he thought there was no great danger, we wished him to set out, for we would rather be in the hands of God than in those of man. " I knew," said he, "that you would entreat me to start from here, and that you are always more ready to follow me than I to take you. Let us go," said he, " and put to sea under God's protection." We took some provisions with us, and set sail, but we soon repented not having followed our captain's advice, and waited for more favourable weather. The sea was furious, and though the wind was favourable enough for our voyage, our bark was so tossed about by the waves that we thought we should perish every moment. Moreover, we all suffered so fearfully from sea-sickness that our captain was moved with compassion for us, and, on arriving before Toulon, he anchored in the roadstead, where we were sheltered from the tempest, that we might recover a little. About five o'clock in the evening, a sergeant and two marines from Toulon came on board our bark from a small boat, and summoned our captain to go with them to the governor, to inform him of the reason

of his voyage. We were trembling with fear, reflecting that it was specified on our passports that
we were to leave the kingdom, without ever returning to it, under penalty of being sent to the galleys
for the rest of our lives, and dreading lest we might
find a governor ill-disposed to listen to our reasons,
who would perhaps arrest us provisionally, and if
he made known our detention to the missionaries
at Marseilles, which town is only ten leagues off,
they would accuse us of disobedience to the king's
orders, which would bring us into great danger
and trouble. Captain Jovas was also much vexed
about it. However, he took our passports and got
into the soldiers' boat to go and speak to the
governor. The captain permitted four of us, of
whom I was one, to accompany him. As we were
rowing to the harbour, a thought struck me, which,
by God's grace, was very helpful to us. At that
time the plague was raging in the Levant, so they
took the precaution of furnishing all those who left
Marseilles, either by sea or land, with a bill of
health. The clerk of the office, who did not see
room enough for all our names in the printed form
that was given in such cases, and in which a few
blank lines were left for the insertion of the names
of those who required it, wrote, for abridgment,
"Allow thirty-six men to pass, who are going to
Italy by the king's orders, and who are in good
health." I asked the captain, therefore, to try if
showing this form only to the governor would not
be enough. He approved of this idea. Having
arrived, the governor asked the captain whence he

came, whither he was going, and what was his cargo. " My cargo consists of thirty-six men, sir, and here is their destination," showing him at the same time the bill of health. The governor at once imagined that it was a secret expedition of the court, the object of which it was not his business to inquire.

There was, in fact, a mysterious air in this affair, for we four, who were in the governor's presence, having laid aside our convict clothes at Marseilles, were dressed, as well as we could provide ourselves at the time, in ready-made clothes, so that the governor thought we were disguised. He told the captain he did not want to know any more, and, addressing us, added that we might rest and lodge in the town as long as we liked, and offered to defray our expenses if we wished. We thanked him for his kindness, and retired much pleased with the success of our little stratagem. We then begged the captain to land our companions, that they might come and sleep in the town, and refresh themselves after the sickness they had suffered in the bark. This he did ; and next morning quite early we all embarked again in our tartane to continue our voyage.

After three days we arrived in the roadstead of Villafranca, which town, as I have said, belongs to the King of Sardinia. Having anchored here, we asked our captain if he would allow us to land at Villafranca, to sleep for that night, and that next morning we would come on board again at his orders. " I will willingly, gentlemen," said he, " do you this pleasure, in the hope that you will not abuse my kindness ; for, being once in the town, you are your own masters, and need not embark again, but if you play me that trick you will place me in the greatest embarrassment possible, for you know the declaration I have signed, not to land you at this port." We gave him our word as honest men to submit to his orders, and to start again when he wished us. Without the least scruple he trusted us, and at once put us on shore. We lodged in four or five inns close to the port. Next day, which was Sunday, we prepared to re-embark ; but our captain told us that he had to go and see some one at Nice, which is scarcely a league distant ; that he should attend mass there ; and that when he came back he would take us on board. I asked him if he would allow me to go with him to see the town of Nice. "Willingly," replied he ; and three of my brethren joining me, we all five went thither.

On entering the town the captain told us that he was going to attend mass, and that we had better wait for him in the first inn which we saw. We walked through a long street, and as it was Sunday, all the shops and houses were shut, so that we saw scarcely any one. We did not perceive a little man coming towards us, who, approaching us, saluted us very civilly, and begged us not to take it in bad part if he asked us whence we came. We replied that we came from Marseilles. He did not then dare to ask us if we had come from the galleys, as it is offering a great affront to a man to ask him if he has come from the galleys, except for the sake of religion. " But I beg you, gentlemen," continued he,

"to tell me, did you leave by the king's order?"
"Yes, sir," we replied; "we came from the galleys
of France." "Alas! gracious God!" he exclaimed,
"are you some of those who were released, a few
days ago, on account of their religion?" We
avowed that we were. This man, quite transported
with joy, asked us to follow him. We did so without hesitation, accompanied by our captain, who
was afraid of some snare for us, for he did not trust
the Italians.

The man led us to his house, which was more
like the palace of a great nobleman than that
of a merchant. Having entered and closed the
door, he embraced us with tears of joy, and calling
his wife and children, said to them, "Come and
see, and embrace our dear brethren, come out of
the great tribulation of the galleys of France." His
wife, his two sons, and his two daughters, all
embraced us, praising God for our liberty. After
which, M. Bonijoli (this was his name) begged us
to prepare to join in the prayers which he was about
to offer. We all knelt down, Captain Jovas as well
as the others, and M. Bonijoli offered up a prayer
on the subject of our deliverance, the most earnest
and the most pathetic that I have ever heard.
We were all melted into tears, Captain Jovas included, who assured us afterwards that he thought
he was in Paradise. After prayers they got breakfast ready. After several pious discourses had
been delivered upon the powerful grace of God,
which had made us triumph over our enemies, and
given us the constancy to maintain and suffer for

the truth of his holy gospel, he asked us how many
of us had been released? We told him thirty-six.
"That agrees with my letter," said he. "Where are
the others?" "At Villafranca," said we. Then
we told him all our story, and by what chance we
found ourselves at Nice. "But in your turn, sir,"
said we, "let us know who you are, and by what
chance it was that you met us in the street." "I
am," said he, "from Nîmes, in Languedoc; I left it
after the Revocation of the Edict of Nantes, and,
under the protection of the King of Sardinia, came
to establish myself in this town, where, by God's
blessing, I have so prospered that I have acquired
considerable wealth; and, although myself and my
family are the only Protestants in the town, we live
in perfect tranquillity as regards our religion. It is
true that our sovereign has always protected me, not
suffering any of his subjects, either lay or ecclesias-
tical, to trouble me the least in the world. And in
reply to your other question, I must tell you that
one of my correspondents at Marseilles wrote to me
on the day of your release, and begged me, if by
chance you should pass through this town, to assist
you as well as I could. You have seen how I met
you this morning in the street, and I am sure that
Divine Providence arranged this happy meeting,
causing me to go out of my house, which I never do
on Sundays." Having mutually edified each other
by admiring the secret ways which God uses to
manifest his power and impart his grace and
mercy to those who fear him and invoke his holy
name, we discussed what would be our best plan of

continuing our journey to Geneva. The obstacles which presented themselves at first seemed impossible to surmount. Captain Jovas produced the copy of the declaration which he had signed at Marseilles, and which forbade him, under the penalty I have mentioned before, to land us at Villafranca.

It would not have been difficult to justify what he had done by the pretext of bad weather, by which navigators are always excused ; still, not to continue his voyage from thence to Oneglia, Leghorn, or Genoa, according to his orders, would be a manifest contravention of them. It was true that we could with impunity break faith with Jovas, being out of the power of France ; but our honour and our conscience opposed such an act. On the other hand, M. Bonijoli appeared extremely alarmed for us if we landed at one of those three seaports— Oneglia, Leghorn, or Genoa—as from thence to Geneva we should have almost insurmountable troubles and difficulties on account of the numerous lofty mountains to traverse, so impracticable for our old and infirm people ; added to which we could not find horses or mules for so large a company except at exorbitant prices, beyond our means. The only thing that would remain for us then to do, would be to freight a vessel to take us to Holland or England, which would be far too expensive for us, and cause us great delay. What, then, could be done to remedy so many difficulties ? There was, it seemed, no course open to us but that of breaking our promise to Captain Jovas.

But this we would not do, even at the peril of our own life. This poor man, during the consultation which we were holding in his presence, remained in the posture of a suppliant, fearing lest our decision should cause his ruin, and lest the missionaries should persecute him to extremity if we took the route from Nice to Geneva. Both M. Bonijoli and ourselves reassured him by protesting before God that we would protect him from all risks; that we should always consider his safety before our own comfort; and that, if we could find no other alternative, we should unhesitatingly re-embark in his tartane. After this assurance, our captain was set at ease; but we all remained looking at each other without being able to decide upon anything, when suddenly M. Bonijoli exclaimed that he had thought of an expedient which appeared to him safe, and that he would at once try it.

At the peace of Utrecht, the King of France had restored the town and county of Nice to the Duke of Savoy; but after the evacuation he left at Nice a commissary to regulate matters of debt, etc., which were in dispute between the court of France and that of Turin. The name of this French commissary was M. Carboneau. He was on very friendly terms with M. Bonijoli; for as the latter was the only Frenchman at Nice, and as his sons and daughters, who were perfectly well educated, were about the same age as the commissary, he had become quite at home in Bonijoli's house, and was on such good terms with him and his family, that he was as if he belonged to the house-

hold. It was in connection with this French commissary that M. Bonijoli framed his project, which
succeeded wonderfully. He begged Captain Jovas
to give him a copy of his agreement, which he willingly did. He then requested us to wait a little,
whilst he went out, and an hour after he returned,
accompanied by the French commissary. The
commissary questioned Jovas with an air of authority, which his office gave him. He asked him
whence he came, whither he was going, and what
was his cargo. The captain having replied to all
these questions, M. Carboneau ordered him, in the
name of the King of France, to land his thirty-
six men, and to bring them to Nice, forbidding him,
under penalty of disobedience to the king, from
leaving the harbour of Villafranca with his bark
except by his orders.

The captain submitted, went to Villafranca immediately, and brought back the remainder of our
brethren. M. Bonijoli, after having given them a
reception worthy of his pious zeal, lodged them in
different inns, at his own expense, giving orders
that they should be well treated. As to us four he
kept us in his own house, giving us the best cheer
possible for the three days which we remained in the
town. These three days were employed in satisfy-
ing the vanity of the commissary. He made us
come every morning before his house, and standing
in the balcony in a dressing-gown, with a list of
our names in his hand, he called us one after the
other, asked us with an air of authority, and with
the manner of a fop, which made us laugh in our

sleeves, whence we came, the names of our parents, our ages, and other similar useless questions, all to show off his little authority, which he estimated as very great, to a crowd of citizens of the town, who assembled before his house to see what was going on.

M. Bonijoli had told us beforehand that the commissary was very conceited, and he exhorted us, as the best policy, to submit to what he exacted from us—though in truth his requirements were a little extravagant, for he made us stand an hour or two before him, uncovered, with a humble and submissive air, which we were by no means obliged to assume to him, and which we should not have put on, being out of the dominions of France, but for the hope that he would effectually aid us in continuing our journey from Nice to Geneva. On the third day of this performance, being satisfied with the importance he had given himself, he sent for Captain Jovas, and placed a paper in his hand, which he told him to read, and tell him if he was contented with it. This very authentic document, being honoured with the printed arms of the king, and bearing in large letters a "*De par le roi,*" said that he, commissary and director for His Most Christian Majesty, having learned that a French bark had entered into the port of Villafranca, which had been chased and pursued to the entrance of the said port by two Neapolitan corsairs, he had gone to Villafranca, and had found that this bark was from Marseilles, and contained thirty-six men delivered from the galleys of France, going to Italy;

and having visited and examined the bark, as well
as the men, he had found that they were quite des-
titute of food, and that they had not the means to
provide themselves with any ; that, moreover, the
Neapolitan corsairs were waiting out at sea, in sight
of Villafranca, to seize this bark ; that, considering this, and the state of these thirty-six men,
without victuals or money, he, the commissary,
always attentive to the interests of the French nation, had, in the king's name, ordered the captain
of this bark, named Jovas, to land these thirty-six
men, that they might, from thence, make their
journey to Geneva, which was their destination ;
and that, notwithstanding the protestation which
the said captain had made, in virtue of an agreement which he had signed at Marseilles, engaging,
under heavy penalties, not to land them at Villafranca, he, the commissary, had obliged and forced
him to do so, in virtue of the authority which his
majesty had confided to him in the county of
Nice, etc.

Having given this declaration to Jovas, he asked
him if he was content with it. "Quite content,
sir," replied the captain. "Very well," replied the
commissary; "you can set sail for Marseilles whenever you like, and you have only to throw any
blame which they may impute to you upon me as
having forced you to obey me." One may easily
judge whether our captain was satisfied. He was
himself released from a much longer voyage, and
his money, which we paid him at once, easily
gained. He left for Marseilles, and in taking leave

of us he promised to inform the two other barks, which he would meet on his voyage, to come to Villafranca to receive the same treatment as he had done from this kind commissary, who had condescended to invent so many false pretexts to please him and us. Jovas kept his word, for the two other barks came to Villafranca, and the same thing happened to them as to us. Thus all the one hundred and thirty-six landed at this port, and journeyed from hence to Geneva.

After the departure of Captain Jovas, M. Boni-joli prepared to send us off. He hired thirty-six mules to carry us at his own expense as far as Turin, with a postillion or guide to conduct us there. We left Nice at the beginning of July. Our decrepit old men gave us much trouble, scarcely being able to ride. With much fatigue we crossed those frightful mountains, the summit of which, called the Col di Tenda, is so high that it always seems in the clouds. Here, though it was the height of summer, we suffered such cold that we were obliged to descend from our mules and walk, in order to warm ourselves. Snow and ice always lie here to a prodigious height. Lofty and steep as this mountain is, there is no difficulty in ascending it, for a convenient road has been made in zigzags to the top. We descended on the other side into the plain of Piedmont, the most beautiful and agreeable country in the world, and arrived at Turin, the capital of Piedmont, and the residence of his Sardinian majesty. We lodged at different inns, and the next morning received the visits of several French Protestants, of whom a great number reside in the city, and who go to the neighbouring Vaudois valleys to attend Divine service. These gentlemen, to whom M. Bonijoli had announced our arrival, received us with zeal and cordiality, defraying all our expenses during the three days which we remained in this great city, after which, having prepared us mules to continue our journey, they petitioned the King of Sardinia to give us a passport to traverse his states as far as Geneva. His majesty, Victor Amadeus, wished to see us. Six of us were admitted to an audience. The ambassadors of Holland and England were present at it. His majesty gave us a favourable reception, and for half an hour questioned us about the time we had spent at the galleys, the cause of it, and the sufferings we had endured. After we had succinctly replied, he turned to the ambassadors and said, "This is indeed cruel and barbarous." Then his majesty asked us if we had money for our journey. We replied that we had not much, but that our brethren, especially M. Bonijoli, of Nice, had had the charity to defray our expenses as far as Turin, and that our brethren at Turin were preparing to do the same as far as Geneva. We had been instructed to reply in this manner. His majesty said upon this, "You can remain in Turin as long as you please to rest yourselves, and when you want to leave, you can come to the office of my secretary of state, and take a passport which I will order to be made ready." We told his majesty that with his permission we would start on the morrow.

"Go, then, under God's protection," said this prince to us, and he ordered the secretary of state immediately to prepare us a favourable passport. This passport not only gave us permission to pass through his states, but ordered all his subjects to afford us help and succour during our journey. Thanks to God, and to our brethren at Turin, we wanted nothing on our way to Geneva.

There was at Turin a young man, a watchmaker by trade, belonging to Geneva, who, wishing to go thither, asked to accompany us; which, being readily granted, he followed us on foot as far as two days' journey from Geneva, when he took leave of us, saying that he knew a footpath which greatly abridged the distance. We wished him a prosperous journey. He arrived at Geneva a day before us, and having related in the town that thirty-six confessors, delivered from the galleys of France, were to arrive the next day, the venerable magistrate of that city summoned him that he might confirm these tidings. The next day, Sunday, we arrived at a small village on a hill, about a league from Geneva, whence we saw the town with a joy which can only be compared to that of the Israelites at the sight of the land of Canaan.

We wished to go on without stopping, so great was our ardour to be as soon as possible in a city which we regarded as our Jerusalem. But our postillion told us that the gates of Geneva were never open on Sunday till after Divine service, that is, about four o'clock in the afternoon. We were obliged, therefore, to remain in the village till that time, when we all again mounted our horses. As we approached the town, we perceived a great concourse of people coming out of it. Our postillion appeared surprised, but was much more so when, arriving at the Plain-Palais, a quarter of a league from the town, he perceived three carriages coming to meet us, surrounded by halberdiers, and an immense crowd of people of both sexes and all ages, who followed them. A servant of the magistracy now advanced towards us, and begged us to alight, that we might salute with respect and decorum their excellencies of Geneva, who came to meet us and bid us welcome. We obeyed. The three carriages having approached, a magistrate and a minister descended from each, and came to embrace us with tears of joy, and with such pathetic expressions, congratulations, and praise for our constancy and resignation, that they far surpassed what we deserved. We replied by praising and magnifying the grace of God, which alone had sustained us in our great tribulations. After these hearty greetings, their excellencies gave permission to the people to approach. Then was seen the most touching spectacle that can be imagined, for several inhabitants of Geneva had relations at the galleys, and these good citizens were ignorant whether those for whom they had sighed for so many years were amongst us. As soon then as their excellencies gave the people permission to approach, one heard only a confused noise;—" My son! my husband! my brother! are you there?"

Imagine the embraces given to those of our party who were among the recognised!

In general, all these people threw themselves upon our necks with transports of inexpressible joy, praising and magnifying the Saviour for the manifestation of his grace in our favour ; and when their excellencies ordered us to mount our horses again, to make our entry into the town, we had the greatest difficulty in doing so, not being able to tear ourselves from the arms of these pious and zealous brethren, who seemed to fear to lose sight of us. We followed their excellencies, who led us, as in triumph, into the town. They had just constructed at Geneva a magnificent building, in which to lodge and board those citizens who had fallen into want. Though completed and furnished, no one had as yet lodged in it. Their excellencies proposed to dedicate it by lodging us there. They led us thither, and we alighted in a spacious courtyard. All the people hastened thither in a crowd. Those who had relatives among our party, entreated their excellencies to allow them to take them to their homes, which was willingly granted. M. Bousquet, one of us, had his mother and two sisters at Geneva, who had come to claim him. As he was my intimate friend, he begged their excellencies to permit me to go with him. And, following this example, all the citizens entreated to be allowed the consolation of lodging their dear brethren in their houses, so that their excellencies were obliged to give way to their ardent hospitality, and not one remained in the Maison Française, as

this magnificent building was called.   As to myself, I did not stay long at Geneva; for, with six
of our brethren, finding the opportunity of a berline
which had brought to Geneva the chargé d'affaires
of the King of Prussia, and which was returning
empty, we made a bargain with the coachman to
take us as far as Frankfort-on-the-Maine.   The
gentlemen of Geneva had the kindness to pay for
our carriage, and gave us money for our expenses.

We seven, therefore, left Geneva in the berline,
and arrived at Frankfort in good health.   I must
not forget to mention the Christian generosity of
the nobles of Berne.   Though we had forbidden
our coachman to say who we were, in order to
avoid the demonstrative kindness of the Protestants
in the several towns through which we passed, we
were discovered, and conducted to an inn, called
"The Cock."   It is a place where ambassadors and
other noble persons are lodged at the expense of
the state.   Having alighted, we found the secretary
of state awaiting us, who welcomed us in as kind
a way as if we had been his own children.

He told us that he was the secretary of state;
and it was well he did so, for we should not have
known him to be such, either by his dress or by his
attendants, so little difference is there in this country
between the citizens and the nobles.   He added
that he had orders to keep us company, and to
treat us with distinction all the time that we could
remain at Berne.   We were magnificently entertained, and the secretary, who only quitted us in
the evening, occupied four days in taking us to visit

their excellencies of Berne. We were everywhere received and caressed as if we had been the dearest members of their families. They begged us in the kindest way to honour them (for so they expressed it) with our presence in their town for several weeks, and as much longer as we wished. But as our coachman entreated us to depart, wishing to return to Berlin, we remained only four days, at the end of which the secretary of state prepared a good breakfast for us, and in taking leave of us placed twenty rix-dollars in the hands of each—a present from their excellencies. We begged him to express our great gratitude to them, and we started in our berline, which took us on to Frankfort, where we arrived at the beginning of August. We were recommended by our friends at Geneva to M. Sárazin, a merchant, and elder of the Reformed Church at Bockenheim, about a league from Frankfort—for as there is no Reformed Church in Frankfort, all those who belong to this church in the town, whether French or German, take part in Divine service at Bockenheim.

We arrived at Frankfort on a Saturday, the day of preparation for the Holy Communion. We alighted at M. Sárazin's house. He was expecting us, and soon all the members of the consistory, French as well as German, assembled there. They received us with demonstrations of inexpressible joy and zeal, and took us in a carriage to Bockenheim to hear the sermon of the Preparation, which was preached by M. Matthieu, the French minister of this church. These gentlemen entreated us to

receive the Holy Communion with them the next
day ; but we did not consider ourselves sufficiently
prepared, especially I, who had never communicated, never having had the opportunity. We
then returned to Frankfort, where M. Sárazin entertained us sumptuously in his house.

Next day he took us to Bockenheim, and on
coming out of church they made us enter the
chamber of the consistory, when we partook of a
frugal repast with all the members of this body,
both French and German. These gentlemen strongly
urged us to remain some days at Frankfort, but we
begged them so much to allow us to continue our
journey to Holland that they consented. M. Sárazin zealously undertook to arrange our departure
and pay our expenses. He bought a light boat
for us, covered with a tent, with two men to row
and steer it as far as Cologne. He furnished us
with provisions, and ordered the boatmen to land
us every evening at convenient and comfortable
places, where we might sleep and refresh ourselves,
and especially to keep as near as possible to the
German side, where the Emperor's army was encamped on the banks of the river. The French
army, which was then besieging Landau, being on
the other side, we much feared falling into its hands.
M. Sárazin, before we embarked, took us to the
Hotel de Ville to ask the magistrates to give us a
passport. These gentlemen, all Lutherans, congratulated us much upon our deliverance. They
went so far as to say that we were the salt of
the earth, a title which humiliated us by the deep

feeling which we had of our own infirmities, which placed an immense distance between the holy disciples of the Lord Jesus, to whom this sacred name belonged, and us, who felt ourselves to be such weak sinners. We testified to this by our reply, giving glory to God, who alone, by his grace, had strengthened our constancy and our resignation to his holy will. These gentlemen appeared pleased with our words, and I saw some of them who shed tears : after having exhorted us to perseverance, and recommended us to the care of M. Sárazin, they gave us a passport for which they charged us nothing.

M. Sárazin conducted us to the boat which he had prepared for us, and we embarked, testifying our great gratitude to this good Israelite for his many acts of kindness towards us. Our voyage to Cologne was rather a long one, because always keeping close to the German bank, where the imperial army was encamped, we were stopped at each fort and picket to show our passport and have it viséd. A week after leaving Frankfort we arrived in good health at Cologne. There we sold our boat, and the next day we left that town by the ordinary passage-boat for Dordrecht, after having visited some Protestant gentlemen to whom M. Sárazin had recommended us, and who gave us a kind reception. We made no stay at Dordrecht, but started at once for Rotterdam, where we were welcomed with every possible kindness by the numerous flock of our fellow-Protestants, French as well as Dutch, in that town. We remained there two days, and then proceeded to Amsterdam, the termination of our long journey.

It would be impossible to describe the fraternal reception given to us in that great city, so zealous for the confessors of the truth of our holy religion. We went in a body to the venerable company of the consistory of the Walloon Church, to testify to them our gratitude for the constant kindness which they had shown us during so many years, by helping us efficaciously in our great tribulation. This pious company had the kindness to reply to our thanks by the assurance of the continuance of their zealous interest in us. Then they appointed two of their members to go and present us to the Dutch consistory, which assembled expressly to receive us. The demonstrations of zeal and charity which we received there are easier to understand than to express. These gentlemen all embraced us, their eyes bathed in tears, and delivered a touching exhortation to us, beseeching us to give proofs of our holy faith, in edifying the church by a life without reproach, which should answer to that constant profession of confessors of the truth which God had given us grace to maintain upon the galleys. Then this venerable company voted a liberal sum to help us to procure what was necessary for us, and thanked the deputies of the Walloon Church for their kindness in presenting us to them.

We remained wandering from place to place for three or four weeks, not knowing where to settle ourselves, so affectionately were we everywhere received. I was beginning to think how I could

employ myself in a useful manner, when the
consistory of the Walloon Church begged me to
be one of the deputies which they had resolved
upon sending to England for two objects, the one
to thank her Britannic majesty for the deliverance
which she had obtained for us, and the other to
give some weight to the solicitations which were
being made to her majesty to obtain the release of
those who still remained at the galleys, to the
number of about two hundred. To this I could not
but consent. I set out, then, for London with two
of our brethren, and in a short time there were
twelve deputies, all liberated galley slaves. The
Marquis de Miremont and the Marquis de Rochegude presented us to. the queen, who admitted us
to the honour of kissing her hand. The Marquis
de Miremont addressed her majesty in a short but
very pathetic harangue, praising her zeal and
power, in having been able to obtain the deliverance of the confessors of the truth from the hands
of those who had sworn to prolong their sufferings
all their lives. Her majesty assured us from her
own royal lips, that she was very glad at our deliverance, and that she hoped soon to release those
who still remained at the galleys ; after which we
retired.

The Marquis de Rochegude, who well understood the politics of courts, judged it fitting to
present us to the Duc d'Aumont, who was then
ambassador of the King of France at the court of
London. Wishing to make this ambassador desire
himself to see us, he waited upon him, and told him

of the deputation of Protestant galley slaves, whom his most Christian majesty had released, who had been sent to London to thank the queen for her favourable intercession with the King of France, adding that the deputies, to the number of twelve, would have already come to offer their respects to his excellency if they had dared to take the liberty to do so. The marquis thought this step might be useful towards obtaining the liberty of those who were still at the galleys. The ambassador appearing very curious to see us, it was settled that the marquis should introduce us to an audience of his excellency on the morrow.

His excellency received us very graciously, shaking hands with us all, and congratulating us on our release. He asked us how long we had suffered the punishment of the galleys, and what was the occasion of our sentence. Each replied to this question separately, for the time and occasion of each were different. We then heartily thanked his most Christian majesty in the person of his ambassador for the favour which he had shown us, beseeching him to deliver those who still remained captives at the galleys. We earnestly implored the intercession of the ambassador on behalf of our brethren, who were no more criminal than we were, and who had obtained the same intercession of her Britannic majesty with his most Christian majesty, for the king had consented that *all* who were in the galleys for the sake of their religion, should be released, yet only one hundred and thirty-six had been set at liberty, and about two hundred retained. His excellency appeared struck at the distinction, which he said he could not understand, unless those who remained had committed some other crime. We protested to the contrary, each alleging the most convincing proofs.

I took the liberty of asking the ambassador to give me his attention for a moment, that I might prove that it was no difference in their crimes which kept our brethren in the galleys. I was the youngest and the least serious of the band, and I made bold to plead this cause before his excellency; but I asked his permission with so much confidence that I should be able to convince him, that with kindness and patience he consented to listen to me. I told him succinctly the cause which had made me leave the kingdom; that being bound in close friendship to a young man of Bergerac, named Daniel le Gras, we had started together, and had both been arrested at Mariembourg, and then both condemned by the same sentence to the galleys for life; that the parliament of Tournai had confirmed this sentence, declaring us both convicted of the same crime; that, in a word, our two names were written on the same paper which contained our sentence, without any distinction either for any particular crime or other disobedience to the laws; yet, nevertheless, I was released and my companion remained, which very clearly proved that the court of France had not released the one hundred and thirty-six only, on account of any difference in their crimes. The ambassador did us the justice of appearing convinced by this example, which he begged me to write down. He said he thought that the minister of marine and his secretaries had made this blunder. He assured the Marquis de Rochegude that he would write to the French court, that it might be made to feel that their abuse, if it was not remedied, would appear, and would in reality be, an injustice. "And in proof that I speak sincerely," said he to M. de Rochegude, "come to me to-morrow, which is the post-day for France, to take my letter yourself, which I will read and seal in your presence, and which you can then send to the post. You will see in it how I have taken the subject of these poor fellows to heart." Then turning to his secretary, the Abbé Nadal, he said, "Here, Monsieur l'Abbé, are honest men, who, notwithstanding their religious prejudices, show their candour and their good faith." The abbé only replied by an inclination of the head, and afterwards showed that the approbation and kindness with which his master honoured us were not to his taste ; for next day, the Marquis de Rochegude having gone to the ambassador to take his letter as had been agreed upon, his excellency received him in the most gracious manner, and told him that he had kept his word, and that the letter was written. But having called the Abbé Nadal, and asking him where the letter was, "What letter, my lord ?" replied the abbé. "The letter," said the ambassador, "on the subject of the confessors at the galleys."

This honourable title of confessors, which his excellency gave us, made the abbé shudder ; and as his master still insisted in demanding where the letter was, he coldly replied that it was upon his excellency's desk. "Give it me, then," said the ambassador. Thereupon the abbé told him that he wished to say a word to him in private ; and having whispered in his ear, the ambassador told the marquis that his secretary had reminded him that he had written about some matters in his letter which did not regard the galley slaves, and that, therefore, he begged him to dispense with showing it to him, but that he might reckon that it should be sent that very day. M. de Rochegude saw through this, and that the abbé had dissuaded his master from sending the letter. Though the ambassador assured M. de Rochegude that the letter had been sent, neither he nor we believed it ; and our brethren were not released for a year after, and then by a new solicitation from the Queen of England. I have described this incident to show that honest people pitied us, and were inclined to render us service, and that it was only the ecclesiastics who hated us and thwarted us everywhere. This Abbé Nadal was both chaplain and secretary to the embassy. During his residence in London he gave several proofs of his animosity against the Protestants. The ambassador was good and moderate, and always appeared very humane towards us, but the Abbé Nadal spoiled him. The abbé had so gained over the officers of the household, and so strongly incited them against the French refugees, that scarcely a day passed that these honest people did not receive affront.

These gentlemen were so bold that they annoyed our people even in their churches ; and one Sunday morning, when the minister, Armand du Bordieu, was preaching at the Great Savoy (as the principal French church is called), when he was in the middle of his sermon, one of the duke's officials had the irreverence to cry out quite loud, " You lie," and then escaped as soon as he could, for this insolence so excited the people that they would have torn him in pieces if they could.   Another time I witnessed the following scene with my own eyes.   An officer of the French embassy, being at the French café near the Exchange, said that the refugees ought to be hanged.   Some one represented to him that he ought to be more circumspect in his language, since, by God's grace, they were in a land of liberty, and protected from the persecutions of France : this insolent fellow replied very brutally, " Do you think, gentlemen, the King of France has not arms long enough to reach you beyond the sea ?   I hope that you will soon find it so."   But a London merchant, M. Banal, a good refugee, was so excited with anger against this officer, that he gave him one of the most violent boxes on the ear which I have ever seen, saying, " This arm, which is not so long as that of your king, will reach you from a nearer place."   The officer put his hand to his sword, but all the Frenchmen who were there fell upon him, gave him a great many blows, and determined unanimously to throw him out of the window of the second storey, which would certainly have taken place had not the mistress of the café besought, with clasped hands, that he might be allowed to go out at the door. This they allowed, out of consideration for the woman, but not without having thrashed him well. He ran to carry his complaint to the ambassador, who, far from justifying him, said that he had deserved what he got from the refugees ; that he deserved a second punishment from the king ; and that he could not understand how the officers of the king could insult anybody. These incidents truly show what the Jesuits and their allies will do ; they sought to persecute us in the safest asylums. One may hence judge of the *favour* with which they treated us when in their power.

I shall finish, as I have promised, my memoirs with the year 1713. Having resided in London for about two months and a half, and having nothing more to detain me there, I left in the month of December, with the approbation of the Marquis of Rochegude. Some of our brethren remained to solicit the queen's aid on behalf of our brethren who were still at the galleys. I arrived in good health at the Hague, where I communicated to those persons who were interested in the subject, what had happened in London, not forgetting the praise which an immense number of persons in that great city deserved, Englishmen as well as French refugees, who had received us in a most Christian and charitable manner. Besides different presents from private individuals, the consistory of the Savoy Church defrayed our expenses during our sojourn in London. I stayed nine weeks at the Hague. The minister, M. Basnage, begged me to go with him to several noblemen, who wished to obtain a pension for us, which their highnesses kindly granted a short time after. We had in no way deserved this benevolence, and it was only their Christian charity which made them bestow it upon us. For my own part, I cherish a gratitude beyond all expression for it, and considering this generosity of their highnesses, I can only admire their piety, their zeal for the glory of God, and their love for their neighbours, which induces them to conform constantly to that holy precept of "doing good to all men, but especially unto those who are of the household of faith."

May God himself be the rewarder of their virtues, and to the end of time may he richly bestow upon their republic his most gracious blessings!

JEAN MARTEILHE AND OLIVER GOLDSMITH.

(Note to p. ix.)

THE French editors seem not to have been aware of the fact that the volume had been translated into English so early as 1758. The preface to the English edition sets at rest all doubt as to the historical character of the narrative. The translator says, "The author, indeed, who is still alive and known to numbers, not only in Holland, but London, has, from prudential motives, thought proper to suppress his name; and the same reasons that have induced him to conceal it equally influence the translator." *

This statement gains additional interest from the fact that the translator, who calls himself James Willington, was no other than Oliver Goldsmith. Goldsmith had but recently returned from his wanderings on the continent of Europe, and he was endeavouring to eke out the scanty pittance which he received as usher in a school by doing drudgery as a bookseller's hack. The work which he did in this capacity was either anonymous, or under the pseudonym of James Willington, who had been a fellow-student at Trinity College, Dublin. Most of his biographers conjecture that he concealed his name from feelings of weariness, disgust, and despair, at his repeated failures in literary composition. More probably, however, he was prompted to this course from a consciousness of latent power, and the hope of occupying a place in our literature which he would not imperil by giving his name to anything unworthy of himself. It is probable that, during his stay in Holland, he may have met Marteilhe. His language seems to imply that he had some personal acquaintance with him. The following extract from the preface is characteristic :—

" Could the present performance teach one individual to value his religion by contrasting it with the furious spirit of Popery ; could it contribute to make him enamoured with liberty by showing their unhappy situation whose possessions are held by so precarious a tenure as tyrannical caprice ; could it promote his zeal in the cause of humanity, or give him a wish to imitate the virtues of the sufferer, or redress the injuries of the

---

* " *The Memoirs of a Protestant Condemned to the Galleys of France for his Religion.* Written by Himself. In two volumes. Translated from the Original. Just published at the Hague, by JAMES WILLINGTON. London, 1758." See *Works of Oliver Goldsmith*, Vol. III., p. 355. Edited by PETER CUNNINGHAM. Murray's British Classics. And *Life and Times of Oliver Goldsmith*. By JOHN FORSTER, Vol. I., p. 134.

T

oppressed; then, indeed, the author will not have wrote in vain."

The *Quarterly Review,*[*] in a very interesting article based upon this volume, and *Les Forçats pour la foi, par Athanase Coquerel,* carries Marteilhe's history down to a point somewhat later than that at which the present narrative breaks off. " His death took place at Cuylenberg in 1777, at the advanced age of ninety-three years. Mention is made of his aged widow, and it is known that he had a daughter, who was married at Amsterdam to an English naval officer of distinction, Vice-Admiral Douglas. In 1785 their son, Mr. Douglas, and his wife, came to visit their French relations in Perigord. 'It is pleasing to find,' says M. Coquerel, 'that the memory of Marteilhe, though lost sight of in France, was respected in England, and that the honour of an alliance with the martyr of the galleys was estimated as it deserved.' . . . It is, indeed, a good lesson for us who live in an easy and tolerant age, in which the exercise of the sterner virtues is more rarely called for, to be reminded of the fortitude of such men as these admirable, though little known, martyrs of the Reformation, who, in the fine language of Sir Thomas Browne, ' maintained their faith in the noble way of persecution, and served God in the fire, whereas we honour him in the sunshine.' "

THE SUFFERINGS OF M. SABATIER.

(Note to p. 172.)

THE foregoing narrative is confirmed, in a remarkable manner, by the statements of a volume, entitled, *Relation des tourmens que l'on fait souffrir aux Protestants qui sont sur les Galeres de France.* Londres, 1708 ; Amsterdam, 1709.   This work, which is extremely rare, was written by Jean Francois Bion, a native of Dijon,

[*] No. 239, July, 1866

and cure of Ursy, in Burgundy. Growing weary of the inactive life of a country priest, he applied for and obtained the appointment of chaplain in the galleys, and served in this capacity on board the *Superbe.* Touched by the courage, patience, and resignation of the suffering Protestants under his charge, he was led, first, to question the truth of a religion which could persecute so cruelly as his own, and, ultimately, he embraced the faith which could endure persecution so nobly. He says, " It was wonderful to see with what true Christian patience and constancy they bore their torments ; in the extremity of their pain, never expressing anything like rage, but calling upon Almighty God, and imploring his assistance. I visited them day by day, and, as often as I did, my conscience upbraided me for persisting so long in a religion whose capital errors I long before perceived, and above all that inspired so much cruelty ; a temper directly opposite to the spirit of Christianity. At last their wounds, like so many mouths, preached to me, made me sensible of my error, and experimentally taught me the excellency of the Protestant religion. God grant it may be effectual to my salvation."

Bion made his escape to Geneva in the year 1704, and subsequently settled in London, where he kept a school, and was minister of a congregation at Chelsea. His narrative not only confirms the general truth of Marteilhe's, and acquits it of any suspicion of exaggeration, but it gives details more horrible by far than any which this work contains. It is evident that Marteilhe enjoyed special privileges and immunities, in which his fellow-sufferers were not permitted to share. Of the punishment inflicted on M. Sabatier, Bion says :—

" 'Tis certain that though there was at first a very great number of Protestants condemned to the galleys, the bastinado and other torments hath destroyed above three parts out of four, and the most of those who are still alive are in dungeons ; as Monsieurs Bancilhon, De Serres, and Sabatier, who are confined to a dungeon

276 Autobiography of a French Protestant.

at Chateau d'If. But the generous constancy of this last, about eight or ten months ago, deserves a place in this history, and challenges the admiration of all true Protestants.

" M. Sabatier, whose charity and zeal equals that of the primitive Christians, having a little money, distributed it to his brethren and fellow-sufferers in the galleys; but the Protestants being watched more narrowly than the rest, he could not do it so secretly, but he was discovered and brought before M. de Montmort, intendant of the galleys at Marseilles: being asked, he did not deny the fact; M. Montmort not only promised him his pardon, but a reward, if he would declare who it was that had given him the money. M. Sabatier modestly answered, that he should be guilty of ingratitude before God and man, if, by any confession, he should bring those into trouble who had been so charitable to him; that his person was at their disposal, but he desired to be excused as to the secret expected from him. The intendant replied that he had a way to make him tell, and that immediately: whereupon he sent for some Turks, who, at his command, stripped Sabatier stark naked, and beat him with ropes and cudgels during three days, at several times; and seeing this did not prevail over the generous confessor, the intendant himself turned executioner, striking him with his cane, and telling the bystanders, 'See what a devil of a religion this is.' These were his own expressions, as is credibly reported by persons that were present. The gazettes and public letters give us an account of the same. At last, seeing he was ready to expire, he commanded him into a dungeon, where, maugre all torments, Providence hath preserved him until this day."

LONDON: ROBERT K. BURT, WINE OFFICE COURT, FLEET STREET.

www.ingramcontent.com/pod-product-compliance
Lightning Source LLC
Chambersburg PA
CBHW021044030726
47496CB00006B/1672